MW01598513

Stray Our Pieces

Jason Graff

Published by Waldorf Publishing
2140 Hall Johnson Road
#102-345
Grapevine, Texas 76051
www.WaldorfPublishing.com

Stray Our Pieces

ISBN: 978-1-64370-012-0
Library of Congress Control Number: 2018955775

For Laura & Warren

ACKNOWLEDGEMENTS

The title *Stray Our Pieces* is taken from the lyrics of the song "Love You" by Syd Barrett and used with permission. Chapter 9 was excerpted in the January 2018 edition of The Write Launch.

1. Neighborhood Friends, Enough

When the front door creaked open, I was on the couch with a book in front of me, but I wasn't reading. My eyes were just passing over the words. Really, I was daydreaming about what I'd like to eat, if only I could find the energy to roll off the couch and take the four steps necessary to get to the kitchen. Too bad, I'd eaten the last Yodel earlier that morning after finding we were out of Pop Tarts. There were some apples but they hardly seemed worth leaving the couch for.

The door banged shut, and David dragged his way over to me. He whimpered until I lowered my book. I did so slowly, trying to arrange my features into a look that might pass for sympathetic. His bottom lip quivered as if snagged on his buck teeth. After burdening my already chubby, awkward son with a retainer, his orthodontist kept promising us those would soon be tucked back inside his mouth. The trembling of his doughy face almost chased the yearning for another Yodel completely from my thoughts.

"What happened? Were you playing football? Was it a hard tackle? Did you get hurt?" I asked, hoping to get it over with quickly.

"No mom," he said whimpering some more, his breath catching. "I'm not hurt...not like that."

"What then? What happened? I thought you were going out to play football with..."

"Mom, something happened. I've...it's...I...he..." he said, then snorted and sputtered, "We, we, we were playing tackle..."

"I knew it! I knew it! I told you not to. Didn't I? It's dangerous. Someone was bound to get hurt."

"But that's not what happened. I just told you I'm not hurt like that," he said, suddenly finding the poise to become slightly indignant. "We were playing and everything was fine. I was catching passes. I was on Kenny's team. We were winning."

"So what happened?" I asked.

I half-rolled from the couch and came to my knees on the floor so I could reach out and stroke his forearm in the hope of keeping him somewhat calm and intelligible. The Kenny stories were easily the most upsetting in my son's repertoire. Kenny Crumbrick was the oldest boy in the neighborhood by a few years but had no friends his own age, at least none that I'd ever seen. His main form of amusement seemed to be engaging my son and his friends in the sort of play that always ended unpleasantly, usually for poor David.

"He told me that when everyone else was out running routes…" David said, body seized by a bout of heaving "…that he and I would run to his house to play video games, just the two of us. It would be our secret, like we were friends. So," he paused to take a deep breath, his body shaking with the effort, "I ran real fast down the hill towards his house before anyone knew what I was doing, just like he said to. When I got to his back door, I pulled on it but it was locked. I turned around and there was no one there. He was not right behind me like he said he'd be." David pressed his fists into his cheeks, tears now dripping over the back of his hands. "They were all still in Denny's yard. I heard them laughing at me. I didn't want to cry in front of them, so I held it in." 'In' was punctuated by a keening wail.

"It's okay," I said and ran my hand through his hair. "You can cry now."

When one of those crying jags started up, his weeping and sniveling set my teeth to grinding, ever so subtly. I don't know when his tears had begun to have that effect on me but, by then, I no longer even felt that bad about my reaction. He'd once cried, not long before that, when the cap got stuck on a tube of toothpaste. When he brought it to me, face slick with tears, holding it up as some totem of tragedy, I took him into my arms, trying not to laugh, which had only made things worse. There was something wrong with him, I sometimes worried or, more often, wrong with me.

Irrationally, I did, for a time, harbor a fear that something I'd done while pregnant might've made him overly sensitive. During the second trimester, I went through a period of craving Honey Nut Cheerios and ate them dry by the handful, by the boxful. I often thought, during tear-stained moments like those, of the fat, soft-voiced little spokes-bee from the commercials and worried that I'd turned my son into a soft-bellied bumble bee, too timid to sting anyone.

Finally, after some determined skull stroking, I got him to calm down. His body still trembled a bit, even after the tears had stopped. I held him to me and whispered in his ear that it was going to be okay -- a truly empty promise. In some ways, the aftermath of those episodes was often worse as David had the habit of going nonverbal. He'd nod or shake his head to my questions but wouldn't really answer. It was as though revealing his emotions in such depth had worn him out, which I kind of understood. Those scenes always left me fairly enervated as well.

When Daryl got home later that afternoon, I rushed to the door, throwing my arms around his neck. I could tell by the way he hugged me back that he was even more surprised than I thought he'd be. It was a good deal more in the way of a greeting than my customary half-mumbled hello. The desire to even offer the hug had surprised me. With my hands still interlaced behind his neck, I told him about what'd happened to David.

"I'd like to do something about that kid," Daryl said of Kenny and left it at that, turning his attention to what I was going to make for dinner.

Daryl Hytner, wellspring of parenting advice and care.

I had trouble sleeping that night. Daryl snored intermittently, which only seemed to bother me when something equally troubling was stalking my thoughts. David's temperament was primary among the innumerable things that I found mystifying about him. I never cried much, not even as a little girl. I guess I never wanted to learn about his emotional life enough to help him and shamefully admit that I kept hoping the whole crying thing would just pass. I didn't want to think of him as being abnormally sensitive, which he no doubt was. I just lacked something. Courage? Insight? Compassion? A desire to truly nurture? My job, as I saw it at the time, was to get him out of the house, so I could have it to myself. Which sounds more than a little selfish, I'll grant you.

Some time during the night, though, under the spell of my husband's crude nasal lullaby, I found some unexpected resolve to actually try to do something. The mother inside of me, lazy and dormant though she often was, awoke. The bullies shouldn't always win, she roared albeit a tad unconvincingly, the bullies should be dealt with.

Early the next morning, I got up and baked a coffee cake -- boxed and premixed. By the time Saturday morning began its slide into afternoon, the cake had cooled off enough for me to put it on a plate and carry it out the door. I walked down the hill to the house where Kenny lived with his mother.

The pock-marked siding was pulling away in places revealing a layer of molding wood turning from grey to black. Their yard was little more than a wild patch of overgrown weeds with faded scratch tickets and crushed cigarette packs clicking in the breeze. I had to part the overgrown shrubbery that hid the front of the house to make it to the door. I rang the bell. A dog began to bark but was silenced by a whimper-inducing thwack.

The lady of the house, Lynn, came to the door wrapped in a green robe, frayed at the cuffs. She carried with her the pungency of cigarette smoke. Her puffy face, tanned and wrinkled, fixed itself into a scowl. She glared at me the way a wounded animal in search of the energy to continue thrashing about would.

"Uh, huh," she said by way of a greeting.

"Ms. Crumbrick. I'm Gloria Hytner. David's mom. From up the street."

"I know who you are," she growled, her mouth an economy of motion, moving just enough to get the words out.

"Yes…well we…we've never actually met, I don't think. I…uh…I brought a coffee cake. It's an easy little recipe, pretty moist. Anyway, our boys play together so I thought we should at least meet each other – face to face. Maybe have a chat?"

My hands began to tremble against the cake tray. I inched my fingers around to get a better grip on the bottom and further forced my smile. She pulled on the door handle and, thinking she was about to invite me in, I made a half-step forward, only to retreat when it became obvious she was checking to make sure the door was locked.

"Chat, yeah," she said. "I got sugar in the blood. I can't eat that cake."

"Oh…I'm sorry. I didn't know."

"Diabetes, I got to prick myself twice a day to check my sugars."

"I'll…um…have to remember and bring something else next time."

"No sugar for me. Not the sweet life down this end of the street."

"Yes," I said, no longer sure of what to do with my deadly peace offering. "Well…um…can I come in or… um…" The longer I stood there, the more withering her glare felt.

"For what?" she asked, squinting at me with her crow's feet flexing their talons across her temples.

"To discuss our boys. They play together and I thought you'd like to…"

"Our boys? What's there to discuss?" she asked.

"Like I said, they play together, rough-housing, boys' stuff. They do it quite a bit and I think maybe we should talk about…"

"I know that. I seen them together," she said, digging out a pack of Newports from the pocket of her robe. She lit one, shooting a cloud of mint-tinged smoke through the screen. "Seen your boy roughhouse alright. Seen him pee in my backyard. Piss in the grass, right out in the open like a dog."

"I'm sorry? David…peed in your yard?"

"Had his back to me, thank Christ, but I know that sound. My dog makes 'bout the when he goes."

"Sorry, I had no idea Ms. Crumbrick. I'll speak to him about that. I certainly don't want him…"

"Mrs.?"

"Huh, I'm…sorry?"

"It's Mrs. Crumbrick."

"Mrs.," I said, by then my entire arm had begun to quiver under the weight of the cake, so I bent over to set it down at my feet. "Sorry, I didn't know which to…"

"I'm still legally married, Miss Hynter," she said, tilting her head back to blow another cloud of smoke right at me. "Not that the name never did much for me, but I don't have the time or money to bother changing it."

"Mrs. Crumbrick, I think we've gotten off on the wrong foot here. I do apologize if I've offended you in any way. That was not, at all, my purpose for this visit. And I will have a talk with David about going to the bathroom on your lawn. There's certainly no excuse for that."

"It's alright. Boys'll be boys. Boys' stuff," she said, the long line of cigarette ash which had been growing unattended finally broke off and exploded on the collar of her robe. "Kenny tells me your boy still sometimes shits his pants. Is that true?"

"I'm sorry?" I asked, aware of the gasp snapping at the end of my question.

"I said, your son still messes his drawers like a baby, according to my son. I asked if that was true."

"David hasn't *messed* his…"

"Not that I think Kenny's a liar or nothing. But

oys'll make up stories about other boys. You know how kids're. Boys'll be boys."

"Mrs. Crumbrick," I said, firming up my tone, "that's not something that has happened in a very long time."

"How long?" she asked with a cackle.

"I don't see how that's any business of yours."

"I thought you came down here to discuss our boys?"

"I did but that…my son's…that's not what I came to discuss."

"Oh, I see now," she said, smirking and crossing her arms over her chest, "you came to talk to me about something Kenny did. Not how your son can't keep control of where and how he pisses and shits."

I should've stepped over my cake and onto the filthy welcome mat that the sun had bleached to a brittle white, looked Crumbrick right in her eyes and told her what I thought of her and her dirtbag son. That with her wrinkled, smoke-worn face, she could've passed for sixty. That it'd been all over town how her husband had left her for some rotund teenage waitress with a lazy eye. That, for all her talk, it was her son who smelled vaguely of shit, the kind of shit that had been building up in an elderly man's colon for weeks. I wanted to tell Crumbrick those things but then it did seem a smidge vindictive after her bringing up David's problems, plus it would've been too much shit talk for one neighborly visit. Instead, I picked up my cake and stepped away from the door.

"I don't particularly appreciate that kind of talk. I thought we might have a friendly chat," I said, pausing to lift up the aluminum foil so that she could smell the delicious sweetness of the cake before I stuffed a chunk of it in my mouth, "but that doesn't seem possible at the moment."

"Don't have no time for friends," she said. "Good
-bye Miss Hytner, come back some time when you can't
stay for so damn long."

2. Shock and Appall

I took my time with the knife, shaving the cabbage thin, as the recipe card instructed. I smiled at the thought of a lathered-up cabbage head sitting atop an apron in a barber's chair awaiting the straight razor, chatting away about sports or the weather or whatever mindless male-centered garbage gets discussed in such places. I tried to make sure each slice of cabbage was of the same length as the shards of carrot that I had already sliced and put into a bowl. I let the hot water run so that I could rinse off the knife after every few slices, keeping the blade clean.

Outside, Daryl ran a wool brush over the grill -- teeth showing, a snarling expression on his face. Having a cookout had been his idea, but now it looked as though he regretted it. Surely, he would've rather been in the garage working on one of his projects. I couldn't help but sympathize. Hell, I would've rather been in the garage laboring over some wood working project.

Standing behind me, my mother-in-law rearranged the phlegm in her throat like she always did before she was going to speak. I took it that she wasn't sure of her words, so she rolled them around and rinsed them off a few times on their way up. Poor Gail always wanted us to be closer but never saw that we had very little in common beyond her son, and, no matter how much she surely loved Daryl, he was obviously not material enough for a whole conversation. The kitchen clock ticked away and I wondered if that made it worse for her, that empty sound lightly echoing, evidence that I didn't need to talk to anyone or listen to music or do anything other than chop at a head of cabbage to be content in her presence.

Silence, or even its approximation, was certainly not among Gail's favorite things.

"Did Daryl tell you about me and Georgie getting a dog?" she dared ask, finally unable to take it anymore. She coughed after she spoke, her voice was still a bit bubbly with phlegm despite her determined bouts of throat clearing.

"He did. You got him from the pound, right?"

"Yep. We did. Well, I did. Georgie stayed at home. She's a poodle."

"What's her name?" I asked.

"She already had a name when we got her, Fluffy."

"Fluffy. Good name for a poodle."

"I kept it 'cause I didn't want her getting confused by being called something new."

I put the cabbage in the bowl with the carrot shards. Then I folded in the dressing from the jar. Once upon a time, when I was young and trying to impress the world, I made my own dressing. Among the first rewards bestowed on me by the onset of actual maturity was the wisdom that store-bought anything was just about as good as whatever I could whip up, and what difference there might've been was rarely worth the work.

"You sure cut that cabbage thin. Takes time," Gail said, bravely marching off in a new conversational direction. "I couldn't do it. I'd be too nervous to just get it done so I could move on to the next thing. Sure I can't help you somehow?"

"No. You're a guest," I said putting the plastic lid on the bowl and giving it a couple of forceful shakes to mix the veggies and dressing together. "You want to go sit out on the porch? I think David's out there."

"Nah, he's out there reading. I don't want to disturb

him. He'd probably rather read than visit with his old Grandma," she said in a tone that I thought invited me to argue with her.

Naturally, I declined. I gave her a smile as I turned to put the coleslaw in the fridge. Her eyes, watery and small, seemed so full of worry, so full of all she hid from the world. My habit of looking her in the eyes whenever we talked probably also contributed to the anxious air that our meetings always had. Half the time, I was really looking at the nose pads of her glasses which were so filthy they'd turned a thick green. It was amazing she could walk around, perfectly happy, while a bacterial crust was accumulating so very near her face. Escaping my gaze, her eyes finally came to rest on the paper cup she'd been holding since she came in. She kept blowing into it even though, by then, it was almost certainly no longer even lukewarm.

"Just the broccoli now and we'll be all set," I said.

"Are you going to make a casserole?" she asked.

"No. No, just a plate of crudité. I've already sliced celery, cauliflower and peppers. It doesn't seem complete to me without some broccoli and a dollop of ranch dip."

"Smart, quick and healthy, that's the way. Because, I was going to say, you may not have time for a casserole," she said, smiling contentedly at her useless advice.

I started on the broccoli, leaving enough of the stalk on each slice to grab hold of for dipping. I thought of pointing out that bit of foresight to Gail, but it would've been too much like making conversation, too much like giving her what she wanted out of our time together. I had to hand it to her; she made sure to do her mother-ly-in-law duties with me, even though I obviously scared the Depends right off of her. She rearranged more mucus in her throat as I reduced the head of broccoli to little dip-delivery devices. I often wondered if the leaves at the end of the stalk were edible. I thought about having Gail test one out but then Daryl nodded at me from the grill. A second later came a hiss, then a puff of blue smoke. My husband jumped back, shock replacing the blank look in his eyes.

"What's that thing in his mouth?" Gail asked, tacking in yet another direction, hoping as always to strike the rich vein of conversation that would get me to open up.

"Who? You mean Davey?"

"Yep. That plastic thing in his mouth. What is it?"

"Daryl didn't tell you?" I asked. "David has to wear a retainer to fix his overbite."

"A retainer," she said as though it all suddenly made sense. "And didn't you tell me once you thought he got that overbite from sucking on his thumb when he was little?"

"No. I didn't say that," I said, arranging the cut vegetables in the slots around the circular divot where the dip would soon be placed. I didn't add that that it'd been her theory because I didn't want to get into another useless debate about toddler thumb-sucking and its long-term orthodontic impact.

"How come it's baby blue?" she asked.

"Did he show it to you?"

"He took it out of his mouth to show me. I asked him to."

"That's the color he picked out," I said, skipping over asking her why she had done that.

"Who? The dentist?"

"No. David."

"Oh," she said and moved next to me to dump what was left of her coffee into the sink. Black, tarred water rinsed over the vegetable shards. "I wonder why he picked that color. It makes him...well...it looks like something a...a girl would pick out."

"I don't think so, Gail. There're pink ones for girls," I said, using the tone which I'd polished over the years. By then, it almost always correctly conveyed my frustration with how pointless our conversation had become.

"It's good that he reads so much," she said. "So many of the kids today are into those computer games. You're right to keep him from getting into that stuff."

"It wasn't too hard with David," I said, returning to a less talk-weary tone. "He really loves those books."

"Which ones are they again? What's it called, *Power Sander and...?*" she asked, her mouth agape, trying to suck the answer from the empty air.

"It's called *Lands of Power and Dust. Power Sander* would be a book Daryl might read."

"Power and Lust?" she asked, trying to make her alarm sound like circumspection.

"No. No, not lust, thank god. Dust. *Lands of Power and Dust*. It's like a, uh, a futuristic novel but with swords and dragons and strange, gross creatures and all that sort of silliness. Boys' stuff."

"My goodness," Gail said, unable to keep herself from reaching across my body to stack the celery sticks in a pyramid shape. "That sounds like quite an undertaking for a boy his age. I certainly didn't read anything like that when I was young."

"Like I said, it's boys' stuff. You and I were both *Anne of Green Gables* gals," I said. "Weren't we?"

Dog meet bone. Big juicy bone.

"That's right. You loved those books, too. Didn't you?" She broke into her toothy, beatific grin, the same one that she'd passed on to her son. To this day, I cannot erase that smile from my mind whenever I picture Daryl.

"I did," I said. "I had the whole set of them."

"Me too! They don't write stories like that anymore. Do they?"

"No. I don't think so. Not for boys anyway. Stories for boys have to have adventure and violence, no feelings, no emotions, just conquests and scenes of bravery."

"Well, Anne was brave," Gail said, her voice cracking as if jumping over a spark from the past, when the struggle not to be treated like just another helpless girl was the adventure. "She had to be to stand up to those Pye girls."

"How do you remember details like that?" I asked.

"Oh, Gloria, I read that first book and the ones that followed over and over again, until the covers all but came off. I could never forget those Pye girls, Josie and the other one...Gertie." We laughed together and she leaned forward to lay a light hand on my shoulder. "I've forgotten a good many more important things over the years but very few things about Anne."

"I read them over and over too," I said. "Those Pye girls. Hated them. They reminded me of these sisters, twins, who I went to grade school with. They made my life hell. Who were they for you?"

"What, Gloria? Who was...what?"

"Who was mean to you? Who was your Gertie? Your Josie? Mine were Nancy and Olivia, the evil twins. The first girls to make me aware that I was big, bigger than the other girls."

Her eyes went blank. Her lips began to quiver. Swallowing with some effort, she shrugged, sadly, limply. After all her prompting and prying, Gail always proved incapable, often comically so, of engaging with me in the kind of the real conversation she seemed to always be angling for. She shrank back against wall, looking at her hands like she wished she were still holding something.

"You want to help me set the table?" I asked, as a kind of reward for her constantly trying.

"Sure, sure. Are we eating out on the porch?"

"Might as well take advantage of the weather. Such a nice day. Who knows how many more we'll have before it turns cold?"

"Very nice for September," she said. "It's supposed to turn colder sometime next week, though."

I handed her the paper plates and boxes of plasticware.

"Smart," she said, giving them an admiring glance, "less cleanup."

Caroline and Denny arrived promptly at 3. They just walked right in without knocking or ringing the doorbell. Tanned and slim, Caroline was someone who projected an air of studied composure as surely as I gave off one of chaos and dread. She cradled a couple of wine bottles in the crook of her arm and offered a brief half hug. Denny was dressed in a red and white checked shirt and a clip-on blue bowtie. The outfit clashed in a way that somehow managed to speak well for Caroline. She was raising a child confident enough to wear whatever he wanted. A boy who cried as easily as David should never try to pull off a bowtie. Denny's golden hair had recently been buzzed down close to his skull. It was a style David had professed admiration for, but when we went to the barber shop, he turned white and began to shake when the clippers got too close to his head.

"Just because it's one of the kids' birthdays doesn't mean we can't party," Caroline said. I produced a cork-screw and opened one of the bottles. "Should we wait for Marge?" she asked when I handed her a glass, which she then drank from without waiting for an answer.

"Is Gregg coming?" I asked, hoping not to seem too obvious about my hopes of catching a glimpse of her handsome husband.

"Flying," she said, and offered an apologetic tilt of her head towards the heavens.

Jonny and his parents followed soon after. Marge handed me a covered dish. Al groused, saying something about an ulcer. I'd known him for almost eight years by then and hadn't heard him speak an entire sentence. He mumbled constantly and always smelled vaguely of gar-lic, so much so that I rarely got close enough to hear him.

Marge, Caroline and I would sometimes get togeth-er for lunch or a walk or to take the boys places together that none of us could face going on our own. No matter where our discussions began at those outings they'd al-ways end in glorifying the little tyrants who ruled our worlds. They'd each gush about their boys in a way that made me feel bad. If I had a similar impulse, it was mut-ed. I usually just listened, thinking the whole time about how their good little boys would often team up with that dullard Kenny to pick on my David. I knew there was no way to make them see they were raising hideous, grubby monsters, so I just mostly kept my mouth shut.

Once, I did venture a brag about how David had tested into the gifted program at school. That earned me sharp looks from them and then some quiet and confused congratulations. It's okay to inflate the degree to which your son enjoys going to church or go on and on about how good looking your Denny is, but revealing the truth about the gap between your son's intellect and that of his friends was in poor taste, apparently. Boo-hoo for those gals and their slack-jawed offspring. The world will always need short-order cooks and parking attendants.

After we finished Daryl's expertly overcooked burgers and blackened, rock-hard dogs, I let Gail light the cake. We sang happy birthday which, thanks to the wine that we ladies had enjoyed and the beers that Daryl and Al had been steadily consuming, was done with more gusto than harmony. When it ended, everyone barked orders at David to blow out the candles. Rather than blow air onto them, however, like a regular human, my darling son produced little globules of saliva from his mouth and attempted with varied success to douse the flames. I was so shocked and appalled that he'd snuffed two out in that fashion, while also missing twice, before I could put a stop to it.

"David," I screeched. The weightless buzz the wine had brought on abruptly left me. "What're you doing? What do you think you are doing?"

"Putting out the candles," he said, a stunned look on his face as though I'd interrupted some sacred right.

"What the!? Why're you spitting on the cake? The cake that now no one else can eat," I said through clenched teeth. "What were you thinking?"

"I didn't want anything to catch on fire," he said. "If I blew air, then an ember might've flown off and landed somewhere and my air would be feeding…"

In a move my mother would've certainly approved of, I slapped the back of his head. Someone gasped. David ducked to avoid a second blow, which wasn't coming. He turned to me with his eyes squinted shut. I glowered at him, daring him to start crying. Maybe it was the wine, but I didn't feel guilty at all, not like maybe I should've. I took the cake, box and all, walked out the back door of the porch over to where our trashcans sat in the wooden pen Daryl had built for them. I made sure to catch David's eyes before dumping the cake.

I noticed the looks being passed between Marge and Caroline when I came back in. It wasn't disgust or even pity written on their faces. I would've appreciated and accepted pity. It was condescension, easy to read in another, hard to hide when you feel it. I blamed and yes, hated David for letting them wear such looks for me in my own home.

Later that night, I stood outside David's bedroom and listened as Daryl tried to console him. He offered an overly patient and detailed explanation as to why something as frightfully obvious as spitting on food was frowned upon, especially when the food is meant to be shared. My husband was the one with the skill, so necessary for child rearing, of being able to talk to our son as though he was a product of some distant, alien culture and needed to be made aware of the odd ways in which we humans behaved. Daryl could also, when needed, strike the kind of compromising bargains with our son that I refused to make. I stopped listening to them when I felt the onset of a headache. I tried to read in bed but the wine had made my eyelids warm and heavy.

3.   Good Night for an Antennae Whipping

As Halloween approached, I found myself less than fully up to the task of finding a decent Greylor costume. David had made Daryl promise to get him one and, as was often the case, fulfilling his father's promise had become my duty. I refused to shell out what they were asking for the officially licensed *Lands of Power and Dust* apparel, which was little more than a vinyl apron made to look like a torso covered by chainmail and plastic mask so thin even David would've struggled to suffocate himself with it.

When I volunteered to make him one, which I did because parenthood was turning me into a masochist, he reacted in his usual measured way. David flung himself down on his bed and wept thick tears at the thought of becoming any less a Greylor, than he had imagined. I pointed out that the ones in the stores all looked so cheap, they couldn't possibly have matched his vision of such a heroic figure. This notion moved him some but not as much as when I suggested just cutting eyeholes in a bedsheet for him so he could go as Greylor's ghost. Faced with that choice, he ceased his whining, though I sensed he wasn't quite yet a total DIY convert.

I battled my soul to keep snideness from creeping into my tone while discussing the various accoutrements worn by the hero. To David, the most important things to get right were the red beard, ruby and sapphire power rings, black leather boots, chainmail tunic and iron sword of powerful length and thickness. It made it hard not to picture my son's hero as a medieval drag queen. Unsatisfied that I had a grasp of these details, David read right from his book about the armor that: "*...shall not be* *pierced by the swords and arrows of mortal man. It with-stands fire as though there is no heat at all. Outliving its wearer, the armor will be passed down through the generations from warrior to warrior and from hero to hero."*

So, Styrofoam basically.

"Is there a picture of him wearing it somewhere in the book?" I dared ask.

"There aren't any pictures of him in any of the books, Mom. It's a book for young adults, not for kids."

"Is there, maybe, a picture of him in the armor on the cover of one of the books?"

"There's a picture of T.R. Ungrin, the writer, on the back of each volume," he said.

In such moments, I wondered if they needed to recalibrate the test that showed my son was gifted.

"Okay, let's try it this way," I said, calmly, though I wanted to scream in frustration. "Is there a passage in the book, other than the one you read to me, that gives some more details as to what the armor is supposed to look like, like maybe what color it is or something?"

"Let me see," he said, picking the book up from his lap.

That was the first time I really noticed that he had the habit of leaving his books lying face down, opened to whatever page he was on, just as I did. When I was a girl, the top drawer of my desk was stuffed with bookmarks that were never of any use. I seemed to get them for every gift-giving holiday. I don't think I ever used a single one. They sat in that drawer until Mother threw them out while I was away at college. At the time, I'd complained bitterly about her invading my privacy but never missed them. Once I cracked a book, it stayed cracked until I finished it.

"What?" David asked, no doubt feeling the odd sensation of my loving eyes glowing down on him.

"Nothing. Nothing," I said. "It's just the unexpected things that make me happy."

"What?"

"Never mind." I tousled his hair like some simple-minded mom on a TV drama, who wants more than anything for her family to be happy and approve of the job she's doing.

Daryl worked late Halloween night, leaving me to accompany David and Denny around the neighborhood. It worked out pretty well, actually, as I hadn't bought any candy anyway and planned to just spend the night watching TV in the basement of our otherwise darkened house. As we set out, I wasn't sure how proud to be of the outfit I'd thrown together for him. Made from costume jewelry, cardboard, tin foil, Styrofoam and copper colored yarn, it looked as though my son had pulled a Viking-style raid on some craft fair. My mild reservations about its thrown together appearance were doused completely when I saw that Caroline had outfitted Denny with little more than a hooded sweatshirt and what appeared to be the antennae from a radio for a sword.

"Is that really what Greylor's loyal companion is supposed to look like?" I wondered to David in a whisper.

"Hucebuse wears alloy armor and boots with iron toes," David said, shaking his head. From the lippy frown on his face, I gathered he found his friend's attempt to be an embarrassment to all the kingdoms in the *Lands of Power and Dust*.

My knights, or more accurately, my knight and his friend wearing a green sweatshirt and wielding part of a no-longer-working radio, led me into the evening. At each stop we made, our neighbors, many of whom I saw only on that night, asked my escorts who they were supposed to be. My son's overly enthusiastic explanations earned the pair nervous smiles and bite-sized candy bars. Those who did know me from my infrequent walks around the neighborhood nodded at David then at me as if to say: "Nice going, housewife, those of us with actual jobs are too tired to do something like that." I grinned through my abhorrence at their silent, backhanded compliments.

By the time we reached the far edge of our neighborhood, it was getting late. The official town-sanctioned time to beg for candy was drawing near its end, but the boys wanted to hit some of the houses beyond the power lines on what might've been thought of as the good side of town, had Roslyndale enough character to have a bad side. By that time, my thighs were chafed and I lagged behind the boys, surreptitiously enjoying the candy I'd been swiping from both of their pillow cases, when they weren't watching. I should've felt bad about taking from Denny's sack, but I wanted to make sure they both got cheated by around the same amount.

I paused for a moment when I heard the distant whistle of the commuter train, then the clacking of its wheels passing just over the hill. It was on its way to the city, and I paused, as I always did whenever I heard it, to wish that I were onboard. Just me alone, going home to my place in the city. It would be carrying me back after I'd narrowly survived a weekend with Mother listening to her gripes, her petty invectives against Daddy. Naturally, I was younger and thinner too. Who says you can't have it all?

That was the only way I could put myself on the train, the only reason the childless, unmarried, younger version of me would set foot outside the city. Seeing Daddy. Trying to save him from Mother, not to mention the Alzheimer's. You know you're getting close to finally giving up completely on your dreams when you can't keep the worst parts of reality from intruding. Younger me. Kidless me. Unmarried me. But still with a sick father. I almost felt guilty for having to think that way in order to make my fabricated life seem plausible.

Guilty. Almost.

There were no streetlights out there where the road dipped and often flooded during heavy rain storms. My knights had disappeared. Then, a figure sprang out of the darkness up ahead. It was barely perceptible, a shadow just darker than the darkness surrounding us. I raced ahead, worrying that karma was about to extract a terrible price for my fantasizing that an alternate, and yet still far from perfect life, would've made me any happier. Before I could see what was going on, I heard a scream. I dropped a half-eaten Charleston Chew and broke into a fat lady sprint, which is at pace with a normal-sized woman's jog. My thighs to one another: "Can I get by here?" "Please do pass, madam, then it shall be my turn." I still couldn't see them but heard yelps and screams as well as something sharp cutting through the air.

"Boys," I yelled, just before I could make out three shapes silhouetted in the light of the first street lamp on the other side of the power lines.

One figure was down on the ground, being whipped by something sharp. I panicked, then I noticed David standing off to the side flinching from the blows that Denny was raining on the fallen figure. When the victim rolled near enough to him, David gave him a whack across the face with his foil-covered, cardboard sword. Here was my reward for hitting him, for teaching him the ways of violence. My son had crossed to the other side of town and become a street thug.

"Stop. Please stop," the figure yelped before finally getting up the courage to remove his rubber ghoul mask. "Fucking quit it!"

Once I realized it was Kenny on the ground, the impulse to intervene, which only seconds before had me actually running, completely disappeared. I also bitterly regretted tossing the Charleston Chew away. Kenny's tiny eyes flashed at me through the dark. He got to his feet, sneering at Denny but more at my son whose cardboard blows had almost certainly been less painful. Breathing with effort enough to sound animalistic, he brushed himself off.

"Why the fuck didn't you stop them?" he shrieked at me.

"Sorry Kenny," Denny said, regarding his weapon, which had been bent in the assault.

"It hurt," he screamed. "Why did you let them do that?"

"He came up behind us," David said, which earned him a deathly scowl from Kenny. "You scared us."

"Didn't you know who it was?" Kenny asked. "I was only kidding."

"I'm sorry Kenny," Denny said again.

"You shouldn't go around scaring people and sneaking up on them," I said. "Someone could get really hurt."

"You're not my mother," he shouted. "Leave me the fuck alone. You don't tell me what to do."

Kenny disappeared back into the night, muttering

more words I wished he wouldn't use around my son. I told the boys they'd better hurry up and get what we came all that way for. All evening, I'd been privy to excited tales of Dr. Morris, who lived at the far end of that street, giving away full-sized Snickers bars. By the time we got to his house, Halloween was, by town decree, officially over. The doctor's wife, a waif with dark hair who walked pigeon-toed, dumped the rest of her tray in each of the boy's bags. I even got two bars. The bounty on that end of town had proven well worth the trouble.

4.   The Only Person Really Even Trying to Ring My Bell

Few sounds broke the idle of a weekday afternoon, when I often took to hiding in my basement bunker, more disagreeably than the chime of the doorbell. The ringing phone I could and, when suspecting it was Mother on the other end, would ignore with near blissful ease but the doorbell was different. It announced that someone was actually there. It imparted duties on me that I strove to dispense with as quickly as possible. To make matters worse, the person who most often made use of our doorbell was as tenacious as she was unwelcome.

I dropped the book I'd been trying to read on the couch, pages open so I could pick up Henry James at the same frustrating place where I'd lost interest twice already, and lumbered upstairs. She kept pressing the button in faster and faster succession the longer it took me to get to the door, until it sounded like one on-going ring.

"Sarah," I said, her finger still on the button, the bell's ring echoing in the pit of my sanity. "What is it? I was just about to take a bath."

Tall and solid, she wore her hair in a severe crew cut that made her look androgynous. Her face was covered in acne. She must've been eighteen then and lived on the next street over with her father, Frank, a master electrician of enough local renown that when we moved into that house and needed work done, we knew we couldn't afford him.

"Bath," she said, her mouth forming the word crookedly. "You were there."

"What if I weren't? Would you have just gone on ringing that bell all day and night?"

"Ah…," she licked the spittle from the corners of her mouth and smiled, "there you are. I knew."

"How?" I asked.

"There you are," she said and laughed that deliriously empty laugh of hers.

I'd first encountered Sarah at the supermarket the summer of the year before. She was flanked by two boys. One wore a plastic helmet; the other was in a wheelchair. All were decked out in bright yellow t-shirts with *Special Olympics* written on them. I didn't see them in time, or I might've taken a more circuitous route to my car.

"Money please," the helmeted boy said, limping as he dragged his right leg over to me. His wrist and hand on that side of his body were curled inward and held close to his chest.

"This is a collection," Sarah said, her voice was guttural as though she had difficulty forming the words. "We're collectors."

"Special Olympics," said the boy in the wheelchair, his voice even more forced, making him almost impossible to understand.

"Collection, please," Sarah said and nudged the boy in the helmet, who shook his can at me.

I was embarrassed to only have a few coins and no small bills in my purse. They made a meager sound when I dropped them in.

"There you are near my house," Sarah said when I went to move past them. The boy in the wheelchair shook his can again.

"Yes, I think I've seen you on your bike. I'm Gloria."

They just stared at me. The one wearing the helmet started shaking his can more vigorously. The coins sloshed from one side to the other.

"I'm sorry that's all I have," I said. "I…uh…hope you all do well in the Olympics."

For a moment, it felt as though I'd been set upon by the world's most convincing team of shakedown artists.

"Thanking you," Sarah said.

"Maybe, I'll see you later," I said, "on your bike."

"There you go," she said.

I gave little thought to notion that my prediction could've been mistaken for an invitation until later the following week. I was pulling out to take David somewhere when she stopped on her bike at the end of the driveway, blocking our exit.

"Seeing you," she shouted, leaning down so that her massive head filled the rearview mirror.

Since then, she'd come by a couple of times a week to visit with me. Our conversations consisted mainly of my trying to make myself understood, while also trying to understand her. Overtime, I became accustomed to her way of talking and didn't have to ask her to repeat everything she said quite so often.

"You're going to wear out my doorbell," I said, checking quickly to make sure the latch that locked the screen door was tight. "It'll break from being rung so much."

"Wha?"

"My doorbell. I said you are going to break the poor thing by making it work so hard."

She barked out another laugh, head thrown back, face pulled tight in a rictus of joy. Never did a visit pass without my spine being chilled by that sound. As much as I found it unsettling, I also feared that she'd strain her ribcage. It seemed too unbridled to be completely natural.

"I. Um basketball," she said, breaking suddenly out of her mirth.

"You...what?"

"The team."

"You made the basketball team?"

"Yeah, huh."

"That's great."

"Come to a game?"

"You want me to come?"

"First one."

"The first one?"

"Yeah, huh."

"Well, we'll have to see when that is."

"Wha?"

"Do you know when it is? What day or date?"

"Wednesday."

"Next Wednesday?"

"Ah..." she opened her mouth but only cracked air escaped. She closed her eyes; her face went red. "Um...I..."

"Have your Dad call me and tell me the date."

"Dad'll call."

"Yep. Have him call me."

With that, I began to slowly close the door. Sarah stood there, staring at me, keeping balance as she sat astride her bike with one hand on the doorframe. She followed me the whole way, turning her head in motion with the door to keep me in her line of sight.

"Sorry Sarah. I've got to run. Got a...a...a roast in the oven."

"There you go," she said, backing away from the door on her bike. "Bye-bye."

I tried to return to my book but couldn't help wonder, as I often did, if Sarah explained to her father how brief our visits really were, for how long she had to ring the doorbell, which I then would accuse her of trying to break, and how I always told her something like I had a roast in the oven before shutting the door in her face. From time to time, I'd run into them together out in the world and he'd always make a point of thanking me for visiting with his daughter. He usually did so with his head down, as if trying to avoid looking at me. At first, I took it that he might've been embarrassed for Sarah but later came to consider he might've been hiding his disgust at the false friendliness that I served up, that our house was clearly barely big enough for a whole chime to be necessary to announce one's arrival and that I seemed to make a lot of roasts, be prone to taking a lot of baths, and be generally in the middle of doing a lot of things.

Whenever I told Caroline and Marge about Sarah's visits, they commended me in a way that made me feel useless. They agreed they were happy to be working and neither would know what to do with someone like Sarah, speaking of her as though she were some asylum seeker who'd mistaken my home for an embassy. Caroline even went so far as to admit that "retarded people creeped her out." I secretly found her admission of that fact nobler than my pretend friendship with Sarah, but still took the opportunity to act shocked at what she'd said. My eyes went wide, my head recoiled as though disbelieving the monster that had just reared up before me.

Once, I even went so far as to claim I was happy not to have a job so that I could spend time with Sarah. I claimed it to be as worthwhile as any job I could imagine. "Any job," I even repeated to more hammer home the point that I found their jobs utterly frivolous by comparison. Then, still riding a lustrous tide of self-righteousness, I rounded up my summation with: "The world needs reminding that people like Sarah are here, too." It must've been as convincing as I allowed myself to hope my performances with Sarah were, because Caroline blushed and shrank a little from the table. Marge made the sign of the cross over herself and bowed her head in deference to me.

It was all total bullshit, of course. I wanted a job desperately. Once a week or so, I logged onto my profiles on various job search sites. Most of the positions I was matched with required skills that I didn't quite possess: experience with payrolls, experience dealing with a diverse customer base, experience negotiating the sale of small arms. Experience with filing and answering the phone seemed my best bet, so I tended to zero in on those jobs.

I appreciated that the term secretary had been replaced by administrative assistant, but it didn't make any of those jobs sound exciting. But look, I told myself, you don't bust out of your cell, kill a guard, then a hostage, and scale a wall only to complain about the getaway car. Marge was a receptionist in a doctor's office for Chrissakes; surely, I would one day find a position of equal or possibly even greater esteem.

I strove to put together a cover letter that indicated my getting a nearly perfect score on my LSATs many years ago was impressive and would be useful. I thought of it as a way to subtly indicate that I could handle filing paperwork and answering the telephone. I tried and tried and tried and somehow the letter never came out right. It always sounded like I was bragging or desperate. Both true. It never sounded like I really wanted those mindless office jobs. Also somewhat true. When I was younger, I used to wonder how I would know when I was old. I thought that maybe it would be when I graduated from college or law school or had been made partner at some firm, but years later I realized it was when I knew my lies would do me no good, when even I could smell the stink of BS on them. Truly, that's the symbol of having arrived at adulthood.

Still, I submitted my credentials to any place that would have me, except none of them did. Sometimes, I got an e-mail back thanking me for my interest and promising to keep my resume on file. Most of the time, though, I'd just be ghosted by the position, the listing would just disappear, leaving me to picture someone like dutiful Marge enjoying a light lunch at her desk and reading bible passages as she ran her fingers over her gold cross and high church hair.

Back then, I still had to admit to myself that Caroline, the stewardess, was in a different stratosphere career-wise. I, after all, had somehow made it that far in life without undergoing the training necessary to point both behind me and to the sides to indicate the escape routes, all while wearing an empty smile that barely hid my contempt for mankind.

After nearly an hour of having been yet again sufficiently chastened and nearly sufficiently humiliated by my fruitless attempts to join the ranks of the city's administrative assistants, I shut down the computer and slid the keyboard back into the desk. The whirring sound of the little engine inside sped up before it stopped completely. As I pushed my chair back, I saw some throw pillows stacked up beneath it. It was one of the crawl spaces David liked to make. He specialized in finding those boy-shaped spots where he could fashion himself a kind of sanctorum. Laying atop a blanket, its pages splayed open, was one of his books. I slid from the chair to my knees and picked it up.

The Beetlewomen backed away. Each of their eight eyes shut tight against the glaring might of Greylor's sword. He continued, in his manly way, to walk towards them. He displayed his weapon. Its blade glinted where it had not been stained by their mucousy green blood.

Queen Zelar screeched at her army to hold their line. She told them to be courageous in the face of Greylor's bravery. She scuttled on her many legs. She charged him. He raised his sword. He drove it beneath her lower jaw. That terrible mandible spewed blood. The rest of the Beetlewomen scuttled away. Their cries of fear echoed through the system of underground tunnels.

Greylor turned to Hucebuse and in triumph said, "The Beetlewomen have learned a valuable lesson. Their future is not here. They must seek their preservation elsewhere. Men! The kingdom remains ours!"

5. Holiday from the Expected

Thanksgiving morning's bitter air reminded me that winter would soon be settling on the valley and that I had wasted another year, mostly locked up inside the house, hiding from the world. More and more, I was becoming a prisoner to the falsely romantic notion that solitude was good for me.

I stepped carefully on the ice-covered walk, holding a platter of deviled eggs. Gail had made me promise to bring them. Her current boyfriend, George, had raved about them after the Fourth of July cookout we had. When he hadn't accompanied her to David's birthday party, I'd assumed they were on the outs. I could never decide if it was reassuring or terrifying to learn that relationships could be as complicated for a widow well past middle-age as they were to the average school girl. Apparently, the breaking up and making up, the joy, too often followed by disappointment and sorrow, never really ended. Unless you were lucky enough to find a person whom you truly could not live without. At one time, I didn't have to try too hard to remember when Daryl was that person for me. But as the days, weeks and years passed, the gulf between us widened more and more, until I assumed or maybe even hoped that one morning I'd wake to find I could no longer see even the outlines of that past life.

Daryl shuffled ahead of me, a twelve-pack of beer in each hand like two tiny suitcases. Somehow balancing the tray in one hand, I opened the car door for him. He climbed into the back, telling David he should sit up front.

"I'll be backseat Dad for Thanksgiving," he said.

"Here, hold this," I said, tapping the tray against his window, "so that the eggs don't spill all over the car."

"A please would be nice." Daryl lowered the window and took the tray with a put-upon-husband sigh.

"Thank you, honey," I said to him, catching sight of David cringing at us in the rearview mirror. Whether it was at my obvious insincerity or just his typical revulsion at any sign of affection at all between us, no matter how hollow, I wasn't sure.

NPR had a program on about the area's native tribes that celebrated the first Thanksgiving with the early settlers. David started talking about having learned about them in school. Daryl seemed to be listening to him in his own distracted way. He murmured at the right times, asked a question or two. I stayed tuned in to them only long enough to ascertain that Daryl was doing a fair enough job to relieve me of the need to pay any attention to my son. The sun was bright, the sky a brittle blue with broken clouds floating across it like tufts of torn cotton.

Most of the trees along the road were bare. There was never that much color that time of year anyway. The leaves still clinging to the naked branches were closer to black than any autumnal brown. A light coating of snow blanketed many of the fields in much the same way it had on my first trip up there, on cold April day, all those years ago.

Back then, I was struggling to get to the end of my first year of law school and on my way to meet the mother of a man whom I didn't yet know well enough to realize was not well-suited for me. I guess the one positive about the state of my life at that time was that I was still too numb from the tragedy whose wave had just broken and peeled back over us to be all that anxious about meeting her. He hadn't yet told her that we'd been talking about moving in together. Maybe he didn't think it would actually come to pass. I know I didn't. I was just a bundle of raw nerves at that time, as likely to start crying as I was to go on breathing. We never talked about that period much after it was over but I can't help but think he saw I needed someone to help hold me together. Perhaps, Daryl slipped into the trap as stumblingly as I did. At the time, moving in together seemed not just a reasonable course of action but the only one that made sense. Daryl had been there for me when I'd needed him most. We'd just be relocating the 'there.'

Daryl had squeezed my hand the whole way on that trip, and a kind sort of light shone expectantly in his eyes. He couldn't wait for me to meet Gail. She was so independent, he'd told me. He'd added that she'd redecorated the house completely as a way to recover from her husband's death. The exact appeal of this fact was never apparent to me. I suppose he was trying to equate his mother with the kind of strong woman I was still trying to pretend to be, the kind of woman Daryl was always telling me I was. The kind of woman, it would, in fact, take me years to really become.

I'd drunk so much lousy train coffee on the long ride north that by the time we made it to Gail's house my stomach was upset. I spent the better part of the afternoon in the bathroom. I still had enough pride about such things back then to feel embarrassed for myself. As I sat there on the basement throne, cringing at every uncouth sound escaping from my body, it all seemed like a passing phase; not just the overstimulating effects of the caffeine but everything that had happened in the months leading up to that. Surely, I would soon leave Daryl behind as a youthful mistake and fully resume the life I'd planned for myself. I just needed him to be there a little while longer or so I hoped.

By the time we turned off the highway and down a winding road that led into the little town center near Gail's house, David had stopped reading the book he'd brought along. Daryl was asleep. With no other traffic around, I ran a red light. David yelled at me about it, which woke up Daryl. He smiled at me from the rear-view mirror, still hoping, I guess, that this family thing was going to come together for us.

Gail greeted us with such a big grin on her face that I feared she and George might've just finished what she once referred to as their 'weekly.' I had to act fast to get the tray of eggs out of the way before she engaged me in a bone-crushing hug. She took the tray from me and gave her son and grandson less effusive, one-armed embraces. The whole time, her awful, little dog was yapping away at our feet.

"Fluffy, quiet," she said.

"Hi Fluffy," Daryl said, crouching down to pet the thing.

"I know George will be happy for the eggs and beer," she said. "He's downstairs getting ready to watch football. Why don't you boys go down and join him? Make it a threesome."

"Ahhh, I hate football," David announced in a whine, flinching at the dog. He slouched away, his arms hanging from his body.

"I know, Davey," Gail said. "But it's Thanksgiving, the one day a year when as Americans, it's our duty to pretend to like football."

"Why?" he asked.

"Because it's traditional," Gail replied.

"But why, what makes it traditional?"

"Come on, champ," Daryl said, coming to his mother's rescue. "You can ask Georgie about it. He'll be happy to answer your questions."

"I don't think I'll have that many," David said. "Are you going to watch football with us, Grandma?"

"No. I can't. Your mother and I have to prepare the meal," she said and handed the tray to David. "Now, take this downstairs and mind your Dad."

Gail was old-fashioned enough to think it ridiculous that I would want to or even –barf—be allowed to watch the game with the boys rather than take orders from her in the kitchen. It was either that or she had the most passive-aggressive style of dragooning people of all time. Not that I had an inclination to join the men downstairs. I didn't need to watch my husband drink in front of the television. I could have easily done that at home. Daryl wasn't even interested in the game per se just getting drunk as the blue glow washed over him, killing brain cells on two fronts as it were.

No one with any sense of self-preservation can actually watch an entire football game. From what I've come to understand, it's really a four- hour block of commercials with some light and mildly amusing violence sprinkled in. The fact that men watch it quite willingly is utterly baffling. But then when it comes to that sport, I fear much of the country suffers from concussion-like symptoms.

My father only ever turned the game on to get away from mother, if only for the duration of a Sunday afternoon. She would act insulted by the very idea of football being watched in her home. So naturally, there came a time when I started joining him in the living room. One nice thing about football on television is that it's so easy to ignore if you aren't at all interested. I'd normally have a book with me and would find a sunny spot on the carpet. Daddy would read his paper, glancing now and again at the television as though trying to decide if it was worth figuring out what exactly was going on.

It was the only day when he did not wear a suit. Even in a sweater and jeans, he was still better dressed than most of the men I've known. When I think him of taking it easy, of what it meant to see him relaxed, it's those Sunday afternoons that spring to mind. Daddy in his chair, smiling and calm, just enjoying a few hours when no one made any demands on him.

By the time dinner was ready, George, in accordance with a kind of national directive, had gotten good and drunk. He almost passed out onto his plate. His head drooped, silverware still in hand, a light snore escaping from his nose. Fluffy the dog regarded him with a disappointed look. When he snapped back to full consciousness, his right hand splattered down into his mashed potatoes. Gail was having trouble pretending she didn't notice what was going on.

Almost on impulse, I shot Daryl a look meant to inspire fear. He smiled with agreeable meekness at me, then swallowed whatever was left in his can but didn't dare to rise from the table to get himself another. I accepted that as sufficient surrender, mainly because I was only pantomiming my disgust for Gail, trying to make it look like I cared too, which I did but only on her behalf. No one really wants to be made to look like a fool by her man.

By that Thanksgiving, I'd just about given up saying

anything to Daryl about his drinking. And, I guess, it'd gotten better rather than worse by that time. I wouldn't begrudge him a holiday or his right to get a little drunk. I just wished he wouldn't do it in front of his son.

When dinner was over, Gail surprised me by saying George would be helping her with the dishes. I lingered in the living room off the kitchen, sipping coffee while my boys, perhaps noting this unusual turn of events in the labor distribution and fearing they might be enlisted next, quickly made their way downstairs. I stretched out on the couch, trying to ignore the bitter taste of the reheated coffee. From the kitchen, I heard Gail spitting whispers, then the heavy sound of metal being dropped, perhaps on George's head. The tension soon became impossible to totally contain. I wasn't even trying to eavesdrop.

"In front of my family," suddenly Gail's screech burst forth like a wounded bird seeking shelter.

George mumbled something in return.

"Of all days," she said, clearly not caring who could hear, "I have one day, one big holiday meal with them."

"What about Easter?" George asked, his voice rising now too.

"George, do you want me to slap you? Because you're acting like an ass."

"What?" he asked, laughing. "Come on, Gail…"

I didn't wait around for the slap. I couldn't be sure it wasn't coming. I didn't think she would but Daryl had made passing remarks about her temper over the years. She was less than half his size and he'd spent his whole life living in fear of her. The carpeting on the stairs allowed me to make a relatively quiet getaway. It wasn't until I was almost at the bottom where the dimness of the stairwell gave way to the blue glow of the big TV screen that I heard Daryl snoring away. He was seated in the mission rocking chair. It'd been his stepfather's. When he first started bringing me there, I noticed how hesitant Daryl was to sit in it.

A beer can was squeezed between his thighs. I gave some serious thought to taking the can from where it was and pouring the beer out over his head to wake him up. His mouth hung slack, his ruddy face beet red. There's your husband, your life partner, a masochistic imp inside of me said, as though I needed reminding. In the interest of keeping him from spilling beer all over the cherished chair, I, in an act that I never found particularly savory and avoided whenever I could, reached between his thighs. With a light tug, I successfully extracted the can. His eyes snapped wide but only for a second, and then he slacked his tongue around and resumed snoring.

"David, are you down here?" I asked, now holding the can aloft. I was again possessed by an overwhelming urge to dump it over Daryl's head.

"Over here, Mom," he said, from a darkened corner.

He'd fashioned a reading space for himself beneath the old rolltop desk. It was still closed and locked up tight. Daryl's stepfather, Ray, had hidden the key to it and died rather suddenly without having told anyone of its whereabouts. Gail could've hired a locksmith or really with a screwdriver and a bit of effort opened it herself, but she never did. The idea that there might be secrets there had intrigued me for a time during the early years with Daryl. He didn't like talking about the desk, a reluctance that seemed borne more of annoyance at my insistent questioning than any real fear about finding out what was inside. Both he and Gail seemed to content to let Ray take whatever was in there to his grave. It's also possible that neither of them really cared that much.

I must admit, I realize now I never really knew enough about their lives with Ray to have any insight. Maybe that was what I hoped to find there, maybe if I had found something hidden about my husband, everything could've been different. I might've seen the side to Daryl that I'd decided was missing. Probably not though. By the end, we were well past the point where a family secret would've pulled us back together.

Beneath this possible repository of family wounds, David had pillows stacked under his head. They'd come from the broken day bed that sat in the corner nearby. He'd taped a flashlight to the underside of the desk. *Lands of Power and Dust Book III* was open in his hands.

"Greylor's onto bigger and more terrible foes than the Queen of the Beetlewomen, I take it," I said squatting down near him and taking a sip of thigh-warmed beer. It'd gone flat but at least dulled the bitter taste left by the coffee.

"No. She's back. Her jaw is bionic now. It makes her practically invincible."

"Really? That sounds like bad news for Greylor's kingdom."

"Actually, it turns out it used to be the Beetlewomen's Kingdom."

"It was?"

"Yeah, the whole first section of book three is about the time before The Great Frost when the Beetlewomen were forced underground. They used to roam the kingdom free and thought of it as theirs."

"Huh. I didn't see that coming, not after he'd defeated them and made that big speech to Hucebuse," I said, taking another sip.

"How come you're drinking that?" he asked, pointing at the can.

"Your father warmed it up for me."

"Are we leaving soon, then?" he asked.

"Yeah, start getting ready. I'll wake up your father."

He crawled out of his spot, handed me the book and put the pillows back where he'd found them. Then, he turned off the flashlight but left it rigged up. I was going to say something but liked the idea of Gail finding it there and wondering what'd happened. I just handed him his book back instead. David looked at me for a second then at the book, then at me again, squinting.

"Mom?" he asked. "How come you know so much about Book Two?"

"I found it under the desk at home. You like them so much I thought it might be good."

"I thought you said it was too male, too macho for you."

"I did but maybe we shouldn't judge what we don't really know about."

He reached up to touch the top of my head. A gesture so odd that I had to keep from flinching as he tousled my hair.

"What was that for?" I asked.

"It's the unexpected things about you that make me happy," he said, sounding certain that he knew it would make me laugh.

I did. We did together. By the desk in the corner, while Daryl snored away in the chair, the two of us laughed until we shook. In that moment, I seriously considered leaving my husband there and just going home with David. I don't think he would've complained. Gail though, whose shrieking could now be heard from up-stairs, was another matter.

6. Membership in the Gasket Fitters' Union

David made a hard turn after pulling the shopping cart free, barely looking where he was going. Luckily, two elderly easy riders on their Rascals moved quickly enough to avoid a collision. The first of them, a rotund woman with a selection of Hostess snacks in her basket, had the temerity to say something about my son being fat under her breath. Rather than respond, I gave her scooter a once over while sneering and shaking my head.

There were cords of wood stacked up just inside the sliding door. I placed a bundle in the cart just as I did every year, usually around the same time, when it smelled the freshest. One of the reasons I let Daryl talk me into buying that house was his claim that the wood stove would make the house cozy during the winter and keep our heating costs down. I mean, the man actually broke out paper and pencil and did some math to show me. It would save enough, or so he claimed his calculations demonstrated, to allow me to think about going back to school sooner than we'd planned. More than ten years later, the stove had yet to be lit.

A bad gasket inside the door prevented it from shutting tightly, which made lighting a fire a hazard. How we missed that, I don't know. It probably had something to do with the fact that Daryl was the one to give it the closest inspection when we saw the place. I blamed myself for being too willing to accept any idea that would help me get back into school sooner. Back then, it seemed like my going back was so inevitable, we didn't really need to make any specific preparations. It was surely going take shape as a result of the resolve I had to finish law school as I'd planned. Lamentably, that force of will seemed to be something I gave up even less begrudgingly than my name when I got married.

"What's that for?" David asked.

"Maybe we'll get the stove going this year," I said.

"I thought it didn't work."

"Your father's going to fix it."

My annual wood purchase was always followed by Daryl's annual display of fake enthusiasm for fixing it. Each year it was, "yeah, yeah, let's finally get that thing up and running" then later "I'll get on that, like, next week." Sure Daryl. Next week. Our lives were always going to get better next week.

I bagged some beans and asparagus. It'd always been such a chore to get my son to eat vegetables, until he found out that asparagus made his urine stink. Boys are so gross. I used that to my advantage as much as I could understand it. On our way out of the produce section, Captain Dave wheeled the cart into my back. The metal of the undercarriage crunched painfully against the bone just above my heel. When I turned around, I found he had his nose in a volume of *Lands of Power and Dust*.

"David, what did I say about leaving that at home?" I asked, not yelling but not minding how loud I was, either. "Watch where you're going and put that goddamn book down."

"I want to read this once more before I lend it to someone."

"Who are you lending it to? Someone who won't give it back?"

"Just someone Mom. Okay?"

"Put it away."

"I just wanted to stay at home," he moaned.

I snatched the book from him and threw it in the

cart. It slapped against the wood.

"Don't you dare," I snarled, when he tried to retrieve it. He pulled his hand back as though a beast had snapped at him, which wasn't entirely inaccurate.

"Why couldn't I just've stayed home?" he whined, the sort of petulant childish whine that gives that tone such a bad reputation.

"You can't stay home alone. Besides, you needed to get out of the house, get the stink blown off of you."

"Why? I want to stay at home. I can. I'm not a little kid."

The shopping trip went into a pretty steep decline after that. At times, I had to practically drag David along. He'd wander off, returning with items that were not on my list nor would I ever purchase. Down one aisle, he tried to sneak a jar of Nutella into the cart. I told him to put it back, not that I wasn't tempted. He tried the same with some sugary cereal featuring a cross-eyed cartoon bird. Then, he tried to tuck a jar of marshmallow fluff into the cart's front corner as I was searching the shelves for the store brand peanut butter.

"Don't you do that," I said, clenching my teeth so that it was like the words vibrated out of my body.

Moving in slow motion, he climbed up on the side of the cart and began slowly lowering the fluff down. The grin on his face made me want to slap him all the way up that aisle and down the next.

"David Raymond Hytner, if you put that in the cart," I said at a volume that in retrospect should've been a little more embarrassing, "I will cut off your fucking hand."

A rare time in which I felt that despicable, violent word was called for. David had never heard me use it. He looked so shocked that I worried he might start crying, but instead slinked away and put the fluff back on the shelf behind him.

The ride home proved agreeably quiet. David tried a whispered protest or two but I shot him the look that let him know my threat was as real as it could've been. When we pulled into the driveway, Sarah was there on the front porch to greet us. A gentle snow had been falling that afternoon, and she'd been waiting long enough that it'd begun to accumulate on the frame and rear rack of her bike.

I hit the button and the garage door went up, offering a full view of the many projects Daryl had only half finished. Most of it was dominated by some kind of canoe which he had begun working on with great excitement the winter before. He'd claimed that we would like where we lived more if we took greater advantage of the natural surroundings. Now, what there was of it sat beneath an old bedsheet, its skeletal metal nose poking out as if still sniffing possibilities that would never be realized. Next to that was a pallet of bricks which in the very distant past were to be the foundation for a fire pit and large outdoor oven. All of this made pulling the car into the garage something of a delicate operation. I'd tapped the passenger-side mirror against the garage frame hard enough to knock it crooked once or twice.

"There you are," Sarah said once we emerged from the car. She stood with one leg off her bike, leaning with her arm against the garage door.

"Hi Sarah," David said.

"There you are, Davey," she said.

Sarah seemed to be the only person who could still get away with calling him that to his face. I don't know if he thought protesting would be useless due to her condition or if he genuinely didn't mind hearing it come from her. In any case, he always made me proud by being nice and polite to her. Sometimes being nice and polite is all that's really required.

"Does your dad know you're out in the snow and cold?" I asked.

"He says 'Sarah, you like snow,'" she said, blinking the snowflakes from her eyelashes. "Tell you about my game."

"Your basketball game?"

"Yeah."

"I'm so sorry I wasn't there. Your dad never called me with the date. Did you tell him to call me, Sarah?"

"Yeah."

"You did?"

"There you are," she said.

"Make sure to tell him to call me."

"We scored," she said. "We won."

"You did?"

"By seven, forty points."

"By how many?"

She blinked again, this time slowly, like a drowsy turtle.

"Well, congratulations," I said. My feet were growing cold. I'd worn shoes rather than my boots. "We should get these groceries inside so they don't get too chilled."

"Supper," she said. "I go better home."

"Okay," I said and could've hugged her, so great was the relief I felt at her quick departure. "Do you want a hat for the ride?"

"There I go. I have hats at home."

"Bye Sarah," David said.

With some effort, she rolled away up the driveway through the snow, her tires caked with white. I wanted to call after her, give her a ride home, but I didn't. It was cold. I wanted to get inside. David stood by the trunk, waiting to do his duty. Between the two of us, we managed to get all the bags into the house in one trip.

"Where does this go?" he asked, cradling the cord of wood in his arms.

"The metal basket next to the stove."

"Is Dad really going to fix it?" he asked.

Had I become what I always said I would never be? What I had only joked about turning into because it seemed like such a horrible fate? Had the fact that I was totally and undeniably a housewife turned me into the kind of person, the kind of woman that waited for some man to do things for her? How had I ingested such a virus? Had I not been reading trashy magazines with enough ironic detachment? Had I been allowing myself to look forward a little too much to the *Afternoon Hour of Justice: Relationship Court with Judge Darlene* followed by *Not So Small Claims*? Had all of it, all the little bits of the stereotypical housewife lifestyle that I'd taken on as a joke begun to have a cumulative effect over the years, until finally I'd become what I thought I was mocking?

"No," I said to my son. "No. You know what, David? I'm going to fix it and you're going to help me."

"I don't want to help do that. I want to finish my book."

"Let the power and dust settle and go put on some of your grubby clothes. This could turn out to be a dirty job."

On a forgotten shelf above Daryl's workbench in the

garage, I found the items he'd purchased for the job long ago wrapped up in a plastic bag covered by a thick coating of silvery dust. Inside of it, I found a rubber tube folded into a figure eight secured by a twist tie and a plastic tube of something called Oven-See-Ment. Helpfully, the back of the tube had some instructions complete with tiny illustrations regarding the task at hand. There appeared to be only seven steps, including the unillustrated final one which instructed one not to use the stove for at least 120 minutes after the job was completed. That seemed like something the gifted David and I could handle. As for the other six…well, I was going to prove something.

Back inside, I found David kneeling before the stove. He wore an old pair of jeans and a sweatshirt with a football on it. Ah, an ode to the moments of the odd pleasure one takes when her kid listens to her and complains with only his overly rigid posture as a sign of protest. I handed him the tube, which he began to squeeze.

"No," I said, reaching over to flip over the tube in his hands. "Read me the instructions."

"Is that all I'm going to get to do?" he whined. "This's why I don't like helping."

"No. We can trade off. You want to scrape the gasket track?"

"What's that?"

"You'll see."

"Can I squeeze this stuff on when it's time?" he asked studying the tube. "Step five."

"We'll see. Just read me step one right now."

"Why do you get to do step one?"

"I'm the foreman, David. This's my job."

"But if we trade off you'll be on the odd steps and I won't get to do the squeezing."

See. My gifted son. I knew something I wouldn't have minded squeezing just then.

"David…." I said.

"Read instructions and hand over the tools," he moaned, "it's all I ever get to do."

"Here," I said, grabbing the tube from him and reading from the instructions. "Pull out the existing length of gasket."

David scooted up to the oven door on his knees. At first, he opened the door just wide enough to stick his hand inside. Then, he opened it as wide as it would go.

"It's that stuff inside on the door. That puffy black stuff," I said and traced the shape around the track.

His tongue emerged from between his teeth, gently perched there like the head of a pink bird, a sign of how seriously he was going to take his task. He pinched the gasket and began to pull. It had rotted through and came away in bits, crumbling to the floor like thick pieces of ash. The more he tore away, the more his face tightened. As always, I wanted to tell him to reel his tongue in so that he didn't bite it off, but knew that might've put at risk the fragile sense of collaboration that was being born there in that neglected corner of the upstairs living room.

"Now, I'll scrape it clean," I said.

"I want to scrape."

"What's the worst thing to be when working with people?" I asked.

"A know-it-all, do-it-all chauvinist," he said in sing-song.

"That's right. See this?" I asked, running my finger along the track from where he had removed the gasket. "We've got to get all the little bits still stuck to the track cleaned off or the new gasket might not fit."

"The new gasket," he said leaning in to run his fingers inside the groove. "What should we scrape with? It says to use a flat-headed screwdriver or small paint scraper. You want me to get one?"

"No. You can stay here and read the next step."

It'd been years since David and I had last worked on anything together. Back then, the adhesive was Elmer's Glue, and macaroni and colored cardboard were involved. As I left him kneeling there, reading the tube, I thought maybe his upright posture had nothing to do with resistance, maybe I was imbuing him with that elusive self-confidence he seemed to lack. That was something Daryl had struggled to do for him, so why should I wait for a man to do that, to do anything. It was even faintly possible that I actually might prove better at it.

Had Daryl taken up fixing the stove as he'd promised, poor David would've been relegated to handing him tools and listening to how important it was to be careful. Daryl didn't think the boy could be trusted to really do anything because he was awkward and clumsy. He'd told me as much. At times, Daryl seemed frustrated that his son was not more like him, wasn't handy and manly. He often claimed that David's personality was something he struggled to really understand.

Oh, the sheer length of the list of all the things that fell into that category.

From the drawer below the workbench, I found a paint-flecked screwdriver. I also had the foresight to grab an X-Acto knife to cut the tip off the tube of oven cement. Still not sure if I could trust David with that part of the job, I tucked it in my back pocket. If our son made a mess or otherwise managed to botch the job, Daryl would be on offense in the *I Told You So* game for longer than I could bear. Giving David confidence was one thing, allowing my husband to have the advantage in our life of war was quite another.

"Here we go," I said, and knelt next to him to begin scraping.

"What's this?" he asked, fingering the X-Acto knife that must have come unstuffed from my back pocket, when I knelt down.

"It's for cutting the tip off the tube of glue."

"Are you going to let me do it?" he asked, sounding as though he suspected he knew the answer.

"I thought you could…supervise me doing it."

"Aw, come on Mom. It's the only fun part of this job. Please let me do it. I promise I'll be careful."

"Do you really promise to be careful?"

"Yes. I said so."

"And not make a mess?"

"Yes," he said. "God!"

"Good enough for me. Now let me scrape."

David was so anxious for me to finish that I could feel him watching. He ran his finger inside the track when I was done with it, making sure it was clean. When he found a bit, he scratched away at it with his finger. I shooed him away and went back to work with the screwdriver.

"Do I glue now?" he asked.

"No. First we have to fit the new gasket."

"Without glue? It won't stick."

"See here," I said pushing the treasured tube under his nose, "it says we have to make sure it fits before we glue it."

"Yeah, I guess we should make sure. Dad says to always measure things twice to get them right," David said, then smiled and let his face fall into the sort of mouth-breathing slackness that best characterized his father.

"David," I yelped unable to keep a slight chuckle from creeping into my voice. "Don't do that."

"What?"

"Pull that face. That's not nice."

"But he looks like that some times. Especially, when he's doing things like this. I think it's the face he makes when he's thinking."

"It's not nice."

"It's just weird," David said. "He looks so stupid when he's supposedly thinking."

I couldn't argue with him. After we made sure the gasket would fit, I let him do the gluing but cut off the tip of the tube myself. Fittingly for all my worries about my son, I managed to nick my own finger in the process. I put a Band-Aid on the wound as he squeezed the glue into the guide track. Then, carefully, we tucked the new gasket in together.

Later that night, I got a fire going. Daryl acted un-impressed with our work when he got dropped off back at home from his day out drinking and retreated down-stairs. David and I sat side by side on the couch upstairs, reading and smiling at the fire roaring away inside the newly fixed oven.

7. Down to a Pack a Decade

I'd been sitting there with my coat on long enough that I'd started to sweat, even though the fire I'd made had long since burned itself out. I listened for noise from David's room down the hall but all was quiet. He was still at the whimpering stage, when I'd left him with ice balled up in a wash cloth. Maybe he'd cried himself out and had gone to sleep.

It had all started less than an hour before. I was sitting there, enjoying a fire, reading the cover story in *People Magazine* about some reality show starlet who'd claimed to have overcome her battles with anorexia, even though the photo spread revealed a tanned, air-brushed bikini body complete with a visible rib cage. Before the cold breath of early winter hit me from the opening front door, I heard the irritating sound of my son crying. By then, my initial response to that sound was pure teeth-gnashing irritation. He'd been outside playing with his friends, which always put his fragile emotional state at risk.

When he'd first stuck his head in the door, I saw a small triangle-shaped wound weeping blood, just below his eye. In that moment, I became what I thought of as the perfect embodiment of motherhood: Mom. Without pausing long enough to hear the tinnitus that was my own mother's voice imploring me not to coddle the boy and make him weak, I was on my knees wrapping my crying son in my arms and holding him close. Shocked by this display, David ceased his crying for a second and went limp before putting his arms around my neck.

"What happened?" I asked.

"K…K…Kenny threw…threw a snowball at me."

"Is that it? A snowball? What else?" I asked, perturbed to find a less grievous injustice had been inflicted than his wound seemed to indicate.

"We were having a snowball fight…."

"Oh, honey. What did I say about fighting? Even play fighting and how it…"

"Mom, I'm not talking about violence in the wider world," he screeched, his mouth thick with mucus. "Listen to me. We were being careful. It was just for fun. Denny and Kenny against me and Jon and I was aiming for Denny with a big one and hit Kenny instead."

"Sweetie, you shouldn't be aiming for anyone," I said, though I really wanted to tell him "nice one."

"By accident, it hit him right…" he said, pointing to his crotch.

"Oh, David," I said, sounding far more delighted than I should've allowed myself. "That's why I say no fighting, not even if you think you're just playing around."

"Then Kenny said…" Now his wailing came in full force, reducing his words to a bunch of unintelligible, water-logged syllables. He squinted as though in pain; tears soaked his cheeks. I released him and led him over to the couch, giving one of its cushions an inviting pat.

"Kenny said what, honey?"

"He said he was going to get me with a real snowball not like the faggy one I'd thrown at him. So he took," sob, sob, sob, "an icicle," more sobs, more sobs, "broke a piece off the end of it," sobbing, sobbing, more sobbing punctuated by an attempt to catch his breath, "and made this snowball around it."

"Which he then threw at you?" I sighed.

"Mmmmm….hmmmm…."

"Okay. Come on, let's get something for that wound so it doesn't swell up."

"Denny and Jonny just laughed at me when I screamed but it hurt."

"Sorry honey. I'm sure it really hurt. Anyone would be crying."

"Kenny threw it really hard. We weren't throwing them that hard. We were just playing."

"I'm sure he did."

After I'd rolled up a handful of ice cubes in a kitchen towel and led him to his room, the motherly feeling began to shift inside of me. Holding my sobbing son would no longer quench whatever it was that now burned. I wanted to commit a violent act against the boy who'd hurt my son. I wanted to give a certain shit-smelling neighbor kid a paddling with a splintery piece of wood.

Putting on my coat and hat, I had one hand on the front doorknob when something made me pause. Surely, this was going too far. I'd apparently suppressed the deepest of my motherly instincts for so long that when they finally emerged they were distorted and slightly monstrous. Let David deal with his playmates on his own, Mother would've advised that's how leaders are made. She likely would've warned me against fighting his battles for him and worried that I was raising a tattler, a squealer, the kind of character who gets shivved during the first act of a prison drama.

As I sat sweating through my layers of clothing, I experienced the most serious craving for a cigarette I'd felt in years. I'd stopped smoking the first time I'd gotten pregnant and kept it up, right through the second time with David. In fact, I hadn't really smoked for pretty much the whole of his childhood. Every once in a great while, I'd sneak one out from a very old, very stale pack hidden in a never-used fondue pot, which sat in the cabinet above the fridge. Those cigarettes must've been over a decade old.

When I'd first met Daryl, I was inhaling nearly a pack a day. During my first semester at law school, I worked part-time as a filing monkey for some ambulance chasers at a midtown law firm. The place was cramped and had either recently been an apartment or still was. To break up the monotony, I'd gotten into the habit of taking a cigarette break with this guy named Doug. He was in the same position I was, doing something that caused us to slowly lose all respect for a profession that we were paying gobs and gobs of money for the chance to join. We'd stand out on the stoop, inhaling one Camel after another, bitching about school, about the numbing mundanity of our work, about the general stupidity of the world. Back then, I was still young enough to mistake an actual compromising of one's ethics for ironically doing so. I'd only lasted at that job for a couple of weeks but the smoking habit lingered.

One cold day later that semester, while hanging out at his place, Daryl and I had our first real fight. Though we'd known each other for only a couple of months, our conversations had already started to become work. Daryl seemed to be forever casting about to find something we could discuss without one or the other of us getting bored or lost or both. I wasn't sure what point he'd been trying to make that day, but he ventured something idiotic and sexist about women artists. And no, Daryl, I did not keep an exact inventory of them all, as that would've required me to transform into some sort of human computing cloud. As I reached for the pack in my coat, I experienced the most burning desire to tell him he was too dumb, too unfeeling to ever be a real sculptor or woodworker or whatever artsy path that was surely leading to some great and final nowhere, but instead just sat there fuming as he went on apologizing, trying to make me understand whatever execrable theory he had about how female artists were "feelers" rather than "thinkers." Deciding I could take no more of his theories, of his talk, of that terrible basement apartment that smelled of mold, I announced I had to have a smoke.

Daryl didn't smoke, never had, but he didn't mind that I did. Who knows how he really felt about it. Even with the vantage point offered by all the intervening years, I still have no idea what he thought about me back then or how he saw our lives fitting together. I suppose he thought of me as his girlfriend and later his wife and that those generic labels were enough for him to recognize his place in our relationship.

He told me that I could smoke inside and handed me an empty soda can to flick ashes into. I told him that I wanted to be alone. He mentioned that it was cold outside. My response was to silently put on my coat and hat while glaring at him. I let myself out and stood smoking next to the trash cans that sat sentry outside his apartment door.

He was right. It was cold; the wind cut bitterly into me. The smoke came from my mouth in thick, galloping clouds. I pulled my cap over my ears and put a glove on the hand that was not holding the cigarette. One thought kept repeating itself; that I should just leave, walk to the subway, down the stairs, hop on the train, go back to my apartment, smoke one more cigarette and then call him and tell him it was over. That it'd been fun but there was no use continuing whatever it was we thought we were doing.

I started to walk away. One step after the other assured me that I was doing the right thing. One step after the other measured my then-brief time with Daryl. I thought it'd been almost worth it. It had been fun enough. But it was over. I was free, for a moment, I was free. It wasn't hard to leave. It would've been easy. At least for a second, it felt that way.

Before I got to the end of the block, I heard the gate creak behind me. And then Daryl was asking me where I was going. Before I could answer, he said he was sorry. He said that he'd made a comment that he thought would impress me. I turned around and there he was, halfway down the sidewalk in his socks, no coat, shivering, saying he didn't want to lose me. He told me I should finish my smoke inside. And then it was the weirdest thing; I just totally lost my nerve. I was in no mood to have a break-up conversation right there, right that minute. I kissed him like a lie and told him he did impress me. I went back with him, which felt right only because it was so easy, far easier just then than leaving and later having to explain myself. I had no idea yet how complicated things would too soon become.

The cabinet where I hid my smokes smelled of stale tobacco. I had to go up onto my tiptoes to reach into the fondue pot. Atop the pack sat a red Bic lighter that was older than my son. If I search hard enough back for details of that night, when I nearly walked away from Daryl for good, I see the same red lighter being used. I pinched a smoke out of the pack. It felt brittle between my fingers, like if I squeezed too hard it might crumble to nothing. When I heard the door to the garage open, I palmed the smoke and slipped the lighter into my pocket while slowly stepping off the chair.

"What's up hon?" Daryl asked, carrying with him the sickly sweet smell of sawdust.

"You're home early," I said, placing my free hand over the one that cupped the cigarette.

"It's started snowing again. Dom was worried about the roads so he sent everyone home. What were you doing?"

"I was just checking to see if we still had the fondue pot."

"I didn't know we had one of those," he said. "It's for melting cheese, right?"

"It was a gift from Karla Krugman. You remember her? I knew her in law school. I think she got it second-hand."

"Oh yeah," he said, entirely unconvincingly. "Where's Dave?"

"In his room," I said and gave him a one-armed hug. I even planted a kiss on his cheek. His stubble stung my lips.

"Everything okay?" he asked.

"He took a snowball in the face earlier."

"In the face?"

"He's alright, a little shaken up."

"Who did it?" he asked.

"Guess."

"Ken Crumbrick."

"Yep."

"I hope you told him to get right back out there and hit Kenny with one right in the exact same spot."

"He was really upset, Daryl. He got cut."

"He'll have to learn to stand up to guys like that

someday. I know I did."

"Why don't you go and tell him the Rick Peterson story again? That will make him feel better. Like it always does."

"Rich. Rich Peterson was the dude's name. And you know what, I just might."

"God Daryl," I said sighing through my nose. "That never works, NEVER. It only makes him feel worse."

"If I keep telling him it, maybe he'll, like, get grown up enough to hear it."

For a while, we stood there close together but far away. The divide kept us from agreeing even when one of us was right. Usually me. I was struck by the keenest sensation that I wanted him to take me in his arms just as he had in that moment of indecision all those years ago. I wanted to feel the reassuring warmth of his body coursing just beneath what was cold inside of me. And if I'd only asked, he would have done so, folded me in his arms and kissed me on the forehead, maybe even whispering a "sorry" as he did it. It was what I'd trained him to do. But by then, I was well past the point of being able to ask for what I needed from him. Another moment that I would add to the list that told me it was over between us.

"I'm going to see if he wants to talk," he said.

"Sure," I said.

"If you're going to smoke put on a hat. It's getting pretty cold out."

I spat out a laugh and nodded, "I will if I do."

He stomped off down the hall, knocked on David's door and entered when there was no reply. I climbed back up onto the chair. I put the lighter and cigarette back in the fondue pot. Clearly, no one would be braving the cold to come and get me that day.

Years, decades later, living on my own in a building owned by a pair of unhappily married, retired teachers, I just started smoking again, just walked down to the bodega, bought a pack and smoked one on the way home. By then, I hadn't heard from David in a while, a few months, which was sad but not as sad as the fact that it didn't really bother me. And as I stood outside my door smoking, I thought of Daryl and realized that I barely remembered him anymore. I hadn't spent more than a handful of seconds thinking about him in what seemed like a long time. I stood on the top step, finishing my smoke and thought of calling my son but then mashed out the cigarette beneath my shoe and didn't.

8. Two Rounds at Mother's

Daryl pulled what he thought of as his dressy jeans from the drawer. They were not faded or frayed or stained. They were not a pair he'd ever worn to work. I was about to protest when I found I really didn't care what he wore to Mother's anymore. In fact, I found myself more annoyed by the thought that it'd ever mattered, that I'd ever pestered him to wear something else, that I'd ever let Mother's remarks about how rare it was to have a blue-collar guy at her home for dinner, especially Christmas Eve, bother me. But then, the immortal mood-ruiner himself trampled all over my self-righteous indignation when he pulled on that skintight, oatmeal-colored turtleneck, which I'd never liked and had really never liked him, over a perfectly fine button-down shirt.

"Daryl," I said, "you don't wear dress shirts under turtlenecks. I can't believe you don't know that by now. How often have I pointed out that very simple idea?"

"I thought it was a good idea to wear a nice shirt under the sweater. Class it up, like, two times over or whatever."

"Look at yourself," I said. "Why hide such a nice shirt?"

"Should I put on, like, a regular type sweater so the collar peeks out?"

"You have a V-neck, a black one. That might be nice."

"How about my jeans? Do they look okay?"

"They do. But do you think you might be more comfortable wearing slacks to my mother's house on Christmas Eve?" I asked out deliriously bad habit.

"You can wear whatever you want to my mother's

house," he said, huffily.

"Daryl," I said, unable to keep my voice from rising, "just go change, please. So we can get going. We're going to be late as it is."

"Do I have a sweater I can wear too, Mom?" David asked, peeking into our room and tugging at his crimson dress shirt that was a little too tight across the chest.

"I think your black one will go," I said, rather than endure a whole scene by telling him to put on a shirt that fit better. "You and Dad can be like twins."

David slumped his way back to his room, seeming decidedly unimpressed by that prospect. I was faster than them both in finishing getting ready. I'd long since stopped fussing with make-up or giving an extra thought as to how I did my hair. The day I realized Daryl would rather caress a piece of wood than me was among the most liberating moments of my life. Even more liberating was the day when I first felt comfortable admitting that out loud to myself.

I never let on during the long four-hour drive how little I minded running late. I wound around the snow-packed roads, tossing cinder and salt clumps in my wake, coasting on each sharp bend without trying to make up time. Mother would never admit it but being late showed the sort of lack of consideration and overabundance of self-regard that she'd raised me to take pride in. A certain kind of person can be late, should be late, I remember her once saying; certain people disappoint you by being on time. Not that she ever gave much indication that I might even toy with the idea of considering myself among such august personages.

I flipped between the stations playing Christmas carols, simply because, like telling my husband what to wear, it felt like the seasonally appropriate thing to do. Daryl didn't complain but instead, tried to passively indicate his displeasure by being distractingly restless in the front seat. He kept adjusting the belt across his chest, fidgeting with his seat, opening and closing the glove compartment. All he ever had to do was ask me to change the station or even take control of it himself. I didn't really even like Christmas music all that much.

Daryl couldn't have known but even by then he still hadn't yet used up all his credit for surviving that first Christmas Eve at Mother's. We'd been living together for more than six months by that point, though I'd led mother to think it was a more recent development. The night before we left, I'd learned I was pregnant with David. I hadn't told Daryl yet nor had I completely accepted the news myself.

We'd gotten up when it was still dark and took a cab to the train station. Daryl, hungover and thankfully quiet, could barely keep his eyes open. I wanted to prepare him for the difficult day ahead but didn't want to scare him either. I'd complained enough about Mother that I'd assumed he knew what we were about to run into. Still, I warned him he'd be under scrutiny by everyone there; they'd all be on her side, so to speak. He yawned at this, scratched at his face and declared himself ready.

I was glad that he slept most of the train ride. It gave me time to wrestle with my latest unplanned pregnancy. Just a quick PSA, especially for David: if you aren't taking precautions specifically to avoid pregnancy, then you should be prepared to deal with one. I always thought of myself as a smart, conscientious woman, but it turns out having unprotected sex only really infrequently doesn't count as adequate birth control.

By the time we pulled into the station, the sun was most assertively up, blinding us with the white world beneath it. Mother was waiting for us, anxious to get a glimpse of the man she insisted on referring to as my "beau." If only the idea that my apparently treacherous womb had a new tenant wasn't so large in my mind, I would've found amusing the prospect of her utter disappointment at realizing that Daryl in no way fit the traditional waspy model conjured up by that term. Stepping from the broiling train compartment into the brutal cold, I took his hand. Mother flashed her lights at us from the far end of the parking lot, after we had somehow made it safely down the ice-and snow-covered stairs. As soon as we got in the car, she made some snide remark about the duffle bag Daryl had packed in case we were forced to stay the night. It was held together with duct tape. I'd prepared him enough not to react to her.

"This is the young man who's living with Gloria in the city. Cohabitating, I think they call it," she announced to her dinner guests later that night. "He's in art school. Isn't that right?"

"Yes," Daryl said, no doubt shocked by the sudden jolt of attention. She hadn't said a word to him since commenting on his bag. "I'm in sculpting, wood sculpting."

"Sculpture. Isn't that something?" she said, her head turning from side to side to make sure she had the table's full attention. "Do you know what I find most fascinating about young people who go to school for the arts?"

"What?" Daryl asked which earned him some nervous giggling from Uncle Ben.

"Mother," I said in a pleading voice that she ignored with a wave of her hand.

"I find it fascinating how they manage to convince their parents it's a worthwhile education for long enough to see their schooling paid for."

"Mother," I said, hurling my napkin down on the table, "Daryl's on scholarship at Peckham."

"Where, dear?"

"Peckham School of Fine Arts," Daryl said. "P-So-fa, they call it…we call it."

"Well, I've never heard of Peckham. May I assume it's not exactly the Sorbonne or even NYU?"

On the ride back to the station after dinner, Mother seemed in unusually good cheer, basking, no doubt, in what she took as a victorious humiliation of Daryl. She even suggested we wait in the car at the station parking lot until the train came, but Daryl got out and walked, as quickly as the treacherous conditions in the station parking lot allowed. I said nothing to her as I got out to follow him.

We waited out in the cold on the platform for the last train back to the city. Daryl's face, drained of its usual glow, gave him a wounded appearance like a little boy who'd been let down by the false promises of the season. He'd barely survived the day. He turned his face into the icy breeze and went uncharacteristically silent as he walked to the end of the platform. For a terrifying second, I worried that he was going to toss himself down onto the tracks. I felt it'd all been my fault for feeding him to that lioness, for not really preparing him enough, for not defending him more skillfully. I wish I'd been her target, that my struggles to finish the first half of law school had been the subject of her barbs. But she didn't know about any of that at that time, because it was bound up in my mind with what had happened during the spring before and that was not a subject I was quite ready to allow her anywhere near. Not for the first it time that year, I'd needed Daryl more than I was comfortable needing anyone, and again he proved up to the task without really knowing what he was doing.

I walked over to him, pressed myself into his back, rested my chin on his shoulder and wrapped my arms around him. The wind whipped a few stray snowflakes in our faces as I told him that I loved him.

I waited until we got back to the city to tell him I was pregnant. I treated it like a Christmas present. And he was happy this time. He looked like he knew somehow. He even said he was ready to be a Dad. I wasn't sure what I was doing, I just didn't want a repeat of the spring before. When he said we should get married, I smiled and swallowed a 'no.' But by then, I no longer had any serious plans to leave him. I just didn't realize how long the sentence I'd been handed was. And just like that the little lies I'd been telling myself and him throughout our time together were no longer quite so small nor exactly lies.

That drive many years later might very well have been the first time that I found myself actually hating Christmas songs. "Little Drummer Boy" with its chorus of castrati rum-pa-pumming made me cringe. "Rockin' Around the Christmas Tree," which came on after that, couldn't have sounded less 'rockin'' if a group of postulants were singing it. By the second verse, I needed to concentrate more than usual to resist the urge to plow the car into a snowbank. But the absolute worst, by far, was "Jingle Bell Rock," which must have come on a half dozen times during the first half of that trip.

By the time we passed a billboard for the Treatskill

Hill Diner, my hate for the first notes chiming from the guitar at the opening of that song had me locking my jaw in an effort to block the sound. The tune, empty and uncertain, made me feel that despite having my family around me I was utterly alone in the universe. My traveling companions didn't complain as they normally did, but instead took turns issuing sighs that bore varying levels of frustration and ennui.

The three of us must've each committed some particularly grievous outrage in our prior lives to be stuck in a car together driving four hours west along the snow-limned hillsides, now and again coming dangerously close to the dark continent that was central Pennsylvania; all the while listening to the seasonal dreck spilling from the car's speakers. In truth, I think we were all glad for the music not least because it kept us from having to speak to one another. For three people who shared the same house, the same shower, the same toilets for God's sakes, it seemed as though we should've had a bit more in common. There was some murmuring from all involved when we got stuck behind a tractor trailer that turned the road in front of us into stripes of grey and black slush. At least, it offered something to look at.

Every time I stole a glance of David in the rearview mirror, he was hunched over the latest installment in the *Lands of Power and Dust* series. I couldn't see much of his face. Daryl once expressed a concern that he was going to do some kind of ligament damage to his neck from reading too much. This observation had come a couple of years before, at a point in our relationship when I still thought I could learn to love my husband in the way a wife should. Which is to say that it came at a time that, while we were not exactly close, I still thought the distance between us could be measured and traversed. I'd enjoyed my life with Daryl a lot more in the second or two before I realized how serious he was in his concern for our son's neck. He wasn't kidding. He actually thought reading could be dangerous to a person's health.

Amongst the many tragedies of the speedy courtship-slash-bewilderingly-rapid-degree-of-codependence experienced by Daryl and I was that I never got to fully vet his literary tastes. He was tall and nice and we got drunk and slept together. He said he loved me, then a few months later I was pregnant for the first time and, about to experience all the attendant tragedy affixed to that event. It'd all happened before I could really peruse his bookshelves. Stray copies of *Sculpture Magazine* lay about the basement apartment he shared with another art student. It usually took him three concentrated bathroom visits, never more than four to get through an issue. I strongly suspected he was only glancing at the pictures.

When the sleigh bells started at the beginning of yet another version of "Deck the Halls," Daryl's face contracted as though the bells were being played against his temples. He'd missed a spot shaving, a little cluster of red hairs sprouted just next to his earlobe like that part of him had been sprinkled with cinnamon. He scratched himself there then let out another sigh, but this one sounded like a moan.

"Can we change the radio for just like a break? I'm fah-la-lahed out," he said.

I smiled and nodded. Daryl flipped through static, an instrumental version of "Silent Night," what sounded like Alvin and Chipmunks singing "Little Town of Bethlehem," before finally finding a station playing Metallica's "Sad But True." Daryl'd had it in heavy rotation the fall we met, it was one of the first and only songs that we ever seriously discussed. I'd hated it and Daryl had been, somewhat tragically, totally into Metallica. That afternoon before Christmas, however, the rhythmic assault was welcome and I even nodded along a little, giving the steering wheel a couple of half-hearted drum taps.

"Metallica," the DJ croaked as the song faded out. "'Sad But True' on Christmas Eve. Maybe that's what Mary and Joseph thought of their plight on this day more than two thousand years ago as they sought shelter, so that she could give birth to our lord, the baby Jesus. Now, let's get into the spirit of the season a bit more with a little 'Jingle Bell Rock' here on the region's hardest rocking, hardest working station WHMG."

"Change it," David cried, leaning as far forward as his seatbelt would allow.

We pulled into Mother's driveway. The snow piled up around her property made a thick white wall of the hedges, except in the one area where they had to be trimmed back to accommodate a fire hydrant. Leaves never seemed to grow there nor did snow stick. It was a brown gash in the white. Mother had spent some time first pestering Daddy, and then our lawn care people about the problem, before accepting it as one of the burdens she had to carry in this world.

With the accumulation of snow on the roof and icicles clinging to the shutters, her house resembled a huge square igloo. Even the garland that she'd had wound around the columns on either side of the front door wore a thick beard of frost. And there, breathing pools of condensation onto the door's glass was the ice queen herself, smiling in her best imitation of someone happy to see us.

"Come in, come in," she said. "Get out of the cold.

It's a white Christmas."

She patted Daryl on the back and David on the head as they entered. She reserved for me one of her awkward half-hugs that, though brief, felt as though it tested every spare ounce of her emotional availability.

"I didn't know if you were going to make it," she said as she helped us shed our coats which she then handed to David. "Davey, would you put these in the den?" Not even a minute inside her house and already a Hytner had a chore. This request was made despite the fact that the huge ornate coat rack in the entry hall stood empty. I guess like all of the things she liked best in that house; it was really just for show.

"She made you put on some slacks did she, Daryl?" she asked, taking a pinch of cloth from his outer thigh.

"Yeah, well," he said, and I could almost see him fighting the urge to slap her hand, "jeans didn't go with what I have on."

"And Gloria, I love you in red. Is this the same frock you wore last year?"

"Thank you, Mother. And you look nice too. The turtleneck conceals," said I, wiggling a finger under my chin to indicate the drooping flesh hiding beneath the fabric there. I did my best version of her smug smile as I watched her adjust the collar of it a little higher.

"I tried to wear one of those but she tells me that, like, they can't be worn over dress shirts," Daryl said. "I figure, a sweater's a sweater."

"Sweaters are something of an enigma in the world of fashion, I'm afraid," Mother said. "In my day, you'd never dream of wearing one to a formal occasion but here we are, each in a sweater on a major holiday. Not all change is bad, I suppose."

"Does this qualify as a formal occasion?" I asked. "Are the other guests in tuxes and evening *frocks*?"

"Everyone else is in the sitting room," she said. Ignoring what had been said without making a show of ignoring it was among her greatest and most-used gifts. "Beer, Daryl? I recently purchased a whole case because I know how you like to drink it."

She bought beer because she liked seeing my husband get sloppy drunk. That way, she could wax philosophical to her other guests about how neither her husband nor father ever touched beer and never got drunk. That told her beer must've been the burden of the working classes. These comments were usually made in a stage whisper, whenever she could be sure I was within earshot.

"No thanks," Daryl said, "I'm driving home."

"I'll have one," I said after a beat so I could watch her expression change from mild disappointment to disapproving shock.

"Do you drink *BEER,* dear?" she asked.

"Sure. I like beer. You've seen me drink beer before. What kind do you have?"

"Uh…expensive…imported…I think it's called Heineken."

"Ah, green bottles. Classy, Mother. Are they in the fridge or have you relegated them to a cooler in the garage so that they don't accidentally rub against Uncle Ben's chardonnay?"

"No. I recently purchased a new, more spacious refrigerator. Two burly gentlemen brought it in through the garage and took the other one away. In a matter of minutes, the whole kitchen was transformed."

"I can't wait to see it," I said.

"I wonder what happened to Dave," Daryl said, wandering away from us down the hall.

"He's probably still in the den. I left a plate of sweets in there for him," Mother said.

"Great, Mother. Candy before dinner," I said, hating how aggrieved I must have sounded as it gave away the fact that she'd gotten to me.

Round One to Mother.

The kitchen was spotless as though it had never been used, which was close to the truth. Her new cleaning lady, whose name Mother surely knew no better than I, was clearly thorough. The new stainless-steel fridge gave the room a cold feel as though corpses might be stored there. I pressed my open palm against its door, hoping to leave a mark. On the counter next to it, several aluminum trays were stacked on top of each other. I wondered how many guests she had lured to the very spot I was standing so she could brag about how she was going to help Chef Bon of Tiny French Catering cook the meal.

Tiny French was the sort of local business Mother loved to patronize, mostly due to locally held belief that it was unreasonably expensive. Inevitably, there would come a point in the evening when she would laud its employees: "The most wonderful life savers when one hasn't the time to pull everything together." Relegating anything and everything to the realm of the afterthought was another of Mother's most practiced skills.

I opened the fridge heedlessly, letting the door swing. It worked well enough to elicit a pathetic squeak from Mother. She wanted to accuse me of trying to rip the door off its hinges. I was always hard on things, apparently, like only boys were. In that spirit, I grabbed a bottle of beer and flipped off the cap. It flew into the air and scuttled across the marble-topped island where she would later surely instruct me to stack the plates for "the girl." I think she deputized me for that role because she hoped I'd be careless enough to chip one which would allow her to shine in the role of gallant hostess, who merely smiled as her oafish daughter ruined yet another piece of valuable china. It was all I could do not to open the beer bottle with my eye socket. I took an overly generous gulp, the glug sound escaping from the bottle finally scoring me some real points in the shape of a heavy sigh from Mother.

"Really, dear. Since when do you drink beer? I've never seen you do it. Way back, years ago when you visited us with your college friends for a few days, I tolerated those wine drinks because that seemed fine enough, I guess, but beer? Beer was never something I thought you'd drink."

"First of all, you've seen me drink beer or at least knew I drank it. What do you think Daryl and I were drinking when we lived together in the city? It wasn't champagne over brunch with the Rockefellers. It was beer in bars, pubs, saloons, dives. And when my college friend Maria came, she was only one who ever visited here, we drank vodka."

"Goodness me, my daughter went from thinking she was a red Russian in college to congregating in public houses. A commonly charted course, I'm sure."

I took another gulp, the bottle obliging with another rude noise that broadcast my relish. I kept my composure even after noticing, for the first time, the sticky, unpleasant aftertaste that it left, as though the beer had gone sour. Smiling at Mother, I sat the bottle down and considered my options. I could tell her right then and there that her overpriced, imported beer was spoiled. Any joy to be had in that scenario was contingent upon her having already fed it to one of the other guests. Such a revelation would cause her embarrassment and I would see her face melt and sag into the horrified mask of the failed hostess. However, if I was the only one drinking it, which was a distinct possibility, she'd tell me how expensive it was and then take solace in the notion that I knew nothing about "good beer," as it was evidently unavailable in the "shambolic taverns" I used to frequent. Or worse, prove to her that my drinking beer was a put-on and that she knew me as well as she believed she did. That would result in lots of smug looks passed my way throughout the evening. Would the risk be worth it? Nothing ventured…

"I hate to say it, Mother," I said wincing now and examining the contents of the bottle in the shaft of low winter sun shining through the kitchen window, "but this tastes off."

"It does? What do you mean?"

"Has it been sitting around?"

"No. Not at all. Not here. I ordered it from Marty's Liquors. The man just delivered it yesterday."

"Well, it tastes stale. Maybe it'd been sitting around Marty's for a while."

"It was very expensive for beer," she said, connoting her belief that any argument was ridiculous as she had already been assured of its quality by the total on the sales slip. "I don't think Marty would be in business if he had expensive stuff like that just sitting around."

"I don't know what to tell you, Mother. It's gone sour." I gave the bottle a sniff, unwilling to pour it out until I was sure of the direction we were headed.

"I'm sure it's been some time since you had a beer, Gloria. I don't think there can be that many taverns out where you've been living. The suburbs are a family place, after all, not like the city."

"Like I said, Mother," I said, now pouring it out, the thin foam washing over itself, coating the basin of the sink, "it's off. You might as well dump all of it."

"There's some lovely white wine in the fridge that your uncle was generous enough to bring. Of course, it's rather expensive as well, but I don't think he'll mind us opening a bottle a little before dinner. I am fairly certain it hasn't gone soft."

"Gone off, Mother. The term is gone off."

"That's what I said. Isn't it?" She sat two wine glasses on the island. From the fridge door, she grabbed a bottle and twisted off the cap. "Try it," she said, pouring a splash into one glass as you might for a child.

I picked up the glass, swirling it limply. "Smell it first dear," she said.

I took a whiff.

"Try to appreciate the bouquet," she said. "We drink first with our noses."

I brought the glass to my lips.

"No not yet, dear. Let the experience settle with you. God, did I never teach you how to properly enjoy wine?"

"Mother, I know how to drink wine."

"I just want you to do it properly, dear."

"I know. I know how important something like that is to you. But the fact is, the wine's already been paid for. I can't send it back. I don't have any other options. I am going to drink it now and either I'll like it and ask for more or I won't and go hunt down a bottle of vodka."

"Fine Gloria, dear, fine. I just want you to be in the

proper mindset to enjoy it. You are, after all, drinking a fine wine in your childhood home, not guzzling beer in some lowlife lounge."

"Believe me, I know where I am every time I step inside this house," I said sucking it down then nodding and shaking my glass at her, which she filled halfway.

"Isn't this nice, dear?" She cradled her glass in both hands. "Mother and daughter back in the kitchen together where we've shared so many happy memories."

"You mean like when you'd yell at the caterers instead of me?"

"Why must you be like this?" she asked, slamming her glass down with enough force that I feared it'd broken in her hand. "Always painting the past black. Black, black, black and blacker. Is it so hard to recall the good times? You were no treat to live with, you or your father. You were the ones. You treated me like I was the help around here. I would've liked to have been treated at least as well as *I* treated the people *I* hired. Believe me."

"Okay, okay. Take it easy. Only kidding, only kidding," I said, hardly believing that she'd already wrung an apology from me.

That woman messed me up but good.

"It's Christmas Eve for goodness sakes," she said in a shaky voice. "It's the time of the year when we are meant to remember the good times we've shared with family. God knows, I work hard enough at it. Do you think I relish having all of these people in my home?"

"Mother," I said in a sharp whisper, "Shhhh, they're in the next room."

She turned away from me, kneading the counter with her knuckles and breathing heavily enough that I noticed her back was rising and falling as though she was struggling for air. I laid a hand on her shoulder. I rubbed her back. "It's okay," I said. She turned away to pour her wine down the sink.

"I shouldn't drink anymore," she said. "I lose my composure."

Round Two to me, then.

She employed me soon after to help her 'cook.' Having a task to perform meant we didn't have to try so hard to conjure any magical mother-daughter holiday memories. She read the instructions on the cards carefully prepared by Chef Bon himself, or so she claimed. I was in charge of organizing things to go into the oven and setting various kitchen timers for each dish. It didn't seem like a two-person job, but she used another one of her superpowers and made it so.

Feeling in control again, she began to regain herself enough to tell me about each of the dishes and why she'd ordered them. By the time the au gratin asparagus went into the oven, it seemed that we had, despite our own best efforts, been creating the kind of memories she so wanted to relive. Then finally, finding the serene bonhomie too much to bear, Mother found her way to a line of questioning whose sole intention was to irritate me.

"Have you given any thought lately to going back to school?" she asked as we basked in the earthy sweet smell of the brown butter bubbling.

"Mother," I growled, refilling my wine glass.

"Oh, are you finally finding you like being a housewife?"

"Maybe I am. Maybe I actually am and just don't know it yet."

"I still don't understand it. You put all that time and energy into becoming an attorney. You were just a year or so from finishing. Why didn't you just press on, despite it all? People do you know? Pregnant women and mothers do it all the time, I'm sure."

"Do you just never listen to me or is this some kind of convenient dementia that crops up regarding this particular topic?"

"I know, dear. I know. That was a rough time for you. You wanted to be careful."

"A rough time?" Now, it was my turn to slam a glass down. "A rough time? You make it sound like the cleaning service I'd hired kept changing 'girls' on me."

"Gloria, that's not how I meant it and you know it. I am simply trying to talk to you about your future and every time I do, you boil everything down to this one…"

"This one what?"

"This one…," she paused to straighten her posture, "…event."

"Event? Like a birthday bash or charity ball?"

"Honestly, Gloria. I can't talk to you about anything. You're always snapping at everything I say. Snap, snap, snap, snap," as she spoke she made a failed and painful sounding attempt at snapping her fingers.

Turning away from her, I dug my nails into the side of the sink and grabbed my wine glass, then rinsed it out. Finally, she did successfully snap her fingers once. I felt that sound inside of me. The weak glow of the afternoon sun caught the lip of the glass in the sink. I wanted to pick it up and hurl it at her. Not hit her with it, just miss, throw it just over her head. But I only filled it with water and rinsed it out again.

"I don't really want to talk about this right now, Mother."

"When then, dear?" she asked, her words coming

slowly as though she was speaking to a child. "It's been more than a decade. That wound can't still be so fresh. David's growing up. Why not think about finishing your education? Getting on with your life?"

"Get on with…what do you think I've been doing?"

"Moving out of the city, setting up home with Daryl, getting married. I understand it, dear. I do. But…you used to talk about doing so much more with your life."

"I said, I don't want to talk about this."

"I just think…" she said, the last word dying in her throat.

"I'm going to tell people that it's time to eat," I said taking the chance her pause offered to cut her off, a tactic she had to appreciate as she'd perfected it. "We don't want Chef Bon's food getting cold."

"I'll do it dear," she said, the ghost of a smirk dancing on her lips.

She was definitely ahead on points through three rounds.

9. Dinner Trashed

Uncertain as to whether or not I could take her failure to look at me as we sat down to dinner as a true victory, I kept up my guard as the food was passed around. Daryl and my Uncle Ben were chatting away about cars or property or having a penis. It had to be one of those three things, because it was all they had in common. To my right, David held his book in his lap, planning apparently to eat with one hand. I didn't say anything. I was already suffering enough from familial battle fatigue. Aunt Helen was seated across from me, sipping wine, working up the courage to speak in front of her sister-in-law. Mother liked that she was so predictably cowed, it allowed her to treat Helen with the open contempt in which she took so much pleasure. Helen's fading crimson blouse with its shoulder pads and square cut made her seem so small, like there wasn't much of a body inside of her clothes.

Ben and Helen were wed late in life when common sense and indeed maybe even dignity suggested that the idea of marriage should've probably been given up on. They'd had a small wedding at the courthouse there town. I'd waited outside the justice's chambers. Only Ben and Mother and Helen along with Helen's sister Pam went inside. I think I'd been told I wasn't allowed to go in for reasons that seemed absurd enough to sound official, though certainly it'd been just another of Mother's lies. Many of which I did find as I aged were told for the same reason that I often lied to my own son -- it just made things so much easier.

See Mother, you were not a total failure in passing along your wisdom.

I'd just finished college, though I didn't go to the

graduation ceremony. To my surprise Mother had not been offended. She'd claimed she'd come to hate "the needless pomp and circumstance occasioned by each passing stage of life." I didn't think it then but have come to see she was still talking about Daddy's funeral. He'd passed during my freshman year. She'd been too broken and undone by grief to deal with any of the arrangements. She'd had a hard enough time when he'd been checked into the care center. She thanked me profusely but in her own way for taking care of all the business surrounding it, and by that I mean she didn't complain or criticize a single thing I did.

I still managed to graduate on time, persevering without even a break despite Daddy's passing. I would move into the city to live with Maria a couple of weeks after that wedding. Everything was going according to my plan for my life, which I would allow nothing to interrupt or so it seemed. When things did fall apart, when the thoughtlessness of youth permanently disrupted my plans with matters that I was not yet mature enough to handle, it would take me a long time to rediscover that same singleness of purpose, the kind which had deserted me when I needed it the most.

It'd rained the night before Ben and Helen's appointed day and through most of the morning but by the time they emerged from chambers, so had the sun. It shone down on the courthouse steps with a golden glow. The newly married couple walked towards their waiting car as though on a carpet of glory. Standing next to me at the top of the courthouse steps, Pam cried and untucked a tissue from the sleeve of her blouse, whimpering something I didn't catch. I tried to take Mother's hand as a way of sharing in the joy of the moment but she pulled hers away, then walked back into the courthouse as though she'd forgotten something.

As I watched Ben hold the car door for Helen, both bathed in sunlight, I experienced, totally unexpectedly, a glowing kind of happiness for this woman, whom I'd met only the night before. Surely, she'd once given up on love, on finding someone and here she was the blushing bride, coming up on fifty. There wasn't a lot of romance in books or on the tube for women of that age. Indeed, the dominant patriarchal forces in society would prefer that women just disappear into the background by the time they pass their child-bearing years. Certainly, Ben was no one's idea of a romantic figure, mistaking as he did owning property for being intelligent, and capitalizing on luck for ingenuity. And so, with Mother having retreated, I did allow myself a moment there on the top of those steps to recall my own girlish notions of finding that special someone, of having my own day that was as intimate and joyful as the one embodied by my uncle and aunt driving away on what seemed a carpet of golden air.

Seated next to Helen at the table were Allen Heart and his wife Dale, neighbors of ours from as far back as I care to remember. Allen was successful, spending time as an ADA in the city and then later as a town supervisor. I think I looked up to him before I even realized it. He had jumped at the chance to write me a letter when I was applying to law schools. His face had gotten puffier since the last time I'd seen him, his hair greyer and thinner. His once-brilliant blue eyes which had hinted at a fiery and incisive intellect had dulled as well, evidence, I guess, of what retirement and too much free time with nothing to fill it can do. The more I studied his face, my long-withered dreams of becoming a public servant, which were suddenly so easy to recall with the past gathered around me, began to make me feel very old.

Something Allen had been eating now floated in his glass. Dale noticed and I could see from her face that she was trying to work out how to remove the sizable chunk of what looked to be a potato doing a water dance in her husband's Chablis without anyone noticing. She gave me her nearly perfect, politician's wife smile and whispered to Allen. Allen brought the glass up, examining it in the light, then dipped his fingers in and after a bit of trying, removed the submerged spud chunk. Dale Heart, whom I once pitied for being no more than a housewife, gave me a conspiratorial, knowing look that said: "You know how it is, being a full-time wife is a full-time job."

"We don't see you around much," Allen said to me, still shaking the wine off his fingers. "How far's the drive out here? Five, six hours?"

"We can do it in four pretty easy," Daryl cut in, always there to take charge and clarify when matters of driving times and distances were being discussed.

"And remind me, you're how far away from the city?" Allen asked, sipping his wine with obvious relish as though it hadn't, only a few moments ago, featured a large chunk of half-masticated potato floating in it.

"About an hour and half by train," I said, after pausing in case Daryl wanted to chime in.

"We never drive in," he added as a follow up.

He could have answered that we never went into the city at all. That it was too sad for the both of us, reminding us of the mistakes that can be made there. We half-planned visits, looked at train schedules and debated driving routes but never followed up. We liked the thought of the city much more than the city itself.

"We were just in there the other day," Dale said. "Too crowded."

"What did you go in for?" I asked my question shaped more by reflex than any true curiosity.

"Went to a show, had dinner," Dale said.

"A musical," Allen added with bored disapproval.

"Patty's in Nebraska." Dale smiled as though feeling comfortable enough to switch from an extemporaneous program to the one she'd planned in advance. "Has a big contract job out there to improve municipal water supplies. Poor gal's been there two years already. When she's done, she might retire from doing all that, the travelling overseas and across the country and stuff."

Patricia Heart was ahead of me by several years at school. She had gone to college on an ROTC scholarship and had worked in government jobs at various levels her whole career. I was never very clear on what she did but she always seemed to be doing things to improve life for people who lived in far-flung unimaginable corners of the world, like Nebraska.

"Do you think she'll stay out there when she retires?" I asked, managing to channel Mother by pronouncing 'out there' in a way that made it seem vaguely insulting.

"Too flat," Allen said, shaking his head as if topography was a concern shared by everyone gathered around the table.

At the far end, Mother chatted away with Gertrude Grimlock, who lived next door and, in my memory, had always been shriveled and sour and mousy. Her husband had died around the same time as Daddy. This tragic coincidence allowed the two of them, formerly no more than neighborly to one another, to form an unbreakable bond of self-pity over being left behind by a spouse, who'd been inconsiderate enough to die. Their conversations always seemed clandestine. They spoke with their faces very close to each other, their heads bowed, voices low. Gertie, as Mother called her, had the habit of balling one fist into the other as she spoke.

"Everything is very good so far," said Ben. "Nice work in the kitchen." He lifted his glass. "To both of you."

"I just heated it up, Benjamin," Mother said. "It's from Tiny French."

"Chef Bon is a treasure," Gertie said. "A real, honest-to-God, hometown treasure."

"Very pricey," Dale purred, "but oh so good."

"Mmmm," her husband agreed through a mouth full of roast goose.

"Sinful," Dale went on, "simply sinful."

"Daryl, my good man, you should have some wine with this meal," Ben said. "It's a crime to wash this fare down with water."

"I have to drive," Daryl said, then slurped from a wine glass full of water. The utter uncouthness of the sound pleased me more than I'd dared imagine it could.

Blue collar enough for you, Mother?

"Not even a beer?" Gertie asked. "I thought you liked to drink beer."

"I'm driving," Daryl said, then pointed at me, "she's drinking."

"The wine goes so perfectly with the food," Ben said, holding his glass up to the light presumably to show that he knew how to appreciate the color of it. "I guessed right."

"Fine wine, fine food, fine people," Helen added.

"Going out to the really nice places in the towns around here probably would've cost just as much as having Tiny French deliver it," Dale noted.

"Oh, didn't Mother tell you?" I asked. "She didn't. Did she?"

"Tell them what, dear?" Mother asked, eyes narrowing, brow wrinkling with years of practiced anger.

"I think you should be honest." I slurped from my glass after speaking, doubly pleased by the sound.

"She's joking. She is going to make fun," Mother said and though she laughed, the expression on her face only hardened.

"No I'm not. You don't want them to know. Do you? There's nothing to be embarrassed about. It's the 'in thing' to do Mother."

"What are you talking about?" Dale asked.

"Now what is this?" Mother's brow crinkling further into an *I Dare You* relief map.

"She didn't pay for any of this," I said. "She got it all from the dumpster *behind* Tiny French. It was totally sealed and everything. So, you don't have to worry."

"Dumpster diver," brayed my husband, following it up with a mule-like laugh.

"A bad joke," Mother said, "she's making a tasteless joke. My daughter often mistakes herself for a comedienne."

"What's that? Dumpster diving, you say?" Gertie asked. Her thick spectacles reflected the candlelight which Mother had hoped would lend the evening the very air that I was in the process of extinguishing.

"Some people save money by eating the unopened food they find in dumpsters," Daryl said.

"Lots of places throw away tons and tons of perfectly good food," our son added.

"You mean people actually eat refuse?" Gertie asked. "No. No. I don't believe that."

"Disgusting," Helen said, putting down her silverware and averting her eyes from the soon-to-be refuse on her plate.

"Who does this?" Dale asked.

"People who don't want to work," Ben said. "Radicals who think they're too good to hold a normal job like everyone else."

"Where do they live?" Allen asked. "They must live in the city. It always smells of trash in the streets."

"It's just a bad joke," Mother hissed. "She read about it in some leftie book or magazine no doubt."

"Eating trash, here....in the United States of America. I can't believe it," Gertie said.

"Jobless rabble rousers," continued Ben, banging his fist down on the table. "Shoving first their laziness, then their dull, dull ideas in our faces."

"Is this a real thing?" Dale asked then turned to me. "Where'd you hear about this?"

"I'm telling you, she read it in some Godless publication or saw it on PBS or something," Mother said.

"Yes on PBS! Did you see it too? Is that where you got the idea from, Mother?" I asked, the smile across my face so broad I could feel my cheeks tightening. "It was on PBS last week."

"Of course not," Mother said. "I do not watch that channel but I know what they show -- championing the supposedly downtrodden in between begging for money."

"We like the nature programs," Dale added.

"I don't have to watch such dreck to know what it's

like," Mother said. "Stories about starving souls who've been beaten down by the system. Illegal immigrants probably…."

"…or drug addicts," Ben interjected, the distaste evident on his face.

"Sure," Mother said, leaning forward to nod at her brother, "them too. Don't forget about them. Oh, they want you to say, look how poor they are? Isn't America awful? I know the shows she watches."

I loved the way "shows" came out of her mouth like I was some sort of subversive receiving coded communiques from Moscow in the 1950s. Everyone had stopped eating except for Daryl, who helped himself and our son to more asparagus. I longed for David to take the awkward silence as an opportunity to tell the assembled how it would make his pee smell.

"And we pay for it." Uncle Ben thumped his fist again, this time with enough force to make his silverware jump. "Our tax dollars pay for that channel to insult our ideas."

"But the nature shows can be informative," Dale said. "We watched one on manatees the other night, which neither of us had ever heard of."

"Manatees? I'm sure they're the liberals of the ocean," Ben said, sputtering out a weak two syllable laugh before taking a sip from his glass.

"Dumpsters. Really," Mother sniffed, "what made you bring up such a thing? Were you trying to be funny?"

"I don't know, Mother," I said as I tried to keep from laughing in her face.

"It's not fit for my dinner table. I can tell you that."

"But Grandma, grocery stores throw out so much food that really can be eaten."

"Chef Bon doesn't," Allen said in the tone of a man used to saving the day with deflection diplomacy. "He donates his to the local food bank."

Everyone made sounds of approval. Nodding and mumbling and sighing.

"It's not the kind of topic I raised her to bring forward at the dinner table, I can assure you all of that," Mother said, cutting a small morsel of food, then placing it in her mouth and chewing slowly all the while staring daggers at me. "What happened to his face?" she asked, once she had swallowed then nodded her head at David. The mark of his snowball fight wound still lingered and she, apparently, felt it was now fair game.

"I got hit in the face with a loaded snowball," David said, before helping himself to the last of the asparagus, fountains of foul-smelling pee no doubt dancing in his head.

"A loaded snowball? What's that? Who threw it?" Mother asked with a shriek. "Your father?"

"No," David said, his voice cracking, "Kenny Crumbrick."

I hoped he wouldn't cry. I wanted to ruin the meal a bit but not to the point that anyone would shed actual tears, except maybe for Mother, alone in her bed, hours afterwards.

"One of your little hooligan friends?" she asked. "Gloria, when you took to the idea of moving out of the city, I didn't think you'd flee to some God-awful river valley town populated by Boys' Town rejects."

"He's not my friend," David announced. "He's just always around."

"Don't play with him then," Mother advised.

"I can't help it, Grandma."

"Can't you?" she asked, sounding skeptical. "Has your mother had words with this child's parents?"

"I have," I said. "There didn't seem to be much his mother thought she could do about it. We just tell him to be...watchful when Kenny's around."

"Watchful?" Mother cried, as though I'd revealed my weakness to her. "Watchful doesn't seem to work. He's lucky he didn't get his eye put out."

Then Uncle Ben rode to my rescue, raising his glass and extolling the most tried and true of clichés to excuse men of all ages the world over: "Boys will be boys, I'm afraid. I have to admit to getting into some roughhousing when I was young. I'm sure the other men here did too."

Daryl and Allen both nodded.

"And if you had been hit in the face with a snow-ball hard enough to wound you, our mother would have found that child's parents and delivered to them such a talking to that it certainly would've never happened again," Mother said.

"I can assure you, Edie, that would have been the last thing in the world I would have wanted. Boys don't want their mommies fighting their fights for them. Do we Davey?"

And so, we'd arrived at the crucial moment. David could've whined about how big Kenny was, about he'd give anything for it to stop. Or worse, about how I used to push him to play outside with those boys, when all he really wanted was to be left alone in his room to read. Instead, he swallowed the last of the asparagus and gave an almost breathless: "Right."

"Forget the mother," I said. "I wanted to go out and hit the kid with an ice-packed snowball myself."

That got a good, knowing laugh from all in attendance. Daryl smiled and reached over to give my hand an appreciative squeeze. I raised my glass to them all, then gave Mother a wink.

Game. Set. Match. Christmas Eve was mine.

10. Getting Over New Year's Eve

As a little girl, trying to have a party for myself in my Missoni junior miss dress with the zigzag pattern of blue and grey, the thought first occurred to me that the New Year began for the entire world only after Dick Clark rang it in. My parents were having a party that year, which is to say Mother was throwing a party. She had many friends, something Daddy never seemed to have any need for. They were all reduced to labels for me: "bridge friends," "the gals from the Country club," and so on. Whenever any of these clumps of humanity visited our house, I was confined to Daddy's study where I was given snacks and allowed to watch the TV that had been rolled in on its wheeled cart out of the hall closet.

That year, I'd neglected my book and glued my eyes to the coverage of the festivities going on in the city, as from what fleeting glimpses I could manage, that seemed to be pretty much what the adults were doing. During the course of the night, I fought off sleep by convincing myself that turn of the year wouldn't be official anywhere until that moment in Times Square when the red apple, which they later changed into a great ball of flashing lights -- those prone to seizures avert your eyes -- descended the pole and triggered confetti and kisses and that certain twinkle in Dick's chocolate-brown eyes. Even long after I'd learned that the New Year actually began a world away, somewhere in the middle of the Pacific, then marched its way west, I never fully shed the feeling that the drunk crowd with their cheap noisemakers, who danced to the lip-syncing acts amid an array of garish billboards were the chosen few who vouchsafed the New Year for all of humanity. Though she'd been the one who'd ordered the television brought in and hooked up for me, Mother forbade my watching that "cesspool of depravity" where the distinct possibility of a "Gomorrah-like orgy" surged through the crowd, which she could tell from the manner in which the "pregnant light of lust lit the faces of those dull enough to stand out in the cold for the sole purpose of enjoying such a spectacle," which obviously contributed greatly to my desire to watch it that year at the expense of other pursuits.

This was how she spoke to me when I was 8. No wonder I am, was, so screwed up for so much of my life. The old gal did have a colorful way with words, I'll give her that. One twisted sister all the way around.

When I finally got to live in the city, I was much too old to appear outwardly excited about New Year's Eve, even as a concept. The world-weary, quarter-lifers with whom I was obligated to spend my time were fond of observing that it was a night for amateurs. To merely suggest out loud that going to Times Square might be fun would've been tantamount to committing social suicide.

Even Daryl, who was from so far upstate it was practically the Midwest and therefore adored the city with an ardor only a true transplant can feel, looked down on Times Square, on the crowds, on the whole scene. I suspected that other outsiders like my former husband claimed to hate tourists because they feared bumping into some pre-urbanized version of themselves on the streets -- a rube doppelganger wrestling with a street map or swiping their Metrocard through the reader in a too-tellingly hesitant fashion, all the while wearing a look of bewilderment on their face that most transplants can never be comfortably certain they've shaken.

At the time my social life, due to school and work,

lacked sufficient vector points to even form a circle. I spent most of my time with Maria. Sometimes my classmates from law school, Alicia and Monique, would join us if they had nothing better to do. All of them would've had trouble taking me seriously ever again had I indicated the slightest un-ironic desire to go to Times Square and be part of the festivities. In their own ways they all spoke about finding the real, authentic city that only insiders of the kind they wanted to be knew about. But they all morphed into recluses as time wore on. I found strange the strength of the conviction they shared that all that was good in the world could be found within a few blocks of their respective apartments. I'd never admit it but Mother was right when she asserted that the city makes hermits of those unable to afford what it really has to offer.

By the time the immemorial year of 1998 was making its approach, Daryl and I had, for about three months off and on, been hanging out or hooking up, or whatever the term was we used back then to make the idea that one was having intercourse with someone whom they were not totally sure they even liked that much sound sophisticated rather than gross and desperate. I wouldn't have considered us a couple yet and mistook thinking that rather than actually saying it for not leading him on.

For all of my complaining and unkind thoughts, I've always thought of Daryl as nothing less than extremely decent at heart. He is a nice person. He deserved better. I'm not the only one who got cheated by our situation.

Back then, his school friends from The Peckham School of Fine Arts or P-Sofa, as it was more commonly and unfortunately known, were much like him. Despite their efforts, they tended to be earnest and naïve, not at all the kind of outcasts who fit in at such a place. I did like them, though, liked being around them anyway. They all blend together now, those white guys with the, what were then, odd piercings and tattoos. The one who had thrown the rooftop party where I met Daryl, knew Alicia in high school and, as I remember, was madly in lust with her. She had the good sense not to sleep with him, while leading him on just enough to ensure a safety-valve sort of social life that enabled her to do things when other, more suitable friends were elsewhere.

So it was that group of P-Sofa boys escorted myself, Maria, Alicia and Monique on that New Year's Eve to a bar in a neighborhood, which back then bordered on pre-gentrified gritty. We may have been too cool for the holiday but not for free drinks. Daryl and the boys had found the place, taking a cue no doubt from their hipper more adventurous classmates. They were excited to find something that seemed so authentic and they wanted to impress us. "I know a place few others know about," was, and I am sure still is, the mating call among a certain kind of city dweller. The place we were headed sat at the end of the block where every other storefront had been boarded up and the sidewalk crunched beneath your feet as you stepped on discarded glass and bits of plastic. "People do hard drugs around here," my too easily excited suburban mind crowed.

The bar did not, as far as I can remember, advertise its name anywhere outside. Inside it was so filthy that I couldn't help but think of running home to take a shower. A dark orange light shining from some indeterminate spot overhead lent the narrow space a jaundiced glow, which no doubt went unnoticed by the local neighborhood clientele. The floor was sticky enough to make walking something of an effort. The air, thick with cigarette smoke, burned my eyes. They served beer which tasted faintly of metal and cheap shots of their own devising which tasted not so faintly of cough medicine. The whole scene took the form of a kind of a litmus test for me, as though I needed to figure out a way of enjoying myself there if I wanted to pass myself off as a true citizen of the city.

We drank for a while and talked. Daryl put his arm around me a couple of times and I didn't shake it off. By then, we'd slept together a few times and though I wasn't sure we'd last that far into the new year, a little cuddling in public didn't seem too out of order. The television perched above the corner at the far end of the bar was turned too low to hear but there was Dick Clark, eyes twinkling with expectation. As the countdown began, we all drunkenly joined in and I noticed Alicia watching without the ironic detachment that such an event normally produced in her. The very same expectant glow that lit my face as a child was clearly evident on hers. I think, though she'd never admit it, she too wondered what it might've been like to be there in Times Square among the revelers for whom having fun appeared so much less treacherous, so much less a chore.

I kissed Daryl that night at the appointed hour. He wasn't too cool for that ritual. At the end of the night, I went with him back to his place so we could be alone. I meant to back him off before the night ended but, as it rolled along I got too drunk to deal with the complications that would no doubt have arisen and once again and fell deeper into something I'd kept planning to get out of.

As I woke the next morning, a hangover gnawing like a wolverine at the meat inside of my skull, I was resolute that that would really be the last time. The wind howled outside, battering the steel grate that covered his windows. I let him hold me and fell back asleep. When I woke again, later in the oafternoon, both my will and hangover had waned appreciably. I was hungry and didn't want to eat alone. So, I put it off doing what I really thought I should do, once again and let him order Chinese for us instead.

Over the next couple of weeks, I would again and again make plans to break it off with him but never follow through. Not wanting to hurt Daryl, I continued procrastinating because I didn't want to be mean, then things got very mean for me. It all eventually led me to my life out there in the valley, where New Year's Eve was spent sitting at the kitchen table in Caroline's house listening for sounds from down the hall. The boys were in Denny's room playing video games, which was far from David's favorite activity. I had to keep an ear tuned in case things took an unhappy turn, since my son was the one person I knew who could actually be bored to tears.

In the few weeks before that winter break I'd noticed something different in him. Sometimes, I could hear him talking softly on the phone downstairs then hurriedly hanging up if I made the slightest move in his direction. I hadn't asked him about it but what little motherly instinct I had was tingling. Of course by then, it might've also been early onset menopause.

"And the pillows in Europe?" Caroline was saying. I'd done a good job not paying too close attention to her. "Forget about it! I bring my own. Unless I'm in Italy, the Italians know about comfort."

"Do you fly there often, still?" Marge asked.

I worked my thumbnail on a globule of something -- syrup, maybe jelly -- that had been left to harden on the table. I'd just done the Jell-O shot Caroline had given me, served in a little paper cup like the kind Daddy's pills came in when he was in the hospital.

"The most heavenly shampoo," Caroline went on, indomitably, "and then, of course, the ivory hairclips are sitting right there on the nightstand!"

She might've been talking about a side trip to somewhere else by that point but I couldn't be sure. Finding myself still sober enough to be annoyed, I knocked back another sip of wine. It was red and a little sweet, making my mouth sticky as it mixed with the residue of the Jell-O shot coating my teeth.

"You can find the most wonderful seafood there. And the portions are so small," she continued, pausing only for a quick sip from her own goblet. "Small plates. American portions really are so grotesque by comparison."

Whenever Caroline managed to make a creditable point, which was infrequent, it always sounded a little rehearsed. Her voice dropped slightly, ever so noticeably, as if she were repeating someone else's words, someone whom she thought to be intelligent in the very way she knew she wasn't. I nodded at that deeply, rewarding her for just coming close to saying something interesting after nearly an hour of nonstop banality.

"So," she said, "what'd I miss around here?"

"The Christmas pageant was very nice this year," Marge began. Her rundown would be mercifully brief, if no less annoyingly trite. "Jonny was one of the wise men again."

"That's wonderful," Caroline barked like an appreciative seal before helping herself to another Jell-O shot. "Sorry, I missed it. We tried to get to Mass more this year."

"We did too," I said, thankful that Caroline had offered a lie that was easy to piggyback on. "It's getting tougher and tougher to get David to go."

"Work's been really rough this year. I couldn't do much about my schedule," Caroline said, changing to a topic for which I couldn't grasp at anything. I was now adrift.

That bitch.

"Father Mike's leaving us in the spring," Marge said, tapping her fingers on top of her Sprite can as though impatient with the apostates before her. "I hear they want to bring in a priest even younger than him. He got all of the altar boys nice gifts for Christmas, their own King James Bibles. Jonny was so excited, he could barely talk about it."

"Their own bibles. Isn't that wonderful?" gasped Caroline, expelling the least believable breath of air that any human had ever released in all of recorded history.

"Yes. It was," Marge said. "It will be so hard to see Father Mike leave."

We all nodded and hummed our hymns of agreement. The slight edge in that solemnity contest certainly did not go to me.

"But I know what you mean about work being crazy. Last week, I scheduled more patients than I ever had," Marge said. "Dr. Boggs told me never to tell anyone 'no' if they say it's a dental emergency but then he gets mad at me if I book too many appointments. He tells me to ask more questions and use my own judgment, but I'm not comfortable badgering people about the problems they're having with their teeth."

Whoa Marge, I just checked my program and I see demonstrating your religious penitence as your area of preferred tedium. You're stepping on Caroline's turf in boring us with stories about work.

"He says it is part of my job," she went on. "He says if I won't do it, he'll have to find someone else who can."

"What an ass!" Caroline hooted, slapping the kitchen table and slurping down the last of her wine. She smacked her lips together in a way that suggested she liked the sticky sweet feeling that was ironically keeping me from getting drunk enough not to be internally critical of my friends. "What else did I miss?" she asked.

"The boys had a snowball fight," I said, taking my cue.

"Mmmm….hmmm," nodded Marge gravely.

"And Kenny almost put David's eye out," I said.

"God," snapped Caroline, scowling her most serious scowl, "they should be careful, those boys of ours."

"They shouldn't be fighting. They're boys," Marge said, giving the table a light slap of her own. "They should be playing."

"I think Kenny might've stacked the odds in his favor a bit, during the fight," I said.

"Really?" Caroline asked. "How?"

"He broke off a piece of an icicle and made a snowball around it."

"Oh my," Marge gasped, leading already in the latest *Look Like You Really Care* contest. "That's…he, he shouldn't do that."

"Gloria," Caroline said and laid an unappreciated hand on my arm. "I know he can be rough but who else is Kenny supposed to play with? There aren't any boys his age in the neighborhood. I just think he can be a bit overly enthusiastic."

"He's a bully," I said and immediately felt good. I'd been cautious not to use that word because we'd all agreed, with Caroline's prodding, that it was a term that could be overused and was, at least in Caroline's eyes, something of a slur. But the elation I felt at having it cross my lips was surely an affirmation that I was right. The charge was out there, and now we would have to deal with it.

"Gloria, we want to be careful how we use that word, especially these days. Dennis has never had a problem with Kenny. I've had him over to the house. He and Denny played video games without any problems whatsoever."

"Maybe you should invite the boy into your home," Marge added. "Let him know you think of him as one of Davey's friends."

"Have you had him over?" I asked, to which Marge meekly shook her head.

"That's a good idea," said Caroline as she gazed upon Marge with wide-eyed astonishment, a look she wore from time to time, whenever she found herself in the unusual position of suddenly truly caring about something someone else had said. "Have him over. Let them play video games. Be the mom that hosts things not the…you know…the one who goes to his house to tell on him to his mother."

We sat in silence and finished our drinks. Caroline and I both had another Jell-O shot. She smiled at me like she thought she was helping me be a better parent, sharing her vast mom wisdom.

"Well, about time for Dick Clark," Caroline announced, possibly feeling enough silence had passed for her ideas to sink into my feeble housewife brain. "Let's go downstairs. See what the menfolk are up to."

"Should we get the boys?" Marge asked.

"They're having fun, we'd only be interrupting," Caroline said. "Boys want to play, not sit with us in the basement."

"She's right," Marge said to me as we crossed the hall for the basement stairs.

She held her can of Sprite in both of her hands in a way that made me want to slap it out of them, knock her to the ground, pin her down and start pouring cheap vodka down her throat. She'd become so timid and withdrawn, so pious lately. I wanted to tell her that no amount of prayer was going to make her older daughter, Marie, write or visit. Not letting Jonny go trick or treating would do nothing to ensure that he turned out any more righteous or dutiful. It only made him seem nearly as odd as David.

Why was Jonny spared Kenny's torment? Why were either of their sons spared? I had to be the one to label Kenny. I had to be the one to end the pretending that all was well in our darlings' childhood. I had to be the one to confront his bitch of a mother. I had to be the one to appear overprotective, as if uncertain of my own ability to raise my son. While they got to be the ones to tell me to watch my words, to assure me they were just boys and this was how boys were raised. I shouldn't hurt poor, stupid Kenny's feelings.

How would you like it? I wanted to scream at them from the top of the stairs as they made their way down ahead of me, how would *you* like it if it was your sons who came home crying, hysterical and wounded? But

I held the wine glass firmly and took each step one at a time like a functionally alcoholic charwoman in some early Irish novel, suppressing all I felt as I sipped away any urge to make a scene, to win my point, to vindicate my son.

The wall of the stairwell was hung with family pictures at eye level every couple of steps. The family was always posed in the exact same way. Caroline stood next her elusive husband Gregg, who was a pilot for the same airline, a fact which seemed both romantic and kind of pitiful to me at the same time. Denny stood in front of and between them, smiling that goon smile of his. Even the backdrop, a fall scene of trees and multicolored leaves remained unchanged. Through the years, little Dennis shed his boyish cuteness and became something more masculine, even threatening. By the most recent one, a couple of steps from the bottom, the sparkle in his dark brown eyes was beginning to resemble the same piercing quality as his father's. Gregg appeared to have aged very little but had tried every manner of facial hair over the years, as if daring any of it to distract from his thick blonde hair and chiseled facial features. And not only had Caroline not aged but had also performed the feat of getting thinner through the years. It was tempting to look down on the poster-sized framed photos as a weakness, a show of vanity, but they were an attractive family and knew it. Why hide it? If I'd graduated from law school, I surely would've framed my diploma and found a prominent place in my home for it.

The fug of cigar smoke and male bonding hit me just as I reached the bottom of the stairs. The basement was Gregg's preserve. The walls were covered by dark wood paneling dotted by shelves that held the spoils of his athletic youth with trophies depicting a man hitting a baseball, shooting a basketball, leaping over an unseen hurdle. At the far end sat a bar with three stools and a tattered Jets pennant peeling from the wall behind it. The room had the frustrated air of a place where it'd been hours since an unforced word had been uttered.

Daryl and Al were both seated in Lazy Boys, their cans of beers sitting on the table between them. Gregg had stretched out on the couch that ran along the side wall. His can was tucked between his thighs and he scratched his exposed and quite muscular stomach. He sat up slowly as though unbothered to be seen in such a position. Caroline sat down next to him while Marge and I took seats on the edge of the fireplace on the other side of the room.

The combination of the Jell-O shots and wine began to make my head spin. I had to fight to keep from closing my eyes and falling asleep. I was close to the TV which was gigantic, taller than I was. Dick Clark's palsied face floated into view like a partially paralyzed balloon float. The wrinkled folds of flesh around his collar were almost lizard-like. The crowd behind him hooped and hollered, yelled and screamed and all smiled as the last few minutes of the year began to wind down. Their excitement melted into thick clouds in the cold air.

"Can you imagine being there? Look at all those people," Caroline said.

"Looks exciting," Marge replied.

"It'd be cold," Al added, sighing and sipping his beer.

"We should all go some year. What do you think?" Caroline pleaded. "If I've learned anything from my travels, it's not to be afraid of crowds. Like in Venice, this one time..."

"Come on, babe. No one wants to deal with those crowds," Gregg said. He never seemed sexier to me than when he was interrupting his wife.

"I bet you it's easy to stay warm standing with everyone," Marge said.

"It'd still be cold," Al added, sighing again and shaking his can next to his ear.

"If we all went together it would be fun. What'd you say Daryl, Gloria? Next year?" Caroline pleaded. "The boys will be old enough to take care of themselves or we could get a sitter."

"It's just, like, not even worth it. You know, getting on the train and fighting all the crowds," Daryl advised. "You'd be in a mob the whole way. Besides, we used to live in the city and the people who really want to do that are the tourists, who don't know any better. There're so many better places to go, if you're going out for New Year's Eve."

"You guys never went down there, huh?" asked Gregg.

"We didn't," I said.

"We tried to stay away from all that stuff. When you live there, it's something, you know, to avoid," Daryl said. "No one really wants to go. I never really knew anyone who did or even, like, wanted to."

"No," I said, closing my eyes and tilting my head back. "No, you didn't."

The six of us counted down the last ten seconds. I watched the ball drop, its lights brilliant and blinding on the gigantic screen. No longer did I really wish to be there amongst the crowd but was glad for those who were.

11. Bests: Motherhood Moments and Orgasms

David was so engrossed in his book that I could've stood his doorway and just watched him, marveling at the concentration he showed, the very sort of which I'd lately found myself sorely lacking. As he read, I caught just a glimpse of something in his face that hinted at the painfully serious young man he'd become. Had I looked hard enough, I might've even glimpsed the man intent on fixing himself entirely, on finding a reason for every problem he had and correcting it. Like most parents, though, I only really wanted to see the person I thought my child could become.

"Alright," I said and poked my head inside his room as though I'd just arrived, "lights out. It's back to school tomorrow."

He tilted his head back. Fixing me in his too-serious gaze, his eyes asked if I was ready to give up some ground.

"Can I just finish the chapter I'm on? I want to get through this before I lend it to someone."

"Who?" I asked.

"Someone from school."

"Who? What's his name?"

"Just someone from school, okay," he whined, "No one you'd know."

"How many pages are left?" I asked.

He flipped through quickly; several pages at a time. "Not many."

"Fine. Finish the chapter and that's it. Understand?"

It could've been my imagination but I swear he flinched when I stalked across his room to lay the trace of a kiss on his forehead. I then pulled up the blanket higher to make it seem as though that, and not the stolen moment of rare motherly affection, was what I had gone in there for.

"Remember you've got school tomorrow. So try and get some sleep."

"Okay, Mom. I said I'll sleep after I finish this chapter. All I have to go is this..."

Between his fingers, David pinched together a slender group of pages. I doubted it marked the end of any chapter but left him to his reading. Backing out of the room, I watched him read a bit more and then shut the door.

One winter, years before, he must've been six or seven, it snowed every day that first week of break. Big wet flakes pasted the ground and soon piled up. That Friday after the biggest of the storms, I awoke to the sounds of Daryl shoveling -- the hollow scrape of metal against the ground, the gentle thud of his labors as he built imposing white walls on either side of the driveway. Work had been called off twice already that week for him and apparently everyone had to go in that day.

I threw on my robe, a hat and gloves and went to the front door where I found a drift higher than my knees leaning against the screen. Out in the driveway, Daryl had almost cleared enough space to back out. I squeezed into some ski pants, leftover from my long-forgotten days of privilege, grabbed the old shovel from the closet and went out to see if I could help. I was anxious by then to make sure he made it to work. Being locked in the house with both of them for days had worn me down to the quick of my sanity, though at least the heavy snow had been enough to get us out of Christmas Eve at Mother's that year.

It was early and he was too grumpy to properly appreciate my offer. He grumbled something about coffee. I was only too glad to toss aside the battered old shovel and retreat back into the warmth of the house. I took my sweet time making coffee. Let him stand out in the cold and the snow all alone, I thought.

Later, after Daryl had left for work, David started pestering me to play with him outside in the big snowbanks. He knelt on the tall living room chair that sat in between the front windows, resting his chin on the back of it and gazing out at the white kingdom nature had laid before him. He'd never seen so much snow before and to think of it, neither had I. Finally, after distracting myself with some morning talk show that I only watched because the host's stupidity made my growing misanthropy seem more intellectually permissible, I relented, put on my snow gear and then already beginning to sweat, helped David climb into his. I had a flash of teaching my son to master the same bumpy White Mountain slopes on which Daddy had taught me -- how fleeting my warmest notions of parenthood would all prove to be.

We had a brief debate about what to put on his hands. David whined that mittens were for little kids and wanted to wear gloves. I explained to him that since he'd lost one of his gloves the week before and we had no others in the house that fit him, he had to wear mittens. I also threw in a bit of Mother, informing him that if he kept better track of his things he'd have them when he wanted them. He began to sob at this obvious, if cruelly phrased, bit of wisdom. There I was, broiling in my jacket and ski pants, trying to comfort my son about the glove he'd lost.

As if diffusing a bomb, I proffered the notion that he could wear one mitten and the one glove still remaining which I'd held onto in case its brother showed up some day with tales of school bus journeys to exotic lands like the Poconos. That calmed him. The building tantrum ebbed away to a whimper almost instantly, like taking a kettle off the heat.

Crisis now averted, I took his big-boy, gloved hand, and we went out through the garage. In the driveway, a car-sized strip had been shoveled down to the concrete. Along either side of it rose great towering ridges of snow, so high that we were well hidden from our neighbors on either side, which is to say from Marge and Al's on the one side and the boarded up house wrapped in exposed, moldering mylar on the other.

"Wow," David exclaimed, "Did Daddy do all of this?"

"He did. Your father got up very early to shovel."

"He must've shoveled like a billion, million inches of snow."

"He shoveled a lot."

As with most things in his life, when it came to shoveling snow, Daryl did just enough to get by. That morning, it'd been a nearly impossible chore to clear just enough of a path up and out of the driveway. If the mountains of snow on either side of the space he'd cleared began to drift much one way or the other, he'd never be able to get the car back into the garage. Taking note, I prepared a short version of the speech I would give him about that should he have to shovel again. He took that almost-done-right approach in other areas of his life as well. In the bedroom, for instance, he'd barely get going before bringing the proceedings to an abrupt close. At least on that morning, his efforts were enough to satisfy our Taurus's needs.

David stood beneath the massive snowbanks, gazing up at them. He jumped up attempting to see over, then pressed his hand into the side where the melting snow had refrozen again and become hard. Towards the end of the driveway, he found a soft spot and began digging it out with his mittened hand. He made a snowball then sent it flying over the icy parapet. I fetched the shovels from the garage.

"Here," I said, handing him the smaller one, the beat-up one that I had attempted to use earlier that morning.

"What's this for?" he asked.

"We're going to dig out the soft snow and make a little cave for ourselves."

A look of bewilderment made steel of his hazel eyes. Sure, his father might've had the digging skills but I'd proven once again to be the creative genius of the operation. David asked no more questions and began moving little shovelfuls across the driveway, trying to toss them atop the opposite embankment. A face-full of it, blowing back at him was normally his reward. I succeeded in not laughing each time. I used my considerable bulk for something other than making craters in the couch cushions for once and sent my loads out into the street. It didn't take long before we had enough space hollowed out so that we both could sit down in our icy, manmade womb.

The distant beep of snowplows was all there was to be heard. I paused to feel what I could nearly finally feel. I was, in that frozen moment, the world's greatest mom. The idea and execution had rendered my son uncharacteristically speechless. I don't remember how long we stayed there in our little snow cave, listening to the quiet world barely moving around us, watching our breaths grow wide and white and then evaporate, but it felt as though we might live forever there.

When he finally spoke, David said he wanted to stay out there until his father got home to show him what we'd done. I suggested we'd get cold and hungry, if we waited that long. He agreed just as he did with everything I said for the rest of the day. I could do no wrong. A temporary condition that as every parent knows passes more and more quickly and becomes rarer and rarer as her child ages.

Years later, when my growing and by then much less agreeable son had finally returned to school after an interminable winter break, I let myself into his room to clean it. If I'd announced my plan to him, he would've protested the injustice of such an intrusion, a misadventure whose veneer of sterilization he would've seen as merely a cover for more nefarious ends.

He was supposed to clean his room to earn his allowance but didn't do a very thorough job. Like father like son, I guess. I already half-pitied his future lovers. When I did clean, he didn't complain much afterwards. In fact, he rarely noticed when the bed had been made, the trash emptied, the dirty clothes picked up from the floor or that the layer of dust coating every free surface like moss had been wiped away. Not even the fresh vacuum tracks were apparently enough to raise his suspicions.

As I began to pick up his clothes, I became aware of my folly in charging Daryl, a man of less than fastidious grooming habits, with having a conversation with David about his personal hygiene. My son's room stunk like old socks that had been used to cover an unusually smelly set of dick and balls. Worse than the smell was the realization that the odor was familiar, a smell I knew well. It was that of my husband. Oh yes, gents, that stench is very much your signature odor once you have been intimate with a woman, trust me. Having kids alone does not kill the romance; but having kids that remind you, without trying, of those very particular olfactory notes, slaughters even the memory of romance.

I doused the air with a generous spray of Lysol as I covered my mouth and nose. Moving quickly, I finished picking up the last of his clothes, wishing I'd thought ahead to put some tongs in my back pocket. By the time I ran the vacuum cleaner, I could just about stand the smell. The lemony air spray managed to overpower that thick dose of budding manhood.

As I dusted, I noticed with a pang of pride how neatly arranged the books were on the shelves above his desk. There were seven volumes in *Lands of Power and Dust* series. One title in particular caught my attention *Lands of Power and Dust Book IV: A Lust from the Future.* It even seemed to be pulled out a little as though waiting for me to discover it. There were many words I would have felt more comfortable encountering in my son's room than "lust." In fact, almost all of them. Carefully, warily even, I slid it from its spot and opened to a page at random.

...unaware of the danger that lay inside the young one's coat. Bedray, that thief of thieves, drew her dagger from its scabbard. Then while she smiled into the boy's laughing eyes, stuck him with it in his belly. Her long blade plunged into his skin. It drew from him a crimson cry. She withdrew the weapon. It was soaked in the boy's lifeblood. Next, she drew it across the soft, gurgling meat of his throat. His body did the dead man's dance. Blood

covered the top of his tunic with its signature stain. He
slid down the wall. Soon, he died there in a puddle of his
own crimson self.

I flipped back to the beginning of the book; searching now for that which I hoped not to find, the action
from which the work drew its title. It made me feel like
an intruder, a snoop who secretly spied on her son. The
thrill of it made me giddy enough that it took a few pages before I was really able to concentrate. I never read
the books you read, Mother told me, when in a moment
of foolishness, I asked for advice as to my son's literary tastes. In truth, secret philistine that she was, Mother
could have ended that sentence before she got to "the
books" part.

From the beginning of the book, it was clear Bedray
had been established in another volume. *"Her hair still*
like a raven's, her chest ever-heaving as she made yet an-
other escape." Along the way, the author, T.R. Ungrin,
dropped some clumsy hints that she had been wronged
and it was the reason she'd turned to a life of crime. *"She*
reminded herself again of the fate that befell many a rare
beauty. It was hard to live without a man in the world.
She was forced to face the cruelties as a woman all by
her lonesome." That's pretty much what we all do, T.R.,
with a man or not.

Against all odds of that genre, the character of Bedray turned out to be smarter and deeper than the male
characters. The *Lands of Power and Dust*, was, much
like the world in which it existed, a place dominated by
dull men and their dull laws. Bedray hadn't been born a
thief but made one by a society too afraid of strong, intelligent women to allow them admittance into the halls
of power. Or at least that was my reading.

By the time I reached the part I had first flipped to, I was on her side. She had to kill that street urchin. He was merely the weakest in a family of more timid, brutish thieves. She would go on to kill his brother for an amulet that had once belonged to her family, a rather elaborately carved piece of jade.

Naturally the insufferable hero, Greylor was tracking her down, helping those she'd wronged, judging her deeds and just making a general tedious ass of himself. There would appear to be one sure way to gain the admiration of adolescent boys, write your hero so he comes off as a self-righteous know-it-all that they can easily imitate.

"*'Her reasons are of no interest to me,' Greylor said, having to once again explain his thinking to Hucebuse.*" Greylor's companion really should've been called Hucebuse the Thick or Hucebuse Who Makes the Hero Look Good Purely By Comparison. *"'I only want her brought to justice. She needs to be made to understand how little she knows of the ways of men. Let her explain to the council, who it was that she feels had wronged her family. For there are women who feel wronged everyplace and they do not all take such bloody revenge. I say this, Hucebuse, if we permit them, the women will run riot and tear our fragile peace to pieces."*

Nary a page went by without Greylor making some equally sweeping, empty-headed pronouncement. As I read, I kept telling myself it was natural, it was after all a book for boys. I could use that mantra to overlook the blood and violence and even the chest-thumping speechifying but whenever a female character showed up if she didn't thieve like Bedray, she simpered and kissed up to the valiant, vacuous hero.

"Greylor," said Isha of New Village, "thank you on behalf of all the women here. We fear Bedray even more than Prince Feelator. He only wants us to abide his laws and pray for new ways in which to serve him. Bedray is dangerous. She has nothing but hate for all womenfolk. We can understand what she cannot."

No, maybe she hated you because you quailed like a bunch of ninnies when she tried to get you to rise up against the patriarchal power dynamic, which obviously oppresses you. She did nothing more than seek one of you to help her steal the key from beneath the prince's pillow and set her and her fellow sister-prisoners free.

Without finishing the book, whose prose grew punishing, I put Bedray back in her place and wound the cord around the back of the vacuum, winding it so tight that I almost snapped the plastic hooks. I'd let myself believe that reading anything, any book, was good. But David was coming of age, and while I hardly expected him to read Andrea Dworkin, I didn't give enough thought to how what he was reading must've been shaping his views on women and men, maybe without him even knowing it. I mean, passages like "*...be made to understand how she has erred in the ways of men*" made my discovery more shocking than finding more conventional oppressive filth like pornography. Strange but with all of this righteous confusion welling up inside of me, when I thought of the best way to handle the situation, the laziest most paternalistic plan came to mind.

Get Daryl to do it. Get Daryl, himself not exactly a Dworkin acolyte, to broach the topic of respecting women. He did, after all, respect me in a way that was admirable. In a way I never really gave him enough credit for.

In truth, part of me was afraid to talk to David about

such matters, afraid he would not understand, wouldn't take me seriously. I was also afraid that in talking to David about it, I would have to reveal that I'd snooped, crossed some line which we'd tacitly agreed upon. I could clean but not use it as an excuse to search David's room for evidence. Getting the talk secondhand with Daryl as the puppet would lend my plan the extra layer of cover I needed. David would never suspect his father had been in his room, certainly not to clean or read. Two things my son was in little danger of ever seeing his father doing.

There's no shame in admitting that ever since David had been born and really probably even before that, sex with my husband had ceased being passionate and took on a more transactional nature. It speaks well for my so-called feminine wiles that even at that late point in our marriage, it was still the best way to get him to do my biding. At least sex with him was still good for something. With Daryl, it'd never been as it had been with my first and best lover Jeremy from my college days. He was slender and somehow flabby in all the places Daryl had once been robust and muscular. Jeremy had weak wrists and sweaty hands. His penis was not even three quarters of a handful. And yet, despite all of that, what I remembered most was how he always got me there and then some, whenever we made love. It didn't take me long with him and then he'd keep taking me over, washing wave after burning wave of pleasure over me.

We'd met in a history class called Major Personalities of the 20th Century and were, along with a perpetually absent lacrosse player, assigned to do a group project on the Lever Brothers. They were British soap magnates, who along with a chemist, developed and sold what we basically have come to think of as modern soap, made of oil and tallow. They were very into their employees' health and welfare, even building a factory town for them named Port Sunlight. These facts are among a slight handful that I have held onto from all my years of education and I owe it all, I'm sure, to Jeremy and the soul-rattling orgasms he used to bring about.

And it also surely had something to do with the fact that the first thing I noticed about Jeremy was that he smelled clean, he smelled good, he smelled like someone who wanted other people to get close to him. I don't mean cologne, not like he was wearing some pumped-up testosterone-tinged deodorant of the kind advertised in the back of men's magazines that falsely proclaim to make ladies cream in their poodle skirts after only a single whiff. I even told him that he smelled nice and clean, like soap, when we first met to work on our Lever Brothers project in the smoky study room at the end of his hall. He blushed, laughed a little and smelled himself. I feared at first that he'd taken it the wrong way or had guessed the truth about how awkward and inexperienced I was. When it came out of my mouth, it kind of sounded like the olfactory equivalent of calling him a nice guy. Before what I feared was a miscommunication could go any further, I reached over and took his face in my hands, pulled him to me and had my first French kiss--the whole time worrying whether or not I was doing it right.

It turned out he was a virgin too, which was such a relief later that day when we got undressed, facing away from each other in his room. Then we each took our first clumsy steps into the world of sex and adulthood. We skipped classes the next day. We didn't leave his bed. I don't know where his roommate had gone or remember if he even had one. Together, we'd set foot in a new world and the excitement of it kept us going, gave us the courage to be naked around each other and try things that I never had the courage to try again. For a blissful 48 hours, it was as if we were inventing sex, laying down new principles and rules for pleasure and what was possible.

All three of the sexual partners I'd had since Jeremy, Daryl and two not altogether regrettable one-night stands, failed to capture the magic of those early days. Maybe it'd just been the newness, the freedom I'd allowed myself that had made it seem so exciting. Sex had briefly once seemed so much like something I wanted to do every day for the rest of my life.

Year later, life's plague known as experience, told me that I need to make sure my engine was running if I wanted to endure a night of forced passion with my husband. That was especially true on that particular day, after having encountered the cologne of my son's scrotum. In the basement, I tried to make myself comfortable in the desk chair before the computer. I had bookmarked a website that had always worked for me in the past, Lustylawyers.net. My favorite tab was *In Chambers, After Hours*. It featured stories about defense and prosecuting attorneys taking their frustrations out on each other in the judge's chambers.

All the stories there began in approximately the same manner. A motion is contested between two lawyers, one of whom was almost always described with words like "hunky" and/or "dashing" and occasionally in some of the tackier stories "sporting a deliciously noticeable bulge." His counterpart was a woman -- I always went for the hetero stuff back then -- was a real plain Jane when it came to erotica. She would often be described as "young" or "inexperienced," too often "unaware of how invitingly her chest heaved." Inevitably, there would come a point where the judge, always a man, would have to leave them alone.

Then, as in the one I read that day, the DA Jane and the defense attorney debated the pros and cons of his motion to exclude evidence obtained as part of an illegal search, which gave way to talk about their backgrounds, their hopes and dreams, how each had found their way to the law. They soon found they had much in common, not least of which was an abiding respect for their profession. Jane pointed out that an argument of inevitable discovery would be sufficient to defeat his suppression motion. Only when he admitted that her logic was unimpeachable did my juices start flowing.

Later that night, after a thoroughly bothersome 135 seconds, Daryl rolled off me and lay beside me catching his breath. There was no aching desire for an encore with my fella, I can tell you that. Panting in the dark of our bedroom, he sounded like a stranger to me, like someone I didn't really care to know. He wheezed and wowed like he had a much better time than I had, which would've almost had to be the case.

"Daryl, you awake?" I asked stroking his arm while doing my best impression of someone basking in the afterglow. "Daryl?"

"Mmmm…that was good, babe. What brought that on? What got you in the mood? Let me know so's I can like do it again."

"I'm in the mood more than you know," I said, now rubbing his thigh, "you just work too much, Mr. Hytner."

"I know but we've got his dental stuff to pay for. I'm just trying to, like, stay on top of the part the insurance doesn't cover."

"Well, if it were cheap then it probably wouldn't be something we'd want to put in our son's mouth." I pulled up the blankets and scooched closer to my heaving, cheapskate stallion. "Have you talked to him about you know…cleaning himself properly and puberty and what was going to change with him? Like we discussed a while back. Remember?"

"It's just like wires and plastic isn't it? How could it be so expensive?"

"He's a specialist. They're expensive. We've talked about that. Remember?" I rolled next to him and gently pinched some of the flab around his waist. "It's a good thing your insurance covers so much it, otherwise we'd have to find some kid with the same size mouth who we could rent the retainer out to during the day to cover the cost."

"Gross. Do people, like, do that?" he asked.

"Exploring the black market of dental appliances isn't something we have to do quite yet," I said, feeling a slight headache coming on. "More importantly for right now, you need to talk to him about how his body is changing, about hormones and all of that."

"I made sure to tell him about showering every day and to keep himself clean and, like, you know, use deodorant and all of that."

"I think you need to talk to him again because I was cleaning his room today and it smelled. Smelled…unhygienic."

"Smelled? Smelled like what? Un-hi…"

"Like sweaty balls, Daryl. Jesus, what do you think it would smell like?"

"I don't know. You always go at this shit sideways.

Can't you just ask me to, you know, talk to him about scrubbing his balls up right?"

"I thought that's what I did."

"Yeah, yeah I guess you did." He rolled onto his side away from me, taking the bedsheet with him. "Can't you be like simpler about it? You know, just say to me: Daryl, dude, our son smells like a giant walking dick; can you talk to him about cutting that down a bit?"

"Is that how I have to put it?"

"Mmmm…"

"It's just that he's coming to an age when he'll be interested in girls soon and I want him to have a chance. There's no bigger turn off than a boy who smells."

"Yeah. I know."

"What do you think he thinks about girls?" I asked, expecting a great deal of further prodding was going to be necessary.

"Dunno."

"Has he ever asked you any questions about them?"

"Nah. Not really."

"Have you told him about the importance of respecting women and treating them as equals? Have you told him not to take seriously the representations of women he encounters in movies and on TV and in his books?"

"Mmmm…hmmm…"

"Men too. Have you talked to him about how inaccurately they are portrayed?"

"Mmmm…hmmm…" he said again, then began to snore lightly.

"Daryl," I said and pinched harder at the flab which I had not let go of.

"Ow! What? What is it?"

"I want you to talk to him about respecting women,

respecting them always."

"I will, I will," he cried and pried my hand open. "I will talk to him."

"What will you tell him?" I asked.

"I don't know. I'll think of something."

"That's not much of a strategy."

"Okay. I'll tell him that nothing in anything he reads is, like, 100% accurate when it comes to men and women. That he won't find the kind of women he comes across in books and movies and all of that in the real world. That women, that, you know, all people, like, are more complex than that. He shouldn't, you know, take the other stuff seriously. He should find out for himself. Like keep his mind open when he meets people, 'cause they'll surprise you."

"Daryl," I said with a somewhat astonished gasp, "that sounds perfect. Just make sure to remind him how important respecting people is, respecting women like he would men."

"Yeah, yeah, I know. I know what you want me to say."

I kissed him and held him to me. The night had been a success.

12. Girly Ambition

Curled up beneath an afghan with my feet tucked somewhere under my thighs on the ratty, sleep-away couch which had been Daryl's bed when I first met him, I watched as Judge Darlene Quincy shamed some lazy twenty-something who was being sued by her former roommate. I felt bad for the girl. She was chunky with dirty blonde hair and sad eyes. There was something lost about her, something about her face made it seem as though she'd always been and would always be dumped on. I turned off the TV, feeling a little depressed that the verdict had gone against her.

With an eye towards commiserating with the failure I'd just been exposed to, I slid from the couch and went over to the computer to resume the humiliation of my job search. This day, I didn't have to swallow my pride quite so often or so deeply, as I found an administrative position with a feminist think tank in the city. I felt truly invigorated for the first time in years, like a whole carton of Yodels awaited me at the end of my task.

I pictured myself getting on the train, opening a book to read on the way and ignoring Daryl and David, who waved their proud good-byes. I entered an office filled with bright no-nonsense women, who could see in me the long dormant promise of doing more than lounging around, vaguely loathing what I'd allowed my life to become. We'd discuss Andrea and Betty and Susan during long lunches and how to overthrow the worldwide patriarchy over drinks after work. Surely, these members of the sisterhood would understand the gaps and general thinness of my resume. They'd know the limited amount of rewarding work open to someone in my situation.

Maybe they'd even pay for me to finish law school, maybe I could find one in the city that would allow me to pick up where I'd left off. I could rise and become one of the most valuable members of their group. I'd take on corporate sexism at the highest levels and help sisters not just break through the glass ceiling, which was after all a part of the male vision of the world that had been forced upon women, but I'd destroy the walls and shatter all barriers and begin to transform the whole capitalist system. Make it more maternal. Castrate it, once and for all.

In dusting off my boilerplate cover letter, I found it to be a little timid for those dreams. If ever there was a time when I could be honest and daring, this seemed to be it.

Dear Ms. Schulman,

I am writing to express my interest in the Administrative Manager position currently open with your organization.

I paused trying to think of a way of presenting myself as someone other than a person who feared having her fem card taken away, who feared she wouldn't be taken seriously. The text that followed read like I was just looking for something to get me out of the house and needed to be rewritten. I highlighted part of the letter after that first line, then all of it up to *Sincerely,* and deleted it. The blank screen mocked me. I started a couple more times before breaking off and erasing it.

The same chain of activity was repeated again and again. I started and failed so many times that I feared I'd lost the ability to string together a compelling series of words. By the time David got home, letting the screen door slam behind him and a cold draft of air to flow into the house, the screen was blank once again.

Happy for the chance to put off another attempt, I pushed myself away from the desk and raced upstairs like my son had returned home from combat. What did my baby do? What did he see? Is he in one piece? Damp footprints led from the front door to his room, where he was sitting on his bed reading, boots still on.

"David," I said, easily finding the energy it took to raise my voice above the appropriate level, "how many times have I told you to take off those filthy wet boots when you come inside?"

He said nothing, slumped from the bed and kicked off his boots, managing to do so without use of either of his hands. He then reclined back on the bed. His eyes hadn't left the page. His boots sat in a heap, filthy water soaking into the carpet.

"By the door!" I yelled, putting all of the afternoon's frustration into my voice.

The whole way down the hall, I fought the urge to harangue him. Being aware of that kind of behavior, *projecting*, or whatever the wannabe shrinks like my old friend Maria called it, often didn't keep me from doing it. Quite the contrary, I often found myself more inclined to trust actions that seemed driven by some deep if only vaguely identifiable instinct. But in that instance, I only glared at David as he put his boots on the plastic mat that was right next to the fucking door. I knew I had triumphed in our game when one of the boots tipped over and landed on its side and rather than just walk away, David stooped to stand it upright again.

Whatever warm feeling I had experienced from that little victory had all but evaporated in the few minutes it took me to walk back downstairs, sit at the desk and return to my task. The cursor still jeered. The blank screen went on taunting me.

Then, it hit me. My challenge was to make it look as though I had been keeping up on the issues much more than I had been. It couldn't appear that I'd softened in my opposition to the patriarchy. And I hadn't really. I'd just slept with my husband in order to get him to talk to our son about respecting women. My logic may have been convoluted, but I was clear in my aims.

Dear Ms. Schulman,

I am writing to express my interest in the Administrative Manager position currently open at your organization. I learned of this job on one of my frequent visits to your website, which never fails to keep me updated on the latest news with regards to women's issues. I fear a lot of us lose sight of these issues once we leave school and start a family. Once we lose contact with each other and each other's struggle, we begin to forget what feminism should truly be about. We start families of one kind or another and forget about the lives of others. In a moment of weakness, I even took my husband's name to avoid an argument with his mother. I have failed again and again to keep our struggle at the forefront of my thoughts.

This is why I think your organization and others like it is so crucial. Keeping women informed and in touch--

"Mom," David cried from the top of the stairs in a piercing whine that told me he was about to raise a point of almost incandescent triviality. "Mom…" If I failed to acknowledge him, he would just continue braying down to me like some stranded baby goat.

"What?" I cried.

"Have you seen…"

"David, how many times have I told you to come downstairs, if you want to talk to me? I'm not going to compete with you in a shouting match," I said, shouting myself. Never let hypocrisy slow you down.

He creaked his way to the midpoint of the staircase, just far enough to allow him to speak in nothing more than a slightly raised voice. David always did have such an innate feel for the nature of compromise.

"Have you seen *Bedray's Final Return*?" he asked.

"Have I seen what?"

"*Bedray's Final Return*. It's book five."

"Aren't you on Book 7 or something?" I asked.

"Yeah. I am. But I like to have them in order on my shelf."

"I'm sure it's in your room."

"It's not. I looked."

"Didn't you loan it to some mysterious friend?" I asked. "The one you never mention by name?"

"No. I did not."

"Did you put it under your pillow so that Greylor will visit you in your dreams?"

"I told you, I don't do that anymore," he screeched.

"David, I don't know what to tell you. I didn't take it out of your room."

"Will you come up and help me look for it?"

"Not now."

"Awwww...please...I'm no good at looking for things. You always say so. You always I say I wouldn't find my belly button if it wasn't..."

"There's only one way to improve on that," I said and then threw my head over the back of the chair so I could shout an emphatic, "Go look," right up at him.

He trudged away, his steps as leaden as he could make them. I reread what I had so far, highlighted it but didn't delete it. I wanted to finish one draft, one personal draft of the kind of letter I would like to write before tearing out the guts of it to make it sufficiently 'professional,' whatever I thought that was supposed to mean.

I've done more than merely study and stay abreast of the current state of our worldwide movement. In raising my son, I have sought to instruct him as to how to negotiate the world, which bombards him daily with sexist messages, distorting the image of women for him as well as other boys like him. One must make certain that their child's conception of her or his place in the world is not perverted or, worse, controlled by the ruling corporate patriarchy whose goal is to perpetuate the status quo.

"Mom, Mom," David's shouting preceded his steps, racing down the hall, back towards the stairs. "Have you been in my room?" His voice was so full of righteous rage that I found myself a little afraid to answer, afraid he would see through any lie. "I know you have," he continued, "because all of my books are straight in a line and I just remembered I had one of them pulled out, pulled out just a little."

"You had one what? Wait…why?"

"I had the one before it pulled out, book four. I was going to reread that one first once I finished book seven."

"Dave, you've got me," I said, rising from my seat and going to the bottom of the stairs. His face was red, his arms rigid and tense at his sides. He held his hands balled up into exasperated little fists. "I had to clean your room yesterday," I said. "Are you just now noticing this? What do you think happened to the clothes on the floor? To the dust that was on every single thing? To the…"

"Mother," he shrieked, using the word for me that I had come to think of as a slur, "I asked you, told you not to go in there. My room is my place. I get to decide…"

"David, let me tell you something," said I bounding up the stairs with enough determination to make my son step back. "I don't really enjoy going into your room. It's not something I relish. I wish, truly, dearly wish that you kept it at least clean enough so that the unholy reek emanating from it did not creep out of that boundary zone and force me to…"

"It's my mess and my smell," he said. His face was so red with rage, so alive. Little snake-like veins popped out of his neck, making him so beautiful to me just then. "Don't laugh," he shrieked, his voice cracking pitifully.

"I'm not. I'm not," I said, only then feeling the breadth of my smile. "You're right. I should stay out of there and I will but we need to agree on something…"

"No deals…"

"David Raymond Hytner, don't push your luck. You've raised your voice to me enough today."

He crossed his arms over his chest and sighed enough that his whole body seemed to deflate.

"Let's make this deal," I said, copying his pose. "You put your clothes in the hamper and really clean, I mean dust and run the vacuum once a week, and I will never set foot in there again when you aren't home. I promise. You'll get that as well as the bi-weekly allowance which you have been getting despite your less than stellar cleaning efforts."

"How about raising it to once a week?"

"It's as good a deal as you are going to get David. You've wrangled a concession out of me without really giving anything up."

"What do you mean by a concession? What's been conceded?"

"It's a good deal, Dave. Take it."

He took my hand and gave it a firm shake.

"Now, as to the location of book five…I'm afraid I cannot say. I really don't know where it went."

"I'll go look again but it's not in there," he said, then retreated back down the hall. The fire in eyes as he turned from me was now just a light. The blood had left his face. The veins had shrunk back beneath the skin. He was my meek little boy once more.

"Good luck," I said.

He went back to his room and I returned to the basement and to the cover letter that had begun to take on housewife manifesto proportions. I managed to make it all the way to *"keep myself abreast of current issues…"* before highlighting the whole of it and deleting. It would do me no good to come across like some overeager, half-informed undergrad. I went back to work, ignoring the doorbell as I tried to figure out how to de-stink my own bullshit a little.

"Mom, Mom," David started again before I could finish my thought.

Having already partially bent to his will once that afternoon, I was in no mood to do it again. So, I just sat there before the blank screen and let it mock me. He continued to call for me even as he descended the stairs. I remained silent and waited until he'd reached the bottom and could speak to me at a normal volume.

"Mom, it's Sarah."

"Did you invite her in?"

He shook his head.

"So, you left her standing out in the chilly air," I managed to make this sound unthinkable, even though I'd never invited her in myself.

"She's asking for you."

"Oh...ah...well...tell her that I'm...that I'm...that I'm busy on the computer."

"But it looks like you're not doing anything," he said, tilting his head to the side to peek around me. "The screen's blank."

"Well, we have...we have to...we have to look for your book."

"We can look for it later. Like you said, I already read it."

"But you want to read it next."

"No, I don't. Book four is the one I was going to read again. It was the one pulled out the most."

"We should find book five now while the trail is warm," I said and got up from the chair. "Tell her I'm busy, then I'll come up and help you."

"Alright," he said.

He went back quickly to deliver the bad news to Sarah. I crept halfway up to hear how he handled it. I didn't want to talk to her but didn't want to hurt her feelings either. They seemed to speak for a while. I heard that laugh of hers echo through the house like an empty shout. David joined her with a giggle. Once I heard him close and lock the front door, I emerged fully from the basement.

"She seemed like she had something important to tell you," he said.

"I know but Mummy doesn't really have the energy to talk to her right now."

"How come it takes energy to talk to her?"

"It takes energy for me to talk to just about anyone these days," I said and hoped he'd have no follow up questions.

"Is it because it's hard to know what she's saying

sometimes?" he asked.

"You do have to listen hard to her."

"You also have to make sure she can understand what you're saying, huh?"

"See, David. I think you know what I mean."

"I do," he said. "I try to talk to her sometimes."

"That's great, David. You should. Just because she's…," I said, then stumbled for the right words just as I'd been doing all day. "What were you talking about just now?"

"I was asking her about her bike. It's nice."

"She certainly seems to get a lot of use out of it."

"Can I get a ten-speed?" he asked.

"Maybe for your next birthday."

"With a rack like hers? Can mine have a rack on the back?"

"We'll have to wait and see."

"Why do we have to wait?' he asked. "Why can't we get one now?"

"Your birthday is when we get you the extra things like that."

"That's like almost an entire year away."

"Well, we can't really afford one right now."

"We can't ever afford anything, extra. It sucks."

No argument from me there.

That night in bed, I sat up as rigidly as I could, two pillows propped up behind my head, a magazine in my lap. It was the posture I always adopted for successive days following sex with Daryl. It was my way of showing him that the flutter of passion of the preceding night had passed. He climbed in next to me then lay on his side trying to look seductive, I guess. I felt his stare. He stroked my arm until I shook my head, murmuring something about being too tired. He rolled halfway over onto his back, letting out a huff that was just loud enough to tell me he got the message and not so loud that it annoyed me.

I noticed with something of a start that he had brought a book with him into bed. He fluffed his pillow and put it behind his head. The book rested on his belly.

"What're you doing?" I asked.

He flashed me the cover. There she was, Bedray, wearing a cloak with a collar that dropped down far enough to offer a glimpse of her cleavage. She sprawled across a divan, one arm caressed the thigh of a man the rest of whom was out of the frame, the other held an open sack that appeared to be full of gold coins. *Land of Power and Dust Book V: Bedray's Final Return*. It wasn't so much the lasciviousness implied by her posture that creeped me out but the steely come hither look in her eyes that were an otherworldly shade of purple. I knew maturity was making me into something of a prude, when my own inner voice echoed that of Mother's: "Is that titillating filth what passes for literature nowadays?"

"Is that David's? When did you get that?" I asked.

"This morning. I went to his room before work and you know, slipped out with this. I'm trying to, like, psyche myself for this talk you want me to have with him about washing his balls and respecting women and so on. I thought I'd try to find out what he thinks about girls. Find some clues."

"He's been searching for that book. I spent half the afternoon dealing with the fact that it was missing."

"I picked this one because of all of them it had the, like, cover that would most make you roll your eyes and give me a speech if I were to, you know, look at it wrong.

Like, if he walked into the house after being out with me and you noticed he had it, you'd just have to give me some talk in that strict schoolteacher voice: 'What were you thinking, Daryl? Don't you watch him when you're in the store with him? Don't you see what you are buying him?' Except in this case, you were probably with him so maybe I ought to be giving you that speech. Not that I would 'cause, like, you never take me seriously about…"

"Brilliant Daryl. But, I don't get those for him. He orders them through the book order at school. All that's on the sheet is a checklist with the title and the amount."

"She is kinda hot," Daryl said, taking another look at the cover.

"You're going to have to explain to him that you took it, Daryl. He was positively apoplectic about it."

"You mean he had a fit or something?" he asked, sounding as though he suspected he might know what apoplectic meant but couldn't be sure.

"Close. He was almost in tears."

"God, the little dude needs to relax. He's always crying. Kids'll really pick on him for that when he gets older."

"I think that's already started," I said.

"Poor little dude."

"For now, just work on getting him to wear deodorant, wash himself properly and not think of all women as greedy purple-eyed whores who go around slitting boys' throats for jewelry."

"She does that?" he asked, taking the opportunity to glance again at the cover.

"In a previous book."

"Shit, don't ruin it for me."

"I can't. I haven't read that one yet."

"So far, this Greylor dude is just giving speeches about, like, honor and being the right kind of warrior and shit like that."

"Yes, he does a lot of shit like that," I said which for some reason earned me a laugh and a sloppy kiss on the cheek.

It was the kind of moment that once, very long ago, would've set off sparks. But now, he just went back to Bedray and I to Gabby, the teen television star that had it all, looks, an album coming out, and her own reality show. Just wait, Gabby, and see if you've still got everything figured out when you're nearing forty with a kid coming up on his teens who doesn't yet know how to correctly wash his own genitals.

13. The Morning of the Chubber

Daryl was still sleeping, arms sprawled, reaching for me but I'd been in my customary spot on the other side of the bed, clinging almost to the edge. "Remember to call Mom," he managed to growl, half-intelligibly as the creaking bed springs announced my escape. He'd told his mother about the day's excursion and made plans for me to meet up with her. I wouldn't have minded except for the fact that my schedule for the day was being partially managed by a man who wouldn't know when to shit if his asshole didn't start to open.

David was sleeping soundly in a tight little ball. It'd been his preferred position since he was a baby. I decided to let him sleep a while longer but we'd have to leave soon to make it in time for the sale. I needed some of the morning to myself so I could collect my thoughts and make sure of my plan of action. That was what my life had been reduced to, preparing my mind for a shopping trip. The fact that I am still alive and have not, as of this writing, offed myself is proof that I no longer spend time meditating on matters such as how best to attack the husky section at JC Penney's.

If I had a favorite time to be in the kitchen in those days, the rare very early mornings on weekends when I was the first one up would've been high on a short list. There was no evidence of Daryl's hasty leave-taking that marred the weekdays. No puddles of coffee on the counter, no crumbs or faint burnt odor from the Pop Tarts or bread that he'd managed to overcook in the toaster. Everything was as clean as I'd left it the night before. I put on the kettle and got myself a teabag and mug. A new layer of snow shone white and crisp in the just-breaking light. Not wanting to wake anyone, I only let the kettle start coughing up some steam before taking it off the heat. I filled my mug. Let it steep. For a few precious moments, I felt like the only person on Earth. The ice stirred in the gutter; tree limbs snapped in the breeze. Nearly perfect, these sounds nestled back into the silence. I wanted to hold onto them, take them somewhere deep inside of me.

I felt the need to hold a line when we'd moved out there by demanding that we not live in a town with a mall. The pretentiousness that led me to make such a demand was based on the thinking that if we just didn't live too close to one, it wouldn't be so much like living in the suburbs and somehow that would equal charm. On that particular morning, many years and long trips with a whiny son to the mall later, I found myself wishing we lived near enough to one to send David off walking with a credit card and a list of what he needed.

Remember to try things on before you buy anything or you'll be walking right back there. Mind the traffic. Look both ways before crossing the highway.

"Why do we have to go so early?" he asked later, pinching crusts of sleep from the corners of his eyes as we backed out of the driveway.

"Told you that the sale ends at 10 and if we wait too close to that time to get there, all the jeans in your size will be gone."

"Why will all the jeans in my size be gone? How do you know for sure?"

"They don't seem to carry a lot in your size."

"I'm fat," he said bitterly, fixing his eyes on the passing road as though his waistline was the filthy snowbank's fault.

"No. You're not," I said. "You just have big thighs. Your thighs are those of an older boy, a teenager. They're mature, mature thighs."

And your ass was positively venerable. Sorry son, it got passed right down the line to you from me, from my dad, from his mother and probably as far back as our family goes.

The overcast sky was a dingy mix of grey and white without any distinct cloud forms. I drove cautiously over the snow-covered roads. Despite the early hour, the traffic getting on the highway was thick. People were always leaving Roslyndale. On that day, we seemed to be the only ones heading west.

David complained some more as we made our way, tossing one or two ideas around that questioned the need for me to buy him clothes. I'd gotten so good at tuning him out by then that I barely noticed, while still contributing enough word-like sounds to the discussion that he couldn't tell. Luckily, the mall in Odenbrook was not far off the highway, so at least I didn't have to see another depressing river valley suburb.

I pulled up to a spot on the backside of the complex where the loading docks and dumpsters were visible. That would allow us to enter Penney's without David seeing the sign that identified the section we'd be shopping in as BOYS' HUSKY. I didn't have the energy it would've taken to soothe his ego again that morning. There was a cluster of cars parked near that entrance while most of the rest of the lot was still empty at that hour. Apparently, all of us fat-ass mommas with our fat-ass kids thought it best to try and avoid advertising the fact that we had to shop in the husky section. Charting the fastest way in so we could lay our hands on the right size of the widest cut jeans and get back out before anyone really noticed was the easiest for all egos involved.

Just outside the loading docks, a young kid with a sparse mustache and pleated trousers stood smoking. His tie hung around his collar unknotted. He breathed smoke through his nose at us as we passed. How early had he gotten up in order to earn something less than a real living wage? I'd be smoking too if it were me. As I opened the door, I heard him slurp from the paper cup he was holding and then spit it out. How much customer service experience could he've had before getting a job there? I'd always thought myself above working retail but was slowly beginning to realize the water table of opportunities available to me had been steadily dropping and would soon be too shallow to safely just dive in.

"We'll get breakfast after this," I said holding the door for my son, uttering the same tragic promise that had likely been made many times at that particular ingress already that morning. "But you have to try stuff on here."

"Aw, Mom, I don't want to try stuff on now, not here. Can't it wait until we get home?"

"No, that kind of defeats the purpose of getting up early and coming here with me. And since this stuff is all on sale, if it doesn't fit, I can't take it back. All sales are final."

"I hate the fitting room. The lighting is all weird."

My little supermodel.

"Don't be such a baby, David. It's just a few pairs of jeans. The less time you spend whining about things, the quicker we'll be out of here."

Unsurprisingly, only mothers had braved the hour and slick roads for this delicate excursion; there wasn't a man anywhere in sight. There were two circular racks with jeans that were well out of our price range. On the wall to the left of the fitting rooms were hutches holding the coveted on-sale jeans with sizes listed on the rim of each hole. Before the wall stood a mother and son. He clutched a pair of the more expensive designer jeans to his chest, while she shook her head. There are few things more heartbreaking than a fat kid with an acute fashion sense. Two other shoppers conversed in a low tone outside the fitting room. "Does it fit right?" was a phrase best whispered in that particular vicinity.

The mother and son pairs moved around each other politely. Being a little overweight around other fat people is like sailing. You have to think and steer ahead to avoid violent collisions. The three boys did not look at each other. When their eyes were not on the floor, they were on the wall of jeans.

As we approached the hutches, I thought of a job for myself, which would use much of my life experience. I could've made a great shopping concierge for overweight kids. I'd been there often enough to know what made the husky section so unbearable. What they needed was someone like me to cheer them on, make them feel good about shopping there. "It's not the kid's section fellas, you're in the husky section now. You have the thighs and asses of men." I could help the young fashion plates find things that flattered rather than just fit. If the store's manager only took a look at the world of rapidly expanding waistlines, he'd see how ahead of things I was. "Look at it this way, gang, you got out of those infant car seats well before your skinny friends." If only we had a second car, I'd do it, I'd find a way to apply for a position there and turn it into a job. No check that, a career.

"Now remember, you're wearing the kind of shirt that should be tucked in, so do so. That way, we can be sure that the jeans fit you right," I said as I began pulling pairs out.

"How many do we have to get?" he asked.

"At least four."

"Four," he gasped as though the number was incomprehensible.

"You're right, six."

"No. No. You said four. I only need four. I'll try on enough so that we can get four."

"Let's get this done," I said. "I want some pancakes."

"Can we go to Stax?" he asked.

"Where else would we go? All you can eat."

One mother and son pair left after an apparently dispiritingly unsuccessful series of sorties into the fitting room. The boy was tragically obese, an absolute mountain of a kid. The mother and son, who'd been arguing, also had left once their fight had ended. She'd snatched the designer jeans away from him. Their generously denimed thighs lightly slapped him in the face, accidently on purpose I was sure. All these rotund boys moving around looked like moons trapped in their mother planets' orbits.

I continued my search, handing jeans down to David. The goal was not just to find ones in his size but also for the size he would no doubt soon be. He held out his arms in front of him like a rack. His posture was slouched and indifferent. He didn't question me about a single pair. Once I'd handed him five or six, I asked if they were okay and if there were any he especially liked. To my surprise, he indicated a white pair. I reached up on tiptoes and managed to pull down a couple that were in his size.

"What made you pick these?" I asked.

"I just like them. They're different."

"Okay," I said.

He'd never expressed any preference for a single item of clothing before, save that which would make him resemble Greylor. I couldn't yet be sure if that turn of events was going to make things any easier but was pleased at the glimpse it offered of a day soon coming when I would no longer need to accompany him on those trips. Boys, if you think shopping with Mommy is torture, try taking your own sons someday.

"Alright, now get into the fitting room and let's see how they look."

Since no one else was waiting for their sons to appear, I hoped things would go smoothly. No matter how obvious it was, David couldn't bear to hear that something was too tight. And telling him not to suck in his tummy was risky. Any remarks that even hinted that an item was too small caused him to lament his size, curse the world and, you guessed it, cry in a way that always seemed cruelly calculated to shame me.

"Fits fine," he said, stepping back into the store minutes later with a pair of stonewashed blue jeans on.

"Tuck in your shirt and we'll see."

He grunted and made a half-hearted effort to get the tail of his shirt beneath the waist of the jeans, managing to make the act look more difficult and unpleasant than it possibly could've been. I mean for holy fuck's sake I merely asked him to tuck in his shirt. His effort redefined the term half-assed and ended with the shirt still half-untucked. That pair did not fit well. When he came out again, he was wearing another pair whose button didn't fasten even with the great gulps of air he was taking.

"If you can't button them," I said, checking to make sure there still was no one around, "you don't have to bother coming out, just set them aside. The label on them is probably wrong."

Finally, he came out with his shirt tucked into a pair that fit reasonably well. They were a little baggy but he'd grow into them. Success.

"How many more do we need?" he asked, starting to remove them while he was still out in the store.

"Well, let's see. We came to get four. We've found one that fits. How many more do we need? What's four minus one?"

"Three," he said after a pause that really was far longer than it should have been.

Again. David. Gifted?

"These fit good," he said, appearing in a pair that seemed to fit. Of course, it was difficult to tell as his shirt flapped down over the waist.

"David. Your shirt." I shut my eyes as I feared the mere sight of my son in that moment would touch off a blistering tension headache.

He reprised his tortured tucker act. Sighing, he began to contort his body as though I'd asked him to slip into a straightjacket. He made noises that almost sounded like curse words, but I let it go as it wasn't worth causing a scene over, even if no one else was around.

"Fine," I said, staying calm. "Two to go."

He came out with another pair that appeared to fit well. I pulled him close to me, which he resisted, and checked beneath his untucked shirt. I resisted the urge to tuck it in myself, just made some noises of my own that were even closer to curse words than his.

"One more to go," I said and glanced away as he

once again began to de-pants himself inside the store.

"We're done," he said, emerging again with his arms spread wide.

This time, he had the white jeans on. They would not have been my first choice but I was so stunned and pleased that he'd shown a preference that I really wanted them to fit. It made it less pleasing then, a good deal less pleasing, to see him again with his shirt untucked. Blood nearly roiling, I went over to him, and taking the hem of the shirt, tugged him to me. Starting from the back, I began to tuck in his shirt so as to save my overworked son the trouble.

"Mom," he complained and squirmed; but Greylor himself wouldn't have broken free of my clutches.

"If you'd just tucked the freaking shirt into your underwear to begin with, like I showed you," I said through gritted teeth, "we wouldn't have to go through this every time you try…"

My frustration and bubbling anger prevented me from being as careful and gentle as I could've been. As I came to the front, where the button was, I went about my task too zealously, my hand going in deeper than I would've liked. My first two fingers slipped past, too far past, the waistband of his underwear. And, for what was surely the most excruciating microsecond of either of our lives, my nails, then cuticles, then the first knuckles of my index and ring fingers were pressing against what was unmistakably my son's erect penis.

Time froze. Stiff.

Yuck.

David's eyes widened. I withdrew my hand quickly. Not nearly quickly enough. He backpedaled into the fitting room, one hand hovering protectively over his crotch. I checked the area again. Shoppers came in the door and passed us, unaware that I'd just accidentally molested my son.

David spent as long in the changing room after that as he had to try on all of the jeans combined. A part of me wished he'd gotten lost back there, slipped into some sort of vortex created by our twin shames and would re-emerge some day in the distant future with no memory of the event whatsoever. Wishing that I would forget it seemed too much to ask. I took a clutch of tissues from the travel pack in my purse and wiped off my fingers.

While I continued to wait, I heard the sound of a commotion developing behind me. I turned to find the tubby fashion plate and his mother planet back and still engaged in a dispute as they reentered the galaxy of the husky section. The boy clutched hard to a pair of twill slacks slung over his shoulder while his mother held two bulging shopping bags. His face was red.

"You're not coming in with me," he said to her through clenched teeth as he passed me.

"Fine, but you have to let me see how they fit," she said.

Due to his size, it was difficult to tell if the boy was older than David. He snorted his way into the fitting rooms, a faint trail of cologne floating in his wake.

"Doesn't want me in there with him anymore," she said to me. "Acts like he's so ashamed to even be seen with me. Like I didn't see him au naturel every day of his life for the first couple of years…whether I wanted to or not."

"Yeah, true," I said.

"I mean, what's he so afraid of?" she asked then stepped towards me and cupped her hands around her mouth. "I mean, I used to wash his wee-willy-winky for him."

"Sorry? Wee-willy-winky?"

"Oh, you know. His…" She pointed down towards her crotch.

"Ahh…" was all I could really come up with.

David had neatly folded the four pairs that fit. Without meeting my eyes, he presented them to me. We went to find a manned register, the husky section being an outpost that apparently didn't require one. In all of the confusion, I guess I'll call it, I forgot to call my mother-in-law. I sent her a text that we were done when we got back to the car. I wasn't sure her phone could receive them. And I didn't care.

Had the seats been upholstered with nails and the floor covered with writhing poisonous snakes, I doubt the car ride to breakfast that morning would have been any more uncomfortable. David didn't speak or glance in my direction. Sometimes, it's better to let things tuck themselves under the rug if they can, or so Mother used to say. I once found that bit of wisdom to be just part of the emotional cowardice that was so typical of her. Funny what accidentally groping your son will do to your outlook on things in the moments immediately following.

When we finally reached Stax Pancake House, Gail was waiting for us at the door, smiling and wearing an idiotic reindeer ski cap complete with antlers. David had once, when he was little, made the mistake of laughing a little too enthusiastically at that cap. From then on, Gail wore it on every cold day that he was to see her. I hadn't quite put the car in park before David was unfastening his seat belt, climbing out and bounding towards her. He hugged her in a way that seemed to surprise her. She gripped his jacket greedily, closing her eyes, knowing it was a moment to savor. I feared he was about to tell her what had just happened. A tragic chain of events unspooled itself in my mind, each iteration of the story told first to her, then surely to Daryl, then a cop, then a judge, then my cellmate. This flash happened in a second, just long enough for me to concoct a tragic ending for myself. I'd always heard kiddie diddlers had a rough go of it in prison.

"Gloria? Is everything okay?" Gail asked.

I put on a smile and commanded my neck to offer a passable nod.

"Where's his…?" she asked motioning towards his mouth.

"His retainer?" I ventured.

"I only wear it at night now," David said.

"But he had it on at Thanksgiving," she said.

"No, I didn't," David said.

"He didn't," I added.

"I must not have noticed," Gail said, then bent down a little and examined his face. "His teeth don't look so b`ucked."

"What?" I asked. My skin, already licked by the fever of my earlier humiliation, went hot and flushed again. "What did you say about his teeth?"

"Just…that…his teeth." She shrank back away from us as if picking up on the shaky current we both must've been giving off like a couple of crossed wires. "They look nice. They're not such buck teeth. They look like they are getting close to…normal."

"Oh," I said, "bucked."

David walked ahead of us like he belonged to someone else, like he wished his real family was already inside, and he was on his way to join them. Throwing open the door, he rushed inside, happy to seat himself as the sign next to the empty hostess station commanded.

"I'm sorry," Gail whispered, wringing her hands then grabbing me by the arm. "I didn't mean anything by that. I just wanted to say how nice his teeth were coming in. Oh, and here you two seemed like you were having such a good morning."

"Let's just hope he gets over it during breakfast," I said and left her to follow me in.

I planned to let David eat as many pancakes as he wanted, soaked in as much syrup as he could actually physically handle. Paramedics be on standby. If fortune was in my favor, maybe it would set off some sort of diabetic coma which, when he came out of it, would leave him with no memory of the morning. Is there an endocrinologist about? I'd let him eat so much that Gail Hytner, who while not the first name in obsequiousness was certainly a top candidate, would blanch and be tempted to wonder aloud if I should be allowing my son to have yet another stack, cascading with yet another slow waterfall of Vermont's honey-brown gold.

As for myself, if a women's correctional facility was to eventually be my fate, then maybe it was time to really just let go of the whole motherhood thing. If I was going to be savaged and beaten by other women for my terrible parenting, then I might as well really earn the beatings.

David examined the menu closely, presumably to cut down on the chance that he would have to speak to me. I did pretty much the same thing to avoid both him and Gail, who just sat there watching us, smiling, hands gripping the table's edge like a trained otter awaiting a fish to be thrown her way. She breathed hard with a creaking sound as though something were flapping around in her chest and throat.

A young girl with "Brittany" on her nametag and washed-out blonde hair barely hid her boredom as she asked if we wanted anything to drink. Perhaps figuring that he was in a strong bargaining position, David ordered himself the "Manly Man Mug" of hot cocoa. I went with tea while Gail was predictably "fine with just water, dear." I'd never noticed before but sitting there in that back booth, watching the snow starting to swirl down, I thought of how she ordered "just water" to drink at every single restaurant that I'd ever been to with her. It made me want to scream.

"Ever try the hot chocolate here, Gail?" I asked. "I hear it's really good."

"No," she said, patting at her little deflated bike tire of a midsection. "Trying to watch my figure. Don't want my belly bulging."

God. Poor Gail. I let myself go completely when I got to be her age. Mine is like a stack of ATV snow tires now.

"George's doctor advised him to lose some weight so we're trying it together."

"It's hot cocoa that they serve here, not hot chocolate," David said, picking up his head just long enough to ascertain whether or not he'd gotten our attention. "Hot cocoa is made from powder, while hot chocolate comes from melted chocolate. But the cocoa is more chocolate-tasting where the hot chocolate is just thicker."

"My goodness! Such a smart boy. I didn't know that. Did you?" she asked me. I shook my head. "Where did you learn about that Dave?"

"Read about it."

"Where? In one of those books you always have your nose in?"

"One of those books," I said. "Does Greylor give a speech about how one is nobler than the other?"

"No. I read about it at school," David said. This time he lifted his head just enough to send a stabbing glare across the table at me.

"'ere you go," said the waitress, arriving just in time with his mug, my tea and Gail's *just water*. He cupped it, blew into it and took a sip. I couldn't bring myself to tell him about the chocolate mustache it'd left him with. Instead, I put my mind to getting through the meal without incident.

I didn't even bother with the radio on the ride home. I hoped the heaviness of the silence would be enough to force David out of hating me so much, at least force him into speaking to me. He'd upset my super sugar coma plan by barely eating three pancakes and giving up on his hot cocoa halfway into the giant mug. He stared out the passenger-side window at the fascinating sight of the miles and miles of snow humped up along the guardrails. Finally, as we turned off the highway, he mumbled something. Rather than respond, I waited for him to mumble it again. When he did, I pulled into the parking lot of a bank that had once been a pizza place that itself had once been a bank.

"What, David?" I asked. He didn't look at me. His focus was instead on the branches of the hedges leading up to the door of the bank that were just peeking out of the snow. "David? What?"

"You didn't have to touch me," he said.

"I am so sorry. I didn't mean to touch you...there...I

was…just…"

"You don't have to manhandle me and tuck in my shirts like that anymore. I'm not a little boy. I can wear my shirts how I want. If I want to not tuck them in and wear them out, then you should let me."

"Oh…kay. I won't do that again. I just wanted to make sure the jeans weren't too snug and that you'll be able to wear them for a while that way we won't have to go…"

"I told you they fit. Why did you still have to do that?" His voice cracked like he was about to cry.

Great. David getting himself out there on the ledge. Soon the car would be full of his tears and my rapidly expanding headache.

"Okay, okay, I said I was sorry. I won't…tuck in your shirts for you. I just wanted to see if the jeans…"

"I told you they fit," wailed David now, sounding angrier but not yet actually crying. "Why didn't you believe me?"

He slid further away from me towards the door and pressed his head to the glass, shaking with sobs. A momentary urge to reach out and stroke his hair passed before I could even get my seatbelt off. With each of his sobs, I sighed to myself, hoping my boredom with such displays would shame him into silence. When he finally stopped whimpering, it felt as though we'd reached some agreement not to talk about it any further. Broaching the subject of erections with my recently weeping preteen would've, just then, been too much for both of us.

I sometimes wonder if he'd recounted that scene to some therapist years later as he tried to work out his intimacy issues. Better some shrink than me.

When we pulled into the driveway, David was still

slumped against the door, his face red. Once I'd come to a stop, he hurriedly got out and raced for the house. On his way inside, he stepped around Daryl and Sarah on the porch without saying a word to either of them.

"How did't go?" Daryl asked as I hauled myself, shopping bags and all, up the walk. All he had on to protect himself from the cold was a robe over his pajamas. He held a cup of coffee in one hand and a soggy stack of mail in the other.

"Back from the shop," Sarah yelped. She sat astride her bike. "The shop where they store."

"It went fine," I said.

"Sarah was just telling me about her basketball team."

"So far, four wins," she said then stared at my bag for a blank-eyed second. "Back from shop."

"Four wins? That's great," I said.

"Daryl's home. There he is," Sarah said.

I couldn't help taking that as a rebuke from her, a show of favoritism. She probably wasn't capable of having such intentions or of being so subtle. At least, I didn't think she was. One thing seemed certain, I was no longer anyone's favorite around that place.

14. Exercising Justice

"Mr. Pettibone," Judge Darlene said, "I don't particularly care what you believe she owes you. You chose to stay at that job and did everything but actually physically force Ms. Darcey to stay at home. Is that not correct?"

"No one forced her, Your Honor," the defendant said, stroking his greying handlebar mustache. "I told her she could work if she wants to but she best keep the house clean and have my meals hot and ready for when I get home."

"Sir, did you or did you not threaten to leave her if she failed to comply with conditions that she'd not previously agreed to?"

"Nah, nah, Your Honor. What I told her was, I couldn't be with no woman who couldn't take care of her man right. Them ain't my conditions, that's just how the world works."

"So you did threaten to leave her if she took a job and could not fulfill these demands?"

"I work hard, Your Honor," he said.

"You also appear to be hard work, Mr. Pettibone."

"We ain't married or nothing," he offered in a final feeble coda to his summation.

"That's not the issue here. The issue here is whether or not your demanding, domineering ways led to the plaintiff passing up viable employment opportunities, only to learn that while doing so you were engaging in a physical relationship with a coworker."

"Your Honor…"

"I've heard enough, sir. I rule in favor of the plaintiff, Ms. Darcey. You're to pay the full amount of the documented damages. If you cannot pay in a lump sum,

I order your wages garnished until such time as the sum is paid."

The defendant then added something which had to be bleeped. In the credits, it stated that Judge Darlene's decisions were final and binding. Those appearing in her *Relationship Court* had waived their rights to due process by any other manner.

I kicked the afghan off my legs and, harnessing all the willpower I could muster, shut off the TV. Life had reached a point of desperation where a television show was now the fulcrum of my day. Before the emptiness could fully settle inside of me and touch off the kind of thoughts which I needed to avoid, I made up my mind to go for a walk. A long one. Full of fresh air. I needed to get out of the house. Another moment spent brooding about the sheer volume of creeps appearing on daytime television would' have threatened to condemn me to the couch, hiding from the world and in turn, being hidden from it.

I went into the bathroom to splash some water on my face. When we moved into this place, it'd been agreed that the basement bathroom was to be Daryl's. He was to use it and clean it. I tried to avoid it as much as I could. The sink was stained in a moldy rainbow of colors from emerald green to black. In the early days and years of living here, I got on him about cleaning it. In time, I found I lacked the energy to both nag him about cleaning his, while also doing a barely halfway decent job of cleaning the family bathroom or the rest of the house for that matter.

I'm not sure of the exact figure but think that close to 90% of all marriages in which neither partner can bring themselves to effectively clean the bathroom fail. Maria and I managed to continue on as roommates after under-grad because she didn't mind giving ours a good going over, even after we'd moved into that tiny apartment that was grimy and damp with a layer of scum in the tub a good inch thick.

I can only think of one time when I even attempted to do a good job of cleaning that part of our lair. It was an icy late February day, frozen rain played like darts against the one tiny window in the living room that we'd subdivided into separate bedrooms. We had no control over the heat. That apartment boiled no matter the season. As I made my way to the bathroom, my nightgown clung to me, pasted to my skin by sweat.

The night before, I'd purchased a home pregnancy test. It'd been two weeks since my period was supposed to come. Most of my life had been lived in abstract dread of that time of the month, the cramping, the headaches, the emotional upheaval but missing one at such an in-convenient time had me praying that it would all come at once, no matter how painful.

When I read the directions on the box, my hands be-gan to shake, and I felt a little ill. I unwrapped one of the sticks and tucked it between my thighs in a position that I hoped would wet it sufficiently, while keeping my hand relatively dry. Under normal circumstances, I would've had no problems peeing, in fact many of my days began with a race to the bathroom, so urgent was my need to go upon waking. On that morning, though, I sat on the toilet for a very long time, until my cheeks were cold and numb but nothing came. I took it as a good sign, figur-ing somehow that if I were pregnant, surely I'd have to pee, surely even the promise of some new weight press-ing down on my bladder would've made it impossible to hold back.

I went to put the unused stick, wrapped in toilet paper, under the sink. In trying to hide it from myself, I moved a sponge whose rough green surface was chalky with the residue of the cleaner Maria favored. Once I'd closed the cabinet, I found I still had the sponge in my hand so I went ahead and scrubbed the sink, tub and toilet. Rinsing the sponge in running water did the trick and so I sat down on the porcelain throne once again to learn my fate.

Marrying Daryl never came into my thoughts during the longest seven minutes of my life. My mind did conjure images of a life with a baby on my own, bringing her to class, nursing her as I studied. I also allowed myself to picture the front doors of a clinic, peopled by religious types protesting. I'd hold my head up high as I passed them. I'd shout to them that it was my body, before going inside.

I almost couldn't look when the time finally came. I picked up the stick, squinted my eyes shut and counted to three. There they were, the two pink lines, one slightly thicker than the other. Before it really registered what was happening, I worried that the two mismatched lines meant something was wrong with the baby or that I was having twins. Then it hit me, I would have to figure out a way of telling Daryl that wouldn't compromise my eternally evolving plan of letting him down easy.

It's just one of those things, Daryl. Let's not get hung up on it. I'll take care of it.

By the time Maria got home, I was a mess. She needed only to follow the trail of balled up tissues to find me in my bed, crying.

"Gloria, bubby, what's wrong?" she asked from the

end of the bed, her cool hand wrapped around my ankle.

I gathered myself, adjusting the collar of my night-gown as if that would help me look more composed. Sniffled once, twice, big sniffles as though I was trying to inhale all of the misery that was being visited upon me.

"Remember when I was worried because I was late?" I asked and broke down.

She leaned forward from the foot of the bed. Took me into her arms. Ran her hand through my hair.

"It'll be okay. It'll be okay," she said.

"What am I going to do?" I asked.

"Have the baby, bubby. We'll get a doula. We'll have the baby right here. Raise her up ourselves. Name her Lilith or Rachel. Don't worry."

She held me as I blubbered on and on. What effect, if any, my tears had on our friendship, I don't know. Maria had certainly never seen me like that. I was the girl who never cried. But overwhelmed and faced with sudden adulthood, I couldn't stop. I cried myself to sleep. She stayed there next to me, holding me, and stroking my hair. It made me wish I had a sister.

The next day, I made an appointment with my doctor to confirm. There was no use telling Daryl anything until I did. The day before the appointment, I called to reschedule for the following week in an effort to put off having to tell him a little longer. My feeling was a gal and her urine should be able to have their little secrets, but on this subject, once the doctor got involved, I knew I wouldn't be able to sleep until I told Daryl. Still, even after I found out, even after the test results were verified, I waited a couple more restless nights before calling him.

When I finally did, I couldn't make the words come

out. I asked if he could meet me the next day at a pizzeria near my apartment. It was the kind of place that sold slices that were so greasy the cheese practically slid right off. I never ate there and didn't want to risk ruining some place I liked with memories of what, no matter how it went down, was bound to be an unhappy scene.

I skipped class that afternoon and got to Nunzio's a good twenty minutes early. The windows were frosted with condensation from the heat, making the outside world opaque and distant. It was like being half-submerged in a dream. I sat in the corner, picking at some garlic knots and sipping a Coke. I had to force myself not to get up and leave once I'd finished eating, so I got another order.

Daryl didn't make me wait, arriving right on time. He waved as he walked by me to order a slice at the counter, carrying with him his customary air of cheerful cluelessness. Before he could slide into the booth across from me, I informed him that I was pregnant and it was his but that I'd take care of it. He was mercifully shocked into silence. His mouth gaped, *I can't be a dad*, written on his face. He still hadn't said anything when his slice was ready. Daryl slid out of the booth to get it and ate half of it at the counter, while giving glances over his shoulder at me like he didn't know what to do.

It made me think the pregnancy was a good thing. It gave me a way out of whatever I had sunk myself into with him. At first, anyway. If I'd only waited a little longer, I wouldn't have felt the need to tell him anything. Everything would've been different; but that's not how it worked out. Instead, I soon found myself unexpectedly relying on him as I never, in my worst nightmares, thought I'd have to. Then we got married and, then we moved out to the suburbs, having endured as much as two people could, once they find their lives no longer work in the city.

Determined to start my walk before motivation totally deserted me, as it so often did, I climbed the stairs from the basement, feeling heavy as though towing behind me the memories that Daryl's filthy bathroom had touched off. The kitchen, clean and quiet, offered no appeal. The Henry James novel I'd been intermittently attempting to read sat on the table face-down, an asymmetrical butterfly with one slender and one very thick wing.

The screen door banged shut. A whoosh of early spring air rushed through the house. David stood in the doorway removing his shoes. I could tell from the choked sniffling sound he was making that he'd been crying. He turned his head and tried to wipe away his tears without me seeing him do it. After unzipping his jacket, he ran by me to his room. He wanted to be alone. That was fine by me. I didn't have the energy just then to attend another of those sulky, pathetic debriefings.

I put on my jacket. Opening the door, I paused to feast on the air's mix of warm and cold, of winter giving way. I was almost free. All that was left to do was announce my departure. I waited for his light sobs to die away completely. No need to appear heartless. Otherwise, guilt, however ineffectual, would hang over my constitutional.

"David, I'm going for a walk. I'll be back soon," I said when it finally seemed safe to make my getaway.

"Oh…oh….k…kay," he stammered in chopping breaths which were characteristic of the middle rather than the end of one of his crying jags.

I swore under my breath, closed the door and, still in

my jacket, went to him.

"David, what's wrong?" I suppressed the urge to add a rueful 'this time' to the end of that sentence. Still, I'm sure I sounded more jaded interrogator than a caring mother. These things often can't be helped.

At first, he kept his face buried in his pillow. Then, lifting his head, he wiped his nose on the back of his hand. A web of mucus clung to the pillowcase. He mumbled through his sniffling.

"Is there something you want to talk about?" I asked.

"He…he…he…" he began, holding back another wave of sobs. "He pulled my jeans and underwear down."

"What?"

"Jonny and I and Denny were getting off the bus and he came up behind me and pulled my jeans down. My jeans and…uh…uh…underwear"

"Who?" As if I had to ask.

He gave me a sideways glance as though wounded by the idea that I would force him to speak the name of the beast. I sat down on the bed. He moved away from me and heaved with more tears.

"Everyone saw me, saw my…" he broke off and the tears came in earnest now, thick and unashamed. His body shook spasmodically. "Fuck Kenny!"

It'd been a tough couple of weeks for his modesty. First, his own mother cops a feel in the husky section, then a bully de-pants him for all of his friends to see. I noticed that he was inching further away from me, moving so that he was almost in the gap between his bed and the wall.

"Is there anything I can do?" I asked, rising from his bed.

"No," he said, regaining hold of himself. "I'd just like to be alone, please."

"Alright. Is it okay if I go for a little walk? I'll be back soon."

"You can…can…can…gah, gah, gah…go."

I rushed back down the hall and out the door, in case he started bawling. Outside, the crisp air chased the lassitude from my bones. My hands and feet soon itched from the unfamiliar sensation of having blood sped through them by movement. It was exercise at a fat girl's pace but exercise all the same.

I expect most mothers would've stayed in the house, listening to their child cry, wringing their hands and racking their brains to think of something they could do to provide comfort. But there was nothing I could or really cared to do for him there in his room. Maybe later, he could talk to his father about it; maybe Daryl had had a similar experience he could share. Boyhood was really, well and truly wearing me out.

The older David got, the more alien and incomprehensible his world seemed to me. Men, I had something of a handle on, they were transparent enough. But boys, at least the one I knew best, perplexed me thoroughly -- a lump of clay that would take what form I knew not. Exposing each other was not something I could picture girls doing. Although, I'm sure somewhere a cruel little queen bitch is pulling up the skirt of some shy, chubby girl who's too sensitive for her own good. Some women believe that if they act like men, it will benefit them. They think that it 's somehow an ideal to aspire to, that it'll help them get ahead, that we should all be trying to be more like men. But the goal as I understood it should not be to join the male world but change it. A world, their world where barbarism and greed run rampant, where grinning hoodlums like Kenny command small armies and trample on sensitive souls like my son, needed to be changed.

The sun hid behind some clouds. There were left-over puddles from the storm that had passed early that morning. The grass glittered with rain-thickened dew. I loved the muddy smell of the air, of life reawakening. It had a defiance to it, the smell of revival.

As I was passing the Crumbrick's house, I picked up the pace. The sound of a blaring television came from the wide-open windows. A yellowed lace curtain flapped forlornly in the breeze. The gutter bent and rusted through as though having just barely survived the winter drooped over the garage door.

I should've marched up to the door and banged on it. I should've had it out with Crumbrick once and for all. A good mother never tires of fighting for her children, at least, I don't suppose they do. In the moment, though, I didn't see the use in having smoke blown in my face while I endured her cross examination.

A laugh echoed from inside the house and floated out into the street. A forthright and joyous sound unlike anything I would've thought Lynn capable of making. It rose from her crackling chest like fireworks. It made me want to be able to laugh like that. To care even less about my son's life in that neighborhood, his and mine. I had to hope things would change. That David would grow up and out of this world. And that I would not be far behind.

At the bottom of the hill, where the Crumbrick es-tate gave way to empty lots alternating with homes in even greater states of disrepair, I turned off of the street onto a trail. It was only a sheet of muddy ground now and come summer it would be overgrown with high weeds but it led to the little public park, which served as a bracing reminder of how old I was, of how long we'd lived there. I hadn't visited it since David was little enough for me to carry him home, which I often did after he'd spent a long day playing there. The park had been something of a selling point back when we were a young family shopping for a home and I still thought I could somehow make that particular F-word work for me. It was where I would go, searching for my happiness as a mother, watching my son go down the slide or pushing him on the swing. All the while, I waited expectantly for some feeling to come over me, for me to discover my contentment in motherhood -- the toughest job that will ever bore you to the brink of raving insanity.

The park no longer seemed as keen to con new mothers into thinking: 'this is where it will happen for me, this is where I will find that magic that everyone else talks about.' The swing set had been reduced from three to one working swing, which dangled from two tangled chains. The wooden stairs of the slide had rotted away to blackened stumps that were too small for even children's feet. It was just as well because the bottom of the metal slide had been almost eaten away by rust. The picnic benches where I used to sit and watch David, almost marveling, yes I once nearly marveled at what Daryl and I had produced, at how this little person had changed my life so suddenly, were by then long gone. Only the concrete base that the table had been bolted to remained. The grass, lush and wildly green, had not been cut for some time, years possibly.

I took off my shoes and socks and rolled up my sweatpants to walk through the wet grass. Behind the bench, it was softer than in other places and not as deep. My feet were soon covered in a thin layer of damp, dewy slime.

I remembered watching David run over that very patch of ground when he was two or three. He'd just learned how to really run and feel free. He took so much joy in the simple act of movement, racing from one end of the field to the other. At the time, I wondered if I'd ever experienced a joy similar to that which was writing itself across his face so boldly.

I took that look as a sign that my child was clearly special with an unmatched capacity for happiness. He would bring that joy into our family. His smile, his love for…well, how wrong I was about all of that. It was merely the field where I allowed myself to plant and sow the earliest of those suburban lies. Those lies about my life and what I could still make of it, if only I tried hard enough.

Daring the damp, I lay down in the grass, spreading my arms and legs. The coolness of the moisture pricked my neck. The clouds were clearing, puffy and shot through with a greyish blue. They moved across the pale spring sky with a hushed kind of urgency. I put my hands behind my head and watched.

Our backyard was mostly dust or mud for the better part of the year. When grass did grown, it came in sparse patches. We tried planting grass in the late summer for the first couple of years we were there but it didn't take. The price to get new turf installed was more than we were willing to spend back then. As the years went on and our financial situation didn't really improve, we came to accept our little piece of wasteland.

When I was a little girl, Daddy and I would lay side

by side in the grass right in the middle of an oval of elm trees that grew in the far back of our property. Sometimes, he'd go out there in his slacks and dress shirt and just lay in the lawn. I'd run behind him and when I joined him on the grass, he'd point out a cloud, ask me what I saw in it, always encouraging me to take my time before answering. When I did, he encouraged me to go further and make up ever more elaborate stories about whatever I was imagining. Not being in a rush, giving space to your imagination was the whole point, he used to say.

If Mother saw us, she'd yell from the house, asking if he was wearing a nice shirt and telling him that he'd ruin it. Usually, he'd just wave at her with both hands like he was saying 'go away' but sometimes he'd sit up, unbutton his shirt and twirl it in the air. The crazed look on his face when he did that always made me laugh.

Once towards the end of his life, I took him out of the care center in his wheelchair. He wasn't speaking much by then. He did raise a shaking finger at the sky, his head tilted back. I told him what I saw. Made up elaborate tales about every shape in the sky. Began to tie the clouds together into a story. I think he was following me and enjoyed it, but there was no way to really tell.

All that time, I'd been telling myself another story. That Daddy and I still had our connection. That nothing had frayed it. It was miraculously free of the static that had clotted up every other part of his mind. After taking him back in, I told the nurses about the clouds, about feeling that he'd enjoyed it. They acted like they understood, but I'm sure it was the type of fantasy they'd heard often enough and were paid to acknowledge as genuine.

As I lay there in the park alone, I struggled to make any shapes or stories out of the clouds. They were too thick and formless, too sad to do anything with. I got up and left.

My back was soaked so I decided to cut the walk short. Stepping over the collapsed wooden fence and looping around the back of the park, I headed for home. There wasn't a paved street there but a dirt path that led up and around the small ridge that sat behind our property. If you followed it long enough, it led all the way out to what had once been a bus stop under an overpass, along the highway. The route had long since been discontinued but the shell of the shelter still sat there, rusting away with a few shards of Plexiglass hanging crookedly in the frame. I could've walked over the rise right into our backyard but didn't want to get any dirtier, so I went down a little more to where the path provided access to Al and Marge's house and their considerably greener backyard.

Once I rounded their house, I saw Sarah in front of ours. She sat astride her bike and stared straight ahead at the front door. I heard David talking to her. He said something that made her howl. I wanted to remain hidden from Sarah more than I wanted to find out what they were talking about so I backtracked and crept along close to Marge and Al's house. A twig snapped beneath me. I spun around and pressed my back against the aluminum siding of the house. Her tires peeled down the street towards me. "Here I am," I'd say if she discovered me. An instant later, I heard her grunt and go whizzing back down the street in the other direction. Still, I waited and listened before walking the last few steps home. I didn't have the energy to deal with her that day.

Daryl still wasn't home. David must've been in his room. I didn't call for him and hoped he'd gotten over the latest Kenny incident enough that he could wait to talk to his father about it. Exhausted, I flopped down on the couch. *Lands of Power and Dust Book VII: Greylor's Promise* lay open on the cushion next to me.

"*And how are we to be certain, Greylor?*" Hucebuse asked.

"*Certain?*" Greylor asked. *He then stroked his mighty beard.*

"*Of their fear, their intentions?*" Hucebuse asked.

"*Their fear! Good, Hucebuse, good,*" Greylor began. "*Their fear is told in their intentions! We threaten them without meaning to. Because we are unified. We have made study of tactics. But we shall not let them fool us with their fear. No. We must continue to show them strength.*"

"*But Greylor,*" worried Hucebuse.

"*But what? What happened today was a trick, a mere trifle. They seek to embarrass us because they know they cannot win.*"

"*So we must remain strong,*" brightly spoke Hucebuse.

"*Yes!*" Greylor shouted. "*Strong and unified!*"

15. Portrait of a Daddy's Girl as Drawn by an Old Woman

After I hung up the phone with Mother, Daryl came racing upstairs. I could tell by the way he had his mouth open with his hands on either cheek in mock horror that he'd heard the conversation. I opened the kitchen cabinet on the other side of which was the calendar I used to keep track of our lives. Rather than use the pencil I usually marked it with, I reach into the back for a red pen instead. I showed it to Daryl. He shook his head some more and pretended to scream and cry. Then, I flipped ahead a page and circled a Saturday. He fell to his knees and pounded the ground. The whole act still made me laugh out loud.

"What's going on?" asked David, who must've heard us from his room.

"Your Grandma is coming to dinner," I said through my laughter.

"Grammy Graham," Daryl said, standing up and smiling at me.

Later, I sat at the kitchen table with *Portrait of a Lady* open in front of me. But I couldn't digest the words. I read for a few pages, then realized I'd not actually been comprehending any of it. It wasn't that I was confused. James's sentences were crisp and clear. I just couldn't focus. I feared I was getting senile or worse, stupid from the untold hours I'd wasted reading trashy magazines and critiquing the legal tactics on *Relationship Court*.

At least with the book open, my boys left me alone. David had returned to his reading, no doubt making better progress. It was sunny and warm out, more like May than March but I'd recently given up trying to get him outside.

My earlier reaction to his performance had put Daryl in a good mood. After I'd stopped laughing, he'd gone out into the garage. I hoped he was going to clean it out but wasn't going to bother to check. The danger of him using the morning's good will as a way of involving me in one of his projects remained high, even at that point in our marriage. It was hard to take any of his complaints about work seriously, since he spent much of his time off at home doing approximately the same thing as he did at work. Of course, he'd claim that making cabinets and artistically sculpting wood were completely different but it seemed to me the only difference was that one was potentially useful and the other blandly derivative. It's hard now to imagine that I ever took him or pretended to take him seriously enough as a 'wood sculptor' to be impressed. He might've felt the same way about me and law school. Against all reasonable odds, he was the one who, at that time, was closer to his dream.

When his P-Sofa friends told me that Daryl was doing something different but in a recognized tradition, I forced myself to hear it as a compliment, even long after they'd stopped forcing themselves to make it sound like one. During our brief courtship, I guess I'll call it, stretching the meaning of that arcane term until it's gossamer, he made a number of things for me. Always offering them up with a look that begged me to be impressed or thankful or at the very least, nice. I don't remember liking one or ever thinking any of it was any good. But I really never knew much about art and yes, was a little flattered to be someone's muse.

I never threw any of those curved, sanded, snooze-inducing forms away. I found places for them in my room, even in the tiny area of the apartment I shared with Maria. If she ever noticed them, she didn't complain. They all went up into the attic when we moved out into the valley. Occasionally, when I came down with one of my infrequent bouts of 'nice wife,' I'd make some noises about bringing some down to decorate the house. He'd agree but never went to get one. We were both thankful enough to have them locked up there. That part of the past was, for him, as easy to ignore as it was to access. It might've reminded him of the hopes he had before we found our lives changed, before the togetherness was thrust upon us.

I don't know exactly how long we'd been seeing each other or how many times we had sex before the day I woke up to find him watching me intently, then telling me he loved me. At the time, it all seemed fast, weird, and not right exactly, but it somehow fit. No boy had ever told me that before, so I thought maybe that was how I was supposed to feel, not turned off exactly but in a state in which I anticipated my own eventual reciprocation. Someone had to be the first to say it to me. I should've loved that person; shouldn't I? We made love again that morning. Back then, I was sure that at some point, I'd catch up and feel more for him.

In the garage, the electric sander stopped. Daryl yelled and threw something. Then came the sound of Sarah's barking laughter cutting through me like a saber. When they laughed together, the echo of the sound in the garage was like that of two mad hyenas on the prowl. I stood up from the table, frozen. I hadn't time to formulate a decent plan to avoid her if Daryl told her I was inside. I thought about locking myself in the bathroom and waiting her out. But I didn't think she'd leave, not if she knew I was home.

She barked out another laugh. It seemed closer. It seemed right on the other side of the door that connected the kitchen and garage. I heard Daryl tell her something. I went to the door. I grasped the handle. To keep it from turning? To keep myself from running away?

"Nah, nah, nah," Daryl said. "Not like the ocean. Different kind of sanding."

"There you sand," she said, "like the ocean."

"There I sand," he said.

"There you sand."

"You know what sand is? Right Sarah?" he asked.

"Near the ocean," she said.

"Sand's just, you know, like rocks that water and wind have pummeled into tinier and tinier stones until they're like so small they're sand grains."

"Pummeled," she said, uncertainly.

"That's how it gets made. And when I'm sanding away at this wood, that's what I am doing. Making it smaller and smaller until it's dust."

"Dust. Now, you dust," she said, laughing, hard enough to make me cringe.

"Yeah, they should just call it that, maybe."

"Sand is dusting. Dusting is dust. There you are, sawdusting."

"More or less," he said. "They all come from bigger things."

"Rocks and stones and woods," she said.

"They all get worn away to, like, something small-er."

"At the beach. There you are, sanding."

"Right."

"There you are."

"Right on," Daryl said. "Give me five."

They shared another hyena chorus after their hands slapped together. I turned from the door to find David watching me.

"She's not coming inside, is she?" he asked.

"No. I think she just wanted to talk to your dad."

"He's good at that."

"At what?" I asked.

"I don't know. He's just good at talking to people."

"Is he?" I asked.

"You said so. You told me he was better at it than you."

"That's not saying much."

"I wish I was better at it," David said.

"More like Dad?" I asked, hoping not to sound too hurt.

"I wish I felt easy with people like he does. There're people I wish it was easier to talk to."

"Like who?" I asked and he blushed. "Like who, David?"

"No one."

"No one?" I asked.

"Mom," he said, like he was preparing to break the lines of communication.

"Anyway, whomever it's for, you'll get better at it as you get older," I said.

Daryl could make you feel understood, even if he didn't actually understand you. Understanding seemed to always be happening when he was half of the conversation. And it might've been a shallow kind, no deeper than that which satisfied his need to sense the most tenuous of connections had been made, but it was completely and totally earnest. It wasn't a ploy or bit of pantomime that he'd learned from some *How to Pick-Up Chicks* article.

When we met for the very first time, it was at a roof-top party, somewhere in one of the boroughs, far away and inconvenient enough to seem practically exotic. A friend of his, who knew my law school classmate, Alicia, had managed to turn renting a dilapidated studio apartment on the top floor of a four-story walk-up to his advantage by cutting the padlock off the door that led to the roof. His landlord lived in Japan, so he didn't really fear being discovered. As I walked up the stairs that evening, my first year law student brain couldn't help but work over the liability issues that might arise as the result of someone serving alcohol more than forty feet above the street in what turned out to be an unsecured location. When I wondered about this aloud, Alicia admitted she was thinking the same thing.

As soon as we came through the door, I felt exposed and uncomfortable. There were no tall buildings or their shadows to hide behind. The air was chilly that September night. The wind blowing in off the river felt sharp as it gusted. I did notice Daryl almost immediately, tall and square with that wavy red hair falling about his shoulders. I remember most, even to this day, his eyebrows which were a shade of strawberry blonde that looked almost unnatural. Over the years, they'd lighten until it was hard to see them but in his youth they were so unusual and beautiful.

I also noticed that he noticed me. He smiled at me and kept smiling as he walked over, a clear plastic cup of pale beer in his hand. Right away, I knew he was, like me, from out of town but also somehow unlike most of the other people there, unlike most of the people I'd met since moving to the city, he wouldn't try to hide it. And he didn't really -- not at first anyway.

He did most of the talking at first. I think he told me all about himself in about five minutes. In the beginning, Daryl's conversation style seemed to be throw everything at the wall and see what stuck. I tried to listen but I kept thinking about the ex-pat who owned the building, hoping he had a good lawyer. Simply padlocking that door would never in the calculus of negligence hold up in court as having fulfilled the burden of adequate precautions. When Daryl pulled me back into the conversation by admitting he'd never been on the roof of such a high building, his eyes kept darting behind me as if truly frightened of my being too close to the edge, which was several feet to my back. Then, soon enough, I found myself joining in, once he admitted how uncomfortable being at parties made him. That is what the two people hiding in the corner of every party are talking about -- how uncomfortable they are to be there.

Slowly, we advanced further into each other's lives from there, despite the fact that I didn't know enough about sculpture or art to know that Daryl didn't really understand what he was talking about. But he was excited and into it. So excited about art school and all that he'd learned and wanted to learn. I gave him a pass on all that. It was refreshing at the time. The nineties had been the age of the slacker and of trying not to smell too much like one was making an effort at anything. How we attempted to prize our ennui, our fatalist conceits that nothing was worth the energy.

That version of Daryl is someone I wished I knew more of. It was like I caught him at the tail end of something. I mean, it's not really talking shit unless the speaker kind of knows how much shit he's talking. Hell, I didn't really even know enough about the law to realize that I was matching his shit with shovelful upon shovelfuls of my own.

At one point, he went off to get his plastic cup refilled from the pony keg of beer some determined soul had dragged all the way up there. He asked me if I wanted some and I said yes, even though I really didn't like beer at the time. Somewhere Mother smirks at me through eternity. I watched him walk away, intending to mingle a bit with the jaded types, wearing their pasted-on city faces, when I found I couldn't leave the spot where I was standing. I moved over slightly but only to get further from the edge of the roof and to stand out a little from the crowd. Part of me worried that Daryl would get lost without me, his double-wide lighthouse, in the line of his sight. While I had no interest in forms speaking through forms or negative space or whatever he was on about before he left me, I liked the way he spoke to me. Liked that it was a give and take. He was good at pretending to be into everything that I was saying, which surely couldn't have been of less interest to him or, really, to any fully intellectually formed human being.

I felt a real twinge of relief when I saw him walking back towards me, plastic cups hoisted above the fray, the breeze lashing an over-sized flannel shirt against his broad chest. Our conversation picked back up and I found myself suddenly riveted by his idea of "sculpture being simply the rearrangement of bodies in space." At the end of the evening, he'd asked me for my number and promised to call me the next day. I'd known he would. Guileless in the best sense of the word.

Satisfied, I suppose, that he wouldn't always be quite

so socially maladroit, David went back to his room. I followed him. He stopped beside his bed, his head back, staring at the ceiling.

"What are you doing?" I asked.

"Thinking," he said.

"About what?"

"How I'll change when I get older. What'll I be like?"

"I think about that too," I said.

"Did you when you were a girl? What did you think?"

I rested my head against the doorframe. Rubbed my socked foot along the wood. He regarded me with me a look that was something like horror at finding my answer to his question was taking actual unabashed thinking.

"Did you think you were going to be like Grandma?" he asked, sounding almost frantic as though my contemplation was worrying him.

"No," I said with a rueful laugh. "No. I think I thought I was going to live in a big house with a chimney and be married to a doctor and have a son almost as good as you."

"I think I'm going to be like Dad," David said, repaying my compliment with a shiv to the heart. "And work with my hands, crafting custom things for people."

"Crafting custom things, huh?" I asked, trying not to laugh.

"Yep. Out of wood."

"But you hate that stuff. You never like helping Daddy."

"He never lets me do anything. He always wants me to sit there and watch and learn."

"Not like the wood stove," I said.

"No. You let me do stuff but it's not the same. I didn't get to use, like, real tools."

"Well, how do you think Daddy learned?"

He shrugged.

"Your dad learned by watching."

"He just, like, watched at first?" David asked.

"Yeah, David, try to observe him when he works."

David let his mouth hang slack and squinted his eyes a bit, a somewhat though not terribly exaggerated mimicking of his father. I laughed even though I knew I shouldn't. He really did look like a mini-version of Daryl when he did that. I used to do a passable, more respectful version of my Dad's tight-lipped pose. It never failed to make him laugh. I don't know that Daryl would've found the same humor in David's impersonation. I never thought they were really close enough for Daryl to appreciate such things.

How I loved being in Daddy's study with him. His island in a house which otherwise had been taken over by Mother. Her love of muted colors, of sterile walls hung with nothing, of rugs and carpets and runners, of air fresheners that smelled like flowers ground down to powder, of dust-free zones, of spaces so clean they made me feel brittle, all gave way to Daddy's gloriously dark, dusty, disorganized office. There, he'd let me spend part of the afternoon after I got home from school with him as long as I was quiet. I'd lay on the button-tufted leather couch reading, my head resting on one arm roll, my feet propped up on a stack of binders. The only sound to be heard was that of Daddy occasionally tapping his pen against the edge of his desk or clicking it three times, never two, never four, always three times in quick succession, until he'd figured out the answer to whatever problem had been consuming him.

Daddy had graduated from law school at the top of his class, but early in his career he'd found that he had a gift for correctly predicting how certain classes of stocks would do in the short term. He could've been a junior partner at a high-profile firm practically right out of school but turned it down to be a day trader. He never used a computer, even after just about every other trader he knew had been using them for years. He had his phone, his paper, his pencil. His charts and quarterlies, some equations that he'd developed. It all allowed him to become, as he put it, "my own man, making my own stake in the world. No bosses. No rules. My time is my time." It wasn't money that motivated him. He likely would've done just as well if not better as a partner with a law firm. Plus, there would've been all those languid afternoons at the golf course, cocktails at lunch, all of the lazy pursuits that he never had any interest in taking up.

I understood from a young age, sitting there reading the well-thumbed pages of my *Anne of Green Gables* books and listening to him thinking with his pen that I was in the presence of a remarkable man. Every once in a while he'd ask me about my book, about Anne, seeming somehow to know everything already that I wanted to say about her. He'd tell me as he held up a fat three-ring binder that it sounded better than what he had to read and think about.

I marveled at those binders for their thickness, their sense of importance. I doubted I'd ever be able to lift something so heavy, let alone read it. The shelves were lined full, not of books he hadn't read, like the libraries in most houses of that sort, but stuffed with those binders he'd created. They were his books, full of facts and figured and trends -- all the secrets of his success. He'd put them together. Written on pages of legal pads, punched through with the hole-punch, stowed in the desk drawer, then snapped into place.

One day, I was laying in my spot reading *Anne's House of Dreams*, the fifth book in the series, which I obsessed over for what seemed like the whole of my eleventh summer. David clearly comes by it honestly. Daddy had opened the French doors behind his chair to let the air in. The smell of the fresh cut grass from the backyard wafted over us. I heard Daddy click his pen as his chair creaked. I sat up to find him bathed in the warm orange light of the late day sun. His head was titled back, a look of contentment on his face.

"Daddy, can I get married in an orchard?" I asked.

It was in Book Five that Anne finally married, the tall, handsome and somewhat difficult Gilbert Blythe. The wedding had taken place in the orchard at Green Gables. The details of Anne being the only bride to ever be married there, of the lone bird singing as they repeated their vows, of the heavenly beauty of the September sunshine made it seem like the perfect setting for such an event.

"If you'd like, honey. I'm sure we can find a nice orchard for that when the time comes," he said. "An orchard. That's where Anne gets married, I guess."

"Do you think I can marry a doctor?" I asked.

Gilbert was a doctor. He came across as such a clever capable man in the books that he became, much like the setting, the only acceptable model for me to follow.

"I'm sure you can," Daddy said. "You can and should marry a man who can give you everything and anything your heart desires. Don't ever let anyone tell you to settle for less. You'll be able to find the perfect man. He's out there for you, your Dilbert…"

"Gilbert," I said, hesitant to correct him.

"Gilbert. Your Gilbert. You can find him, the man of your dreams and don't let anyone tell you different."

"Were you the man of Mother's dreams?" I asked, shaken a bit by the very notion that he might not have been.

"I'm close. I think your mother thought she was marrying more into a life that came with a certain amount of…social status."

"What's that?"

"Let's just say, she probably expected I'd have more friends."

"Oh," I said, only faintly understanding what he'd meant.

"But you won't settle for anything other than exactly what you want and you shouldn't."

I nodded at him. He smiled. In that moment, it seemed destined. He'd set me on my course to find a tall, dark, charming, kind doctor of my own. I don't even think that I really knew what he meant by settling but I knew it wasn't good. The same words that buoy us as children often haunt us as adults.

16. Rats, the Mall

The archway above the Odenbrook Mall's main entrance was soot-stained a greyish brown. A halo of cigarette butts ringed the trash can nearest the door. I gave private voice to the thought of what a nice mall it used to be. Had that whisper been spoken any place other than my head there would have been just cause to relieve me of my belt, shoelaces, as well as any sharp objects. I should've then been given a handful of pills and told to rest for a while in a bright padded cell.

A small counter for Mac's Doughnuts was placed just off the main concourse, making it impossible to go from the entrance to the stores without walking near enough to smell the glazed sugary cloud wafting from it like so many angels' kisses. I'd been trying, with some very limited success, to eat healthier around that period, but always only found it honorable to give in to my weaknesses from time to time -- the sum total of which, after all, is who we truly are. The chocolate cake, thick and moist, broke apart begrudgingly as though glued together with sugar. I devoured it as I paid without even walking away to sit down. I immediately ordered another which I planned to enjoy in a more civilized fashion. The girl behind the counter, chunky in the same way I'd been in my youth, handed the second one over with the commiserating smile of someone who had witnessed stronger wills than mine broken in that very spot.

I could hardly be blamed. The yogurt and Grapenuts I'd scarfed down for breakfast hadn't cut it. My problem was, and is, that I have too much respect for the work that goes into making good-tasting food to eat anything else. Portion control became my strategy as I aged. It's going okay. If I eat a portion of food that's too big, I've learned to control my self-loathing to the point where I can totally ignore it.

I managed to find a reasonably clean table which only required me to brush away some crumbs. Behind me was one full of old codgers slurping their coffees as they went about solving the world's problems. Some vague utterances about a woman's place being in the kitchen were quickly agreed upon with some light chuckling. Had I caught wind of that claptrap when I first burst through the doors with my stomach protesting the morning's insufficient repast, I might've been tempted to say something.

By the time I'd finished eating, I found they hadn't changed the topic. So I picked up my tray, bending down to offer the one, whom I took to be their leader, given the way the rest of them bowed their heads when he spoke about "...the natural state of family life being thrown out of balance by all these career gals," a generous view of my cleavage. I made sure to catch him stealing a glance, then sneered him into shame.

I was only able to savor his defeated blushing for an instant before remembering I was there to buy Daryl a birthday gift. By then, we hardly made much of such events. He'd taken to getting me gift cards so I could get something I really wanted, while I handed him his gifts still in the bag from where they were purchased with the receipts inside, daring him to do the same. As I meandered down the concourse in search of what I yet knew not, I was almost run down by an elderly couple speed-walking. I pivoted once, then again to get around them. They didn't excuse themselves but kept chugging towards the fountain in the middle of the mall; all elbows and heads-down-determination in their matching grey sweat suits, both of which had 'Alaska' embroidered at the top with a picture of a moose on his and a leaping salmon on hers. He'd topped off his ensemble with a sweat band that almost completely covered the crown of hair around his skull. Actual shoppers were a definite minority at that hour. Walkers, all of advanced age, raced about. Many moved at a pace that I was ashamed to think would've left me breathless. More than their energy, I envied them for the guts it took to wear such bold sweat suits out in public.

Without much idea of what I might be looking for or any real desire to find it, I popped into a few stores before walking straight back out. I felt a twinkle of inspiration on encountering some dress shirts whose prices had been greatly reduced at a slightly scruffy Brooks Brothers. One was periwinkle with white pinstripes, the other white with black pinstripes. There were both cut in a way that would've been flattering on Daryl and better, threaten to shake up the starving artist look he was still striving for even now that we were one or two missed paychecks away from it possibly and tragically being true. I could already hear him wondering aloud when he'd have cause to wear such a shirt and realized that I no longer had the will to fill in the blanks for him.

The concourse was, by then, like the late stages of a marathon with only a few clusters of struggling stragglers making their way around the circuit. There were more real shoppers now, a few scattered teenagers hand-in-hand, families arguing, pulling each other this way and that, mothers attempting to drag along recalcitrant children. A woman was being forced to navigate her way through the crowd with a towheaded boy literally kicking and screaming. She clenched her jaw in way that made it seem that she wanted to scream at him, scream at all the world with her voice working its way up to an angry boil. It's strange how uncomfortable we're made to feel for correcting our children in public, for shaming them in front of others. It seems like the one place that tactic would be most effective.

Passing the fountain as I continued the loop, I saw a boy playing with a man I took to be his father. The boy was a few years younger than David and the man a few pounds lighter than Daryl. They chased each other around the raised step that ringed the fountain. There was such a sense of joyous abandon to what they were doing as they reveled in the senseless danger of it. The walkers and shoppers going by offered chuckles or admiring glances. I wondered if a mother would've been viewed in the same way. Fathers are encouraged to be reckless with their sons but I couldn't imagine a woman receiving such tacit approval from the public. We were to be serious and careful with our children. I can see now that I had trouble enjoying such moments with David because it's not something women are encouraged to do, so even imaging it can be difficult. Fathers are permitted to be boys but mothers must always remain adults.

I approached a pimple-faced teen with a chirping walkie-talkie on his hip. His mall security uniform was wrinkled and a size too big for him. He looked the other way when he saw me coming, as though an incident at the Lady Foot Locker needed his immediate attention.

"Do you see that over there?" I asked, drawing his attention to the antics at the fountain.

"Are they yours?" he asked, fiddling with the nob on his walkie-talkie. "Ask them to get down."

"No, they're not mine," I said. "Should they be doing that? Someone could get hurt."

He slouched away from the blue glow of the pretzel stand. Making little effort to affect any sort official air, he approached the father and son and asked them to stop their horseplay with an almost apologetic tone. The man suspecting I'd ratted them out, shook his head at me from across the way. I moved on at a touch higher pace than I customarily walked.

I headed for JC Penney's, a sure sign I really wanted to take no pleasure at all in my visit. After walking about ten feet into the store, I got Daryl the first thing I came across, some cologne that was half-off. It smelled like something he'd never wear, never want to smell like. It smelled smooth and cool, like it would be worn by an office jockey at an insurance company or maybe, a chain restaurant GM or, even better, a first-class steward on a passenger train. Perfect.

As I was making my escape back through the food court, staying as far from the doughnut stand as I could get, I saw Kenny Crumbrick and some boys his age, occupying two pushed-together tables near the Panda Express. They slurped noodles from square cardboard plates. One wore a huge black earring that made his earlobe droop, fat and heavy. He let loose with a loud belch, which was followed by an even louder cackle. The two other boys with their sandy blonde hair and pinched faces could've been twins.

I hadn't had the pleasure of seeing Kenny since he'd pulled down my son's pants. And I wanted to keep it that way. My mind flashed violent scenes of a confrontation with him as I approached, all involving flying cartons of egg noodles. I kept my head down as I neared their table, letting the seams of the tiles guide me to the door.

"That's crummy, Crummy," fat earlobe said.

"Crummy like your mummy," one of the apparently poetic twins added.

"Crummy like your slummy mummy," added the even more poetic of the pair.

They laughed their insidious teenage boy laughs as I slunk by. Heavy earring even half-winked, smiling broadly when he caught me in a glance. It was almost as if he could tell I'd been listening and more, that I didn't entirely disapprove. His teeth were the color of butter, his gums a painful shade beyond red. Kenny kept his head down, very low, very close to his plate. He slurped with an angry sucking sound but didn't respond.

Not until I was safely outside, crossing the parking lot, heading for my car did I feel ashamed of my performance. I'd passed up the opportunity to be the kind of hero-mom not seen much outside of afterschool specials. The kind who would've saved her son's tormentor from his own tormentors and won him over in the end. I could've slapped the small plastic bag containing Daryl's cologne down on the table and come to Kenny's defense. Put my hand on his shoulder and braved the responses of his peers no matter how crude or upsetting. Kenny deserves your respect, I could've told them. He's not had an easy life. His mother's struggling to raise him all on her own. He was born stupid and smelly but it's you who are turning him into someone cruel. So if you find you can't respect him, just leave him alone. His life's hard enough. But I'd already meddled in the life of two strangers and that seemed sufficient for one day.

In our driveway, Sarah sitting astride her bike made pulling the car in difficult. As I inched towards the opening door, she glided along with me. Even as I pulled so close that, to a passing motorist, it might've appeared I intended to run her over, she still didn't move out of my way.

"Sarah," I said, putting my window down. "Can you move? I want to pull in."

"There you are," she said, smiling her crooked smile.

"Yes. Here I am. And there you are. Would you please move out of the way?"

"Way out, out of the way," she cried while backing up her bike into the narrow strip of muddy ground that bordered the driveway.

"How're you? How's basketball?" I asked, once I'd gotten out of the car.

"Is he sanding? Is he making dust?" she asked, trying to look around me into the garage.

"Oh, Daryl," I said, feeling a surprising pang of jealousy. "I don't know where he could be. Would you like to wait while I find him?"

"No. Go home now."

"He must be around. We only have the one car."

"Go home now," she repeated, biking across the muddy grass and back up to the road.

I wanted to stop her, tell her about the old people walking. About the father and son whose fun I'd ended. About Kenny. Just to tell someone. But she already was out of sight by the time I walked back up to the top of the driveway. For once, I almost felt that I needed to hear that laugh of hers in all its unbridled boisterousness.

Inside, I heard whispering coming from David's room, like someone was trying to hush someone else. I crept down the hall, floorboards creaking below me as if delighting in their attempt to ruin my stealthy approach.

I peeked around the doorway of his room to see the kind of sight I would've rather never seen. One so shocking, it'd been to that point unimaginable.

There he was, my husband, on the bed with our son, his head supported by a pillow against the footboard, reading. They were reading together. Daryl trying to prove once and for all that his intellect was at least at a young adult level -- *Lands of Power and Dust* under his nose. David had his head propped against the headboard; a book I'd never noticed before in his hands. One side of the cover showed a young man wearing armor standing in a field of flowers, a large white sash covering part of the right side of his body, the other half had the book's title in somewhat heavy script: *Sir Gawain and the Green Knight.*

"Readers together," I said, holding the little shopping bag behind my back. Pride choking inside of me. That should've been an activity I shared with our son, not Daryl.

"I'm trying to catch up to Dave with old Greylor here."

"That's...great." There was no hiding the surprise in my voice. "What are you reading, David?"

"It's about knights in old England. I just started it today."

"A friend gave it to him," Daryl said with a cartoonish raise of his eyebrows.

"Dad," David whined the whine reserved for me, the vowel elongated and screeched out.

"Who?" I asked.

"Someone from school."

"Does this someone have a name?" I asked.

"You don't know...this person," David said. "Was

Sarah still outside?"

"She was. She seemed in a hurry."

"She must've had to go home," Daryl said.

"Did you talk to her?" I asked.

"I couldn't," Daryl said. "I just…I couldn't."

"He made me go to the door. I talked to her," David said.

"I hope you were nice to her," I said.

He mumbled something close enough to a 'yes.' I then left them to their reading. In our bedroom, I stashed Daryl's gift under the bed. I gave a thought to taking my book and joining them. But I went downstairs to watch TV instead, numbed by the scene of what had been stolen from me.

17. One Glass of Wine Only Makes Me Sleepy

After weeks of waiting, I received a boilerplate response from the women's collective. It thanked me for my interest, bragged about the number of responses they'd received, and, with a copious use of the word "unfortunately," informed me that my candidacy was not advancing to the next phase. I didn't expect them to disclose any particulars behind their decision, however, I did think my honest, forthright and passionate cover letter should've at least earned me a *PS - We know how you feel, sister.*

I shut down the computer and then threw myself onto the floor, crawling under the desk and unplugging the whole contraption. It made a winding down sound that soothed me for a moment. The wood glue around the joints of the desk's undercarriage had hardened into a globular crust. Closing my eyes, I tried to sleep there.

Daddy's desk had been one of my first favorite places to hide from the world, when I was a little girl. Mother never searched for me there. At most, she might've had whomever was unfortunate enough to have been sent over by the cleaning service poke around the house in an effort to locate me.

Those anonymous voices come as the faintest of memories, calling my name from the hall that connected the kitchen with his study. They often sounded afraid that I might answer. Sometimes, they'd make it as far as the study's doorway. I'd hold my breath, tuck my knees into my belly and try to make myself as small as possible. I'd only exhale once I heard their feet clicking away back across the kitchen tiles. Safe again. Alone. There was never a second search party. Mother would ask for help in finding for me only once. Just to appear as though she cared. I often stayed there until Daddy came home.

"Mom," David called. "Mom." Again and again. He was never one to call off a search. "Mom."

I crawled out from under the desk. Rising, I dusted the lint from my clothes as he made his way down the stairs, one lead foot after the other.

"Is any there milk?" he asked.

"Uh, I don't see any," I asked after a mock inspection of my surroundings. "Did you try the fridge?"

"What were you doing down here?"

"I was on the computer."

"Doing what?" he asked.

"Looking for a job," I said.

"Do we have any milk?" he asked again, having given this possible change in our lives his deepest consideration. "If we don't, we should."

"Should we?" I asked.

"Milk's something you should always have on hand. We learned about it in home ec."

The fact that schools were still forcing students to take home economics was, to me, the surest indication that the public education system still remained one of the biggest barriers to the cause of gender equality. Ironically, were one to be tasked with recruiting young women to appreciate the necessity of the feminist cause, I can think of few experiences that would prove as effective as being in Miss Crowley's ninth grade course on the subject back in the analog days when I was a young student. When I first laid eyes on her all those years ago, well before the actual horror of being a housewife had been made real, I thought she looked as though she'd been born old and bitter, born to teach women how to labor through their misery. Wrinkles crisscrossed every inch of her face. As she shuffled around the classroom, zigzagging between the sewing machines, her tiny head bobbed forward and she croaked out words in a brittle voice.

"Boys and girls, you may not understand the importance of sewing but you may learn, as you mature and have to pay for your own things, that the world's expensive," she'd say. "You may wish to know how to repair items rather than throw them away. I know that our world today's becoming more and more disposable, and there's, sadly, nothing I can do about that. But some of you may find once you have to start paying your own way in the world that simply, tossing out a garment whose hem has fallen out or has a repairable hole is foolish. You may find sewing to be an economically wise choice.

"This class is called home economics for a reason. Girls, it's the one place where you will likely make the most difference with regards to your family's overall fiscal health. You'll also learn to keep a house that is neat and that serves well-prepared food. Boys, you can use some of what you learn here to help out. It's not all the woman's job to keep the home. You boys will also learn to appreciate all the work your poor mothers do and the work your wives will likely be doing. This class isn't just for girls."

The purpose of the course seemed to be to assure that we, the class of 1993, would be ready for the world of the 1950s, a place only glimpsed in flickering black and white nightmares on the television screen. Miss Crowley, evidentially, still envisioned our future days ending next to our partner in a separate bed with a nightstand between us.

"I have to find out what you consider to be essential," David said. "It's homework."

"You have homework for home ec?" I asked.

"Ms. Wallis, said we should ask our mom's about this stuff, cause the dads're generally clueless and this area would be one where you'd be the expert."

"She's probably right about that, I guess."

He mumbled a yep and gave me a gesture that was between a nod and a shrug. Lately, I'd noticed that the clarity of his speech seemed to be ebbing away almost as fast as his enthusiasm for being in his loving mother's company. He spun the Lazy Susan around and around until he found the cookies that I'd managed to keep from eating. Then, he flopped down in a kitchen chair and stuffed one in his mouth, attempting to swallow it whole. Flipping open a notebook, he started to scribble as his mouth struggled with the cookie. I turned away. It was disgusting to have to watch him and listen to the cookie disintegrating in his mouth at the same time.

"Will you check the fridge for that milk please?" he asked, spraying the table, I'd cleaned only an hour before, with chocolate-flecked crumbs.

It suddenly occurred to me that old Crowley was being proven correct. I had little, if any real power in my own home. I merely cleaned, cooked and kept track of things. My son sat there, cudding away on a cookie and ordering me around like he was beginning to realize it as well. Beneath the sink, behind the elbow pipe, I found an old bottle of wine.

"What're you doing?" David asked through a still half-full mouth.

"Getting a bottle of wine."

"Are you going to drink it?"

"No. I'm going to stain my teeth with it but to do

that I have to drink it."

"But it's…it's…"

"It's what David?"

"It's still daytime, and I need to ask you these questions."

"I'll be back later," I said and headed for the door. "Across the street. You're more than capable of finding out what we keep in the fridge. If you have a question, ask your father when he gets home. Who knows, maybe he isn't as clueless as we think."

"Dad?" he asked.

"Sure, why not?" I resisted the urge to start drinking form the bottle right there in front of him. "Worth a shot."

If he objected to me going out of doors in my slippers or thought it odd, he didn't mention anything. The ground was damp enough that my feet were cold and wet by the time I made it across the road. I didn't even know if Caroline would be home. I just had to get out of the house and was fully prepared to ask Denny if he minded me drinking by myself. I could go down to Gregg's bar and pretend I was far, far away.

Of course, the nonprofit would've had no interest in someone like me. I wasn't a feminist. I wanted to be one. I'd dedicated so much of my life to escaping the politics and patterns with which I'd been raised, yet I never really knew where I was heading. And suddenly, one day, there I found myself standing on a porch in a worse-than-anonymous river valley suburb with a bottle of cheap merlot in my hand, hoping a stewardess will answer her door so that my day wouldn't be made any more pitiful by having to drink alone.

"Gloria," Caroline said, pulling back the door. She

had her uniform on. My heart sank. She was about to leave, I was sure. On her way to Nevada or Europe or somewhere equally strange and exciting. I would've settled for just going to the first destination with her. "Uh-oh," she said, loosening the kerchief from around her neck, "wine in the middle of the afternoon. How did you know I just got back from the UK? Were you watching from your window?"

"You just got home?" I asked.

"I've done my turns for the month. I could use a glass of that, or six. Come on in," she said, holding the door for me and saying nothing about my damp slippers. "Gregg won't be home tonight and Denny's at baseball."

"Gregg's flying?" I asked, hoping that I didn't sound too eager for our wine-tasting to have no curfew.

"He's not nearly done his month yet," she said. "I can't tell you how much I'm looking forward to next year when I'll have enough seniority to get the bids I really want. This trans-A treadmill really wears me out. It's not as glamorous as I'm sure you imagine it to be. Not by a long shot."

I sat down at the kitchen table, not having to wait long for a full glass of wine to be presented to me. Caroline trudged across the linoleum a little theatrically. She shuffled her feet and gave me a look from under self-consciously heavy eyelids. As she took her seat, she moaned as though in pain. Even after crossing an ocean, though, she still looked so much better than me. Of course, spending part of my day in near catatonic depression beneath the desk in the basement probably didn't exactly count as a beauty treatment.

"Oh, that's nice," she said, taking a sip. "So. Haven't seen you in a while. What's been happening, Gloria?"

"Tough day. Just wanted to wine and bitch."

"Shouldn't have one without the other. What's the bother, m'lady?" she asked in less than successful cockney accent that she'd probably picked up from the TV in her London hotel.

"I just feel…feel…stuck. You know? I'm in the house all day, waiting for the time to make and then eat dinner so I can watch TV and then go to sleep, only to wake up and do it all over again."

"Really? I love being home. Especially now, when it's quiet. The boys are gone. It's all mine. It's my house. My space."

"Try doing it day after day after day, year after year after year with nothing else, nothing at all to look forward to."

"Huh. Yeah, that'd be hard. I guess, I've always had a job," she said, holding her glass up against her cheek. "Ever think about going back to finish college?"

"Law school, you mean. I finished college."

"You should go back and finish that. Be a lawyer. Maybe you could have one of those commercials. *Have you been injured by transvaginal mesh?*" she said, snickering.

"I think I'm a little late for all of that."

"I'll tell you on days like today, I wish I had done law school or something. There were five screaming kids at the back of this plane. And they had some lungs on them, let me tell you. We had a new girl on the crew and the whole flight she keeps asking me what to do with the kids. She's young, so naturally she thinks I know everything," she said, pausing to sip her wine. "So I tell her that in my experience, it was the parents' shame that would quiet them and if these parents had none, well then, she was screwed. I told her to grab herself some aspirin. Drug of choice on this job."

Her snickers turned to snorts as she threw her head back. The wine tasted bittersweet. I could feel it coating my tongue like it was leaving some of its blackness behind. I tried joining her with a laugh of my own. How fake it must've sounded.

"See, that's the kind of stuff you're lucky to miss out on. And I'll tell you what else. Be happy that Davey didn't go out for the baseball team. Those games can run late. There's one tomorrow night and I don't know how I'll stay awake for it."

I wanted so badly to jump on her throwaway comment about her wishing she'd gone to law school. I wanted to point out that going to law school would've meant finishing college first and that by finishing college I didn't mean working her way through the rest of the brothers in whatever frat house I was sure she frequented. I finished my wine. She didn't seem bothered by my departure or worried that I was leaving my bottle behind.

"See you, Gloria," she said to my back. "Maybe we should all go back to school, huh?"

The rubber heels of my slippers slapped across the wet blacktop. The sound began to haunt me as if I were being stalked by my own boredom, so I walked on the grass as soon as I could. I heard yelping and the clashing of what sounded like sticks coming from behind the house. There, I found Daryl and David engaged in a sword fight. The bottoms of both of their jeans were caked with mud.

"Hey, what're you two doing?" I asked.

"I got home early today. Work's a little slow this week so we just knocked off," Daryl said, then turned to swing his sword slowly at his son.

"I'm Greylor," David said, leaping away from Daryl's slow-moving slash.

Their weapons were made of lacquered wood and had been sanded to sharp points. They were careful, gentle even, when their swords clashed. Still, the sound of their coming together was violent. A certain kind of mother would have warned them to be careful, to tell them not to get so close to each other. I just sank down to sit on the concrete step on the backside of the garage.

"We're recreating Greylor's duel with Sackenbush from the first book," Dave informed me.

"I'm Sackenbush, the dastardly Prince of Pathes," Daryl said, waving his sword over his head.

"What can I be?" The wine had gone right to my head making it ache too much for me to care about the dirt on their jeans. "Can I be Bedray?"

"She's not in this scene," David said, letting his guard down to consider the casting choice I'd presented him. "You can be Princess Estrella. She's who I'm fighting to save."

"You better fight hard," I said. "What do I get to do?"

"Nothing, just sit there until I fatally wound Sackenbush. Then you will scream my name and an apology for ever doubting me. 'Greylor!' You'll say. 'No enemy is your equal. Now, I see that.'"

"I think I can do that," I said, emphasis clearly on 'think.'

"But you can't move around much. You're in a cage, Mom."

I said nothing, just let my fat behind grow wet and cold on the damp concrete. I tried to watch, not to appear as pathologically disinterested as I felt. Not even when David lay down in the mud to fool Sackenbush into thinking he was dead did I object to how boring and dirty their play was. Daryl made such a convincing dupe. The role he was born to play. Then came the final move and while Sackenbush turned to me, winking lasciviously, suggesting more of what made me uncomfortable about those books, David leapt to his feet and ran his wooden sword under Daryl's armpit. He dutifully squeezed his arm against his side. The mud mark from where the sword had been tucked almost appeared to be a blood stain on his shirt. Greylor came to where I sat and using the butt end of his sword knocked the imaginary lock off my imaginary cage.

"You are free, Princess. Sackenbush no longer will hold sway over your land or people," David said, deepening his voice. "Tell your countrymen about freedom and how you are wanting them to never be fooled by charlestons like Sackenbush ever again!"

"Gee thanks, Greylor. You're the greatest!" I said and rose from the stone step, my slippers now officially ruined. "And I think you meant charlatans."

"Mom," David whined.

"Oh, sorry." I bowed my head and cleared my throat. "Greylor! Nobody's equal to you. I see that."

"That's not quite it," David said.

"Close enough," Daryl said and I wanted to thank *him* for saving me. "What's for supper?"

"How about we order a pizza, Sackenbush?"

"You didn't make anything?" Daryl asked.

"I was being held prisoner in this cage."

"Pizza!" David yelled and raised his sword high in triumph.

While the boys rejoined the great philosophical debate of our time, pepperoni or sausage, I lay down in bed. Daryl made a half attempt to gather input on toppings from me, calling down the hall to ask if 'roni was alright. I must've dozed off for a while because the next thing I knew the doorbell was ringing. Daryl called the delivery man sir and thanked him. I listened as they got out the plates. They each called for me, twice. But I just stayed there sitting up in bed. They each called again then gave up and started eating. Laughing at something together, they sounded more like a family without me.

That particular event and others like it were brought up by Daryl's attorney during our divorce proceedings as evidence that I'd checked out of life with my family. I'd left my son and gone off to drink wine. I'd come back and fallen asleep. It shocked me because I'd foolishly thought no one had ever noticed or cared what I did. That moment, sitting there with Judge Franklin and my soon-to-be ex-husband's snarling lawyer both judging me with their eyes was the closest I got to regretting my decision to call it quits with Daryl.

In a movie or TV show, I would've looked past Ms. Hodgkins, Daryl's lawyer and told him that I just wanted someone to say something, for someone to ask me more than what was for dinner. If he'd only noticed, we might have talked, and things might have been different.

"Weren't you often disengaged from them, Ms. Hytner? Weren't you often only too happy to be alone, to let the rest of your family do what they could to take care of themselves?" asked Hodgkins.

"That's not true," I replied. "I just got tired of my life sometimes. Doesn't anyone here get tired of their families? Of their lives? "

"Your Honor," Hodgkins said.

"Ms. Hytner, please answer the question with a yes or no. Leave the soliloquies to your counsel. You may proceed, Ms. Hodgkins."

"Ms. Hytner," she began, turning her back to me and walking away before turning again, one of those dramatic pivots only make-believe lawyers use effectively, "why did you spend so much time resting? What were you tired of?"

Back then, I didn't know what the truth was. It certainly wasn't the answer I gave that day in court or the one I must've been saving to use in the Lifetime movie of my life. It was as most things were, a part of the purgatory where we all live, the limbo that makes up most of our existence. We can only suffer through it and hope to explain it to ourselves later.

18. A Day Circled in Red

Daryl had picked up a half shift the Saturday we were having Mother over for dinner. He'd managed, showing shocking foresight, to arrange for me to have the car. One of his co-workers -- Tiny? Goose? Shemp? -- was driving him to work. I could never keep them straight, probably because Daryl only used their ridiculous nicknames. As I lay in bed trying to will myself upright, I thought of the day to come, of the shopping, of dealing with David as I shopped, of dealing with David *in addition to* other people as I shopped. Once it struck me that he probably wouldn't allow a pedophile or a burglar into the house nor burn it down, I decided the day we both had so yearned for had finally arrived. I could leave him at home alone. When I announced this plan to him, the momentous nature of the occasion eluded him. His initial response was indistinguishable from a grunt. I wouldn't have received much of a reaction at all hadn't I told him to not allow anyone in the house, which earned me a screeched "Mom, I know."

I would love to report that soon after leaving the driveway, I began to cry and regret that the passing years had brought me to the point of admitting my little one was growing up, but I didn't. I turned the radio up, instead and sang along with Whitney Houston. Once at the supermarket, my auditory senses, which had been so accustomed to my son's whining, began to fill in the gaps with Mother's voice. "You're not getting canned beans, are you? Dear, those are for soldiers." "Premade pie crust? I didn't raise you to be lazy. Besides, do we need pie? There're only four of us." "Come to think of it, that chicken you got is awfully big. Well, I guess you can always have leftovers. I'd watch how much chicken you eat, though. Filthy animals."

I put the big bird back in the freezer case, scraping my knuckles on frozen carcasses in search of a smaller one. Sometimes, relenting to her voice, when it'd already so successfully drowned out my own, was the only way to make it stop. More frequently than I'd ever admit, she was right.

Being alone in the car was like a preview of my future life when I didn't have to try so hard to placate those around me. I listened to music and, figuring Mother would be late, took the long way back home without having to hear any complaints or answer any questions. When she finally did arrive nearly 45 minutes after the appointed time, I was still getting things ready and could fully enjoy the fact that now, in my home, I was making her wait.

On entering our door, she complained about the roads and the general location of our house, then ordered David to go get our gifts from her car. For me she bought flowers that had started to wilt and smelled of gas station convenience mart. David got a tiny Nerf basketball and hoop. It might as well have been a suppository for all the use he was going to get out of it. Still, he was polite and thanked his grandma with a kiss on her dry over-rouged cheek. For Daryl, there was a twelve pack of beer.

"I don't think he'll mind if I have a couple," I said as I put the beer in the refrigerator.

"Are we not having wine then, I take it, Gloria?" Mother asked.

"No, we are. I can handle both."

"I hope you don't overindulge and find it clever to start introducing improper topics as you did on Christmas Eve. Really, it was too much."

"Dumpster diving," Daryl said with a smile and cracked open a can of Heineken.

"Mother, it was just a joke. I didn't mean for you to be offended," I lied.

"A joke? Is that what it was? A joke? It was utterly and wholly inappropriate for my home."

"I guess you'll get your chance for revenge at my home tonight."

"My mind doesn't work that way, dear. I believe the dinner table to be a place of morals and courtesies. Just as I've always taught you to think. Or endeavored to, anyway."

Caught in the crossfire, father and son exchanged glances then slunk down the stairs, trying not to be noticed. I put the dying flowers in a vase and placed it on the table. The biting silence between Mother and I covered the room like a warm, comfortable blanket.

"Dinner will be a few minutes. Would you like to join me in the kitchen or go downstairs with the boys?"

She said nothing and went to the top of the stairs. "What are we doing down there?" she asked.

"Just watching a show about big cats," David said.

"Big cats?" she asked. "You mean like Garfield from the comics page?"

"No, jungle cats. You know, like lions and tigers, panthers. The predator cats," Daryl, already annoyed with Mother, said in a raised voice.

"I think I'd like a glass of wine," she said and sat down at the dining room table.

I poured her a glass and sat the bottle before her. She turned it so that the label faced her. Observing, I'm sure, that it wasn't the kind of wine her brother Ben would've deigned to drown a rat in, she sipped with a smirk. She was waiting for me to ask for her opinion but I wasn't in any mood to fall into one of her traps, if only to prove I could climb out.

"I hope they don't come to the table babbling about what jaguars like to eat," she said.

"I think after your little greeting speech, they'll steer clear of such topics."

"No place settings?" she asked, leaning back in her chair to examine the table. "Are we just going to eat off the table with our hands?"

"Yes. I thought it would be a nice change for you."

"Gloria," she huffed, "if you would like me to assist you by setting the table, I would be more than happy to do it. Just show me where you keep the china and place settings and such."

"The placemats are in the china cabinet behind you. In the drawers."

"We have choices, I see," she said as she began digging. "Blue or white?"

"Blue."

"Wise choice. Your husband has a habit of making a mess of things when he eats, doesn't he?"

When we first started going out in public together as a couple, I kind of didn't mind the fact that Daryl ate with such gusto. I liked the thought of how disapproving Mother would've been about me dating someone with such "working class manners." "Not that I have anything against those people," she'd often say. "It's just that mixing together socially can be something of a feat. We are used to doing things a certain way and they, well, they have theirs. It's like we're from different countries, really."

"How long have you been in this house, now?" she asked, turning sideways in her chair, trying hard to look like she was not being judgmental, just confused.

"Ten years, almost eleven. We moved in not long before your grandson turned 1."

"Plan to stay here much longer, do you?"

"We have no plans to move out at present, Mother."

"It'll be time to trade up soon. Don't you think?"

"No. We're very happy here," I said.

"Small, though. Maybe you like that. Cozy is what I bet the broker called it. God, even if it were just you and your father and me here, we'd have been at each other's throats."

On each visit, she asked the same questions about our home, as she inspected it through barely disguised stink eyes. She also managed to make the same disparaging remarks framed always as memories she could never see herself making in such a place. I suppose they simply didn't make buildings big enough to keep her from anyone's throat and vice versa.

I still couldn't get the fork through the biggest of the boiling potatoes. And in the state she'd put me in, I managed to exert considerable force into the stabbing. I watched the steam that had condensed on the fork's handle dissipate, hoping it would calm me. I was in no mood to keep or settle scores.

"I don't like my food spicy. Simplicity is best, dear," she said, not giving up her search for the edge of me that she could catch.

"I know. That's why we're just having chicken and potatoes and salad."

"Nowadays everything has to be spiced up with all sorts of goofy, foreign things."

"Really? Like what?"

"Oh. I don't know. I don't know what the stuff's called."

"Daddy liked using spices when he cooked."

"Your father. Don't get me started on him and his hobbies," she said, now closely examining the place-mats. "Saw something on television once and thought it made him a gourmet chef."

"He told me he wished he'd been born Italian. He thought a talent for cooking was in the blood."

"Your father? From swarthy stock?" she tut-tutted, "I'll tell you if he had been, I never would've married him."

"The kitchen smelled so good that time he grew that little herb garden in the windowsill. Remember?"

"If he'd been Italian, you would've never been born," she said as though I'd failed to properly consider the existential weight of her earlier comment.

I rechecked my tester potato. The fork went right through this time. It was hard to tell if it was really ready or if I'd just gotten stabbier. I added more salt and let them go a little longer.

"I always loved it when he let me watch him cook," I said.

"Yes, your father let you watch him a lot. You could've watched me if you wanted."

"Do what?"

"I was known to make food from time to time."

"Were you?" I asked.

"I made a cake for you when you were four."

"I don't think I was interested in cooking then, Mother."

"It was a good cake and much enjoyed as I recall.

Yellow cake with chocolate frosting."

"One time, I'll never forget, Daddy let me hang the pasta on those wooden pegs he used anytime he made it from scratch."

"Noodles all over the kitchen," she sniffed.

"Mother, come on, you liked his cooking."

"Oh, the cooking was fine enough. I didn't care for the messes he made."

"Why?" I asked. "Because it took whomever the cleaning service sent over too long to clean up the next day?"

"It was embarrassing to have people see my house like that, even if they were only from the maid service."

Steam billowed up from the sink as I dumped the softened potatoes into a strainer. It fogged up the window and frosted over my reflection. I'd begun to sweat from the heat. My bangs clung to my forehead.

"Shall I get the silverware then?' she asked.

"Sure."

She tromped into the kitchen, opening every drawer except the first one she'd passed, which was where I'd always kept the silverware, ever since we'd moved in. I could hear her tsk-tsk-ing at what she no doubt viewed as my poor kitchen organization. I let her hunt around a bit before trying to help her find them.

"The first drawer," I said, once she had opened almost every other one.

With a great clattering of metal, she gathered up the spoons and forks and knives. I mashed the potatoes in what I'm sure was record time for me, using the full force of my frustration to pound them until they were practically pureed.

"I hope you didn't use too much butter," she said.

"Overly rich food aggravates my stomach."

"I used margarine."

"Margarine?" questioned Mother. "I guess that is lower in fat. But then I also hear that it's bad for the skin."

"Where did you hear that?"

"My doctor said so."

"Really?" I asked in a mildly incredulous tone.

"Yes. Yes. Dr. Marks told me," she said as though warming up to the idea that a conversation in which she was told that information had actually taken place.

"Bad for the skin, hmmm…" I said as I removed the aluminum foil tent that covered the cooling chicken. "I'll try to keep that in mind, Mother."

"Butter is more natural, after all. Margarine is chemically made."

"You have a point there."

"Natural foods…are better for you. I try to eat…a… natural diet," she said, struggling suddenly to negotiate the ground I'd ceded to her.

"I think I know where you heard that," I said and began to slice the chicken. There was no use letting Daryl do it. By the time he was through, it would've gone cold and appeared as though vultures in serious need of orthodonture had been feasting on it.

"Where, dear? Where do you think I heard that?"

"It's something Daddy always used to say."

"Your father?"

"I remember him saying it once when you complained that you didn't want him to dig up the backyard and put in a garden."

"I do not remember that, Gloria," she said.

"You didn't want him tracking mud all over the

house on top of it all, you said."

"You've a great memory for his wisdom, don't you dear?" she asked. "While mine always seems to be in question."

"Dinner's ready," I yelled down the stairs.

David and Daryl came trundling up, one heavy pair of feet after the other. Their eyes were both puffy, their faces red as though they'd fallen asleep. How anyone who really cared for me could nap, while I was trapped in the kitchen with my lifelong nemesis was beyond my comprehension. I put the platter with the chicken before her. Mother kept her head down, muttering to herself, a scowl stitching together the wrinkles around her mouth and coursing across her sagging cheeks.

"I'll have one too, honey," I said to Daryl when he grabbed a beer from the fridge. "Mother, would you like me to pour you another glass of wine?"

"Have a beer, Edie," Daryl said, using his term of endearment for her that she took the most visible contempt in hearing. 'Mom' would've been a very close second coming from him.

"Beer?" she gasped. "When have you ever seen me drink beer?"

"I just, you know, thought you might like to switch things up," he said as he handed me one.

"No, thank you. I will take a little more wine. Just enough to freshen my glass."

More than just freshen her glass, he filled it almost to the top. Mother smiled her smile of barely tolerating someone. Where was Daryl when I needed him to annoy her 10 minutes earlier?

"I don't usually take such a big glass. The wine should have room to breathe," she said.

"Breathe?" David asked. "Why does it need to breathe?"

"You want the bouquet of it, the smell to have room to open up inside the glass. Smell it," she said and forced her glass under his nose.

"Smells kind of like flowers floating in perfume," David said, taking a tentative sniff. "I know why they call it a bouquet."

"A budding wine connoisseur in our midst," Mother chirped, triumphantly.

"I'm not old enough to drink," he said.

"But you have clearly been born with a nose that will be of great value to you when you get older."

David took a sniff of the air, trying, it seemed, to divine the extent of this gift. We passed the mashed potatoes around. As we began eating, there was a blessed silence. I could breathe. I could eat. I hardly wanted to stab anyone.

"Your mother and father apparently prefer beer, which smells, to me, of poster paste," Mother said, before the brief interval of peace could ruin her meal, "of the kind I'm sure you used in school when you were a little boy."

David reached for my beer but I scooped it up before he could get his hands on it.

"Go ahead. Let him smell it," Daryl said.

I handed it to my son.

"Take a sip," Daryl said.

"Can I have a sip? Can I?" David asked, turning to me with the can close to his lips and a smile on his face that dared me to stop him. He didn't wait for permission.

Daryl hooted his approval at this, pumping his fist in the air. Mother merely sighed and took a defeated sip from her glass. She made a point of being dainty about it, picking it up with only her thumb and ring finger. Always setting the example, that one. Years later, when we met for one of our increasingly uneasy late Sunday brunches in the city, David told me of how he'd recounted that very scene to his latest therapist.

You are all, each one of you headshrinkers, welcome by the way. How rich did that damaged young man make you?

David had theorized to the therapist that that early moment of peer pressure coupled with the taking of a substance may have laid the template for the pattern he would recreate for the rest of his life. I know, it's the kind of shit you'd almost *have* to be getting paid to listen to. I mean, who was supposed to be the peer and from where was he feeling the pressure? After he'd finished explaining this, David dug his palms into his eyes. His posture bent in a way that reminded me of the same about-to-cry kind of vulnerability that he carried with him as a boy. I spent days mulling over that bullshit before I dismissed it. Kids do really say the darnedest things, even long after they've grown up.

"Tastes like wet cement, doesn't it?" Mother asked of the beer.

David scowled and nodded. We all laughed. An odd sound, the four of us laughing together as though Mother had quit being herself for a moment. The ceasefire lasted only until she felt compelled to observe that the chicken was a little dry.

19. Finally Meeting that Someone from School, Ms. No-One-I'd-Know

"Is that okay, Mom?" David asked. "Mom? Mom? Is it okay?"

I stood, blinking in disbelief, the tattered copy of Virginia Wolfe's *Orlando* raised before me like a shield. Had they been holding hands right there in my living room? Where did this girl come from? I may not have been as ready for David to grow up as I'd always thought. It was as though he'd brought home an alien with a slender neck and giant green eyes. She had a little snub for a nose and gorgeous cascading blonde hair. I couldn't help but notice the little nubs of breasts just beginning to stretch the fabric of her sweater, a kind of mirror that reflected the changes which were surely underway but I'd failed to notice with my son.

They exchanged a quick glance. Shared a shrug. They were on the same wavelength, locked together, it was easy to see. Two geeky kids trying to survive the hurricane of life in a public school full of nasty brutes. I might've been happier but for the look in her eyes, something knowing, aware seemingly of how she had the upper hand with boys like my son. Something more, like, dare I call it, motherly instinct told me this slender girl was trouble. I didn't like that she stood taller, straighter than my son and exuded such an easy confidence. She'd obviously been told over and over how smart and lovely she was. One day, she'd enter a world that would allow her to wear her glasses and read her books and have her opinions. No one would talk down to her. But I didn't like her mostly because I'd never heard about her before and here she was in my house with her outwardly apparent sense of self as evident as the breast nubs she was sporting.

"Mom, Mom, can Victoria…"

"Sure," I said pausing at the hushed and half-strangled quality of my voice. "She can stay for dinner."

"We're going to study," Victoria said, holding up a history book in front of her as a shield of her own. Her tome was larger, thicker than mine and, in that way, more indicative of the balance of the threat.

"Study?" I asked. "But it's Friday."

"We have a big history test on Monday. Mr. Keir said anything covered over the whole year up to this point was fair game," David said. "The whole year. It's, like, ridiculous."

"Such a freak," she said. "He smells like really, really bad b-o."

"It really isn't nice to call him a freak. I don't think he can really help how he smells," I said. "I'm sure he would if he could."

David went red. His eyes widened. He began to speak but it sounded like his tongue was stuck to the roof of his mouth. After taking several gulps of air, he softened his face into a pathetic pleading look. Victoria held her book up higher so that she was peeking out from just over the top of it. She used the edge of it to push her glasses up her nose.

"Sorry," she said. "I just meant that…."

"Usually something like the way someone smells," I said, "when it's someone, an adult, who's smart enough to be a teacher, more often than not they have a good reason and haven't just been neglecting their hygiene."

A sudden rush of satisfaction filled me. I had chastened the young Bedray. David's eyes were searching me, pleading even more pathetically for an end to the interview.

"Try to be nice to Mr. Keir," I advised, dropping my book as a way of showing that I was winding up my summation. "I think going around smelling like that would be hard enough to live with, don't you?"

"He's a great teacher. We learn loads in his class," Victoria said, eagerly. "Don't we?"

"A lot," David said, almost in relief at being prompted.

"You're studying the American Revolution?" I asked.

"Yeah," Victoria said, further pleasing me with a bout of nervous laughter, "it's basically the story about how these landed, white British males consolidated their power here in America."

"We learned about the Indian tribes that lived here in the valley, too," David said, now actually squirming where he stood, unable to hide his discomfort any longer.

"Mr. Keir knows loads about local history," Victoria added.

"Really? Like what for instance. What did you learn about the area?" I asked.

"The Nochpeem and Wappinger tribes were the ones who originally settled this area most thickly," David said. "Can we go to my room now?"

"Sure. We'll eat in a little bit. Spaghetti okay?"

"My mom makes really good spaghetti," David said, and grabbing her hand, practically dragged Victoria down the hall.

In the kitchen, I put the thawing sauce that I'd made the weekend before in a pot and turned on the heat. It was still hard in the middle. I crept from the kitchen to the hall, trying to hear what was going on behind the closed door of my son's room. No honest mother ever truly feels bad about eavesdropping like that. It's part of the job. The one part I was really good at. Mothers, who go on and on about respecting their children's privacy, are the ones failing their sons and daughters. If you're not interested enough in what your child's doing to be sneaky, you're not interested enough in your child. And keep in mind, this comes from a mother whose interest in her own son waxes and wanes on an almost daily basis.

"He said it was going to be three of five essay questions," David said.

"From the handout, right?" she asked.

"What handout? I didn't, like, get one."

"Yes you did," Victoria giggled, "everyone did."

"I can't find it."

"I have mine," she said.

"What happened to, like, the one he gave me?"

"God, Dave," she snorted, which lured me into taking a couple more steps down the hall, "how do you get such good grades without paying attention to what's going on?"

"I pay attention."

She laughed. That was followed by what I thought sounded like a kiss, which drew me even further down the hall. I was almost at his doorway when I heard the sizzle of the sauce cooking and a faint smell of it burning. I raced back to the stove, trying to be as quiet as I could. As I stirred the sauce, I reached over and turned on the radio. The news came on, all tragedy and crackling static. I tried to listen, tried to keep my mind on the sauce but was soon standing just at the end of the hall again.

When I leaned forward from that spot just a little, the floor creaked. When I leaned back, the quality of the sound I received from his room diminished considerably. Victoria's voice was softer than my son's with a tone that was foreign to my ears as well, so I had trouble filling in the gaps when it dropped below a certain decibel. I steadied myself on the knob of the open door to the basement, turning my head carefully, slowly -- my ear like a radio telescope trying to pick up any sounds or signs of life.

"Babe, whatcha doing?" Daryl asked from the bottom of the stairs.

"Coming to see you," I said and turned from the hall to start my way down. I had forgotten he'd been given that Good Friday off and once he was out of my sight that day, I didn't spend any time wondering what he was up to or even where he was.

He cocked his head to the side as I made my way down. He spread his arms wide. He had a beer in hand and was dressed in a flannel shirt and sweatpants. The very outfit of a man happy not to have anywhere to be. I gave each step my full weight and realized I wouldn't be able to avoid hugging my husband. He didn't even wait for me to make it all the way down, grabbing me from the bottom step and holding me tight. Our flabby torsos pressed together like two air bags. He scraped his face against my cheek and lifted me in the air.

"Put me down," I said. "You'll hurt yourself."

"You're like, just a thick soul sistah," he said and barked out a laugh.

"That's insulting to so many women in so many ways."

"Oh, c'mon," he said, then pointed to the vent above

us and whispered, "Were you listening?"

I turned my head towards the vent then at him. A mischievous smile lit his face. He'd had enough beers for his eyes to twinkle. His breath was heavy and warm. I nodded. He took my hand and pulled me to him so that we were standing very close to each other, directly beneath the vent.

"They're okay," Victoria said. "I'm not all the way through the last one you loaned me."

"Aren't they cool?" David asked.

"I guess. The plot overall's pretty good and the plot in each one interlocking with the rest is interesting, I guess."

"I've read all of them at least twice," David said, breathless with enthusiasm. "I practically know what word's coming next when I read some sections of them."

"Don't you think Greylor is a little bit, I don't know, kind of arrogant?" Victoria asked. "Kind of full of himself?"

"What? No, he's not. He's the hero," David said, sounding equal measures perplexed and wounded. "It's, like, his wisdom that frees people. The swordsmanship is just so the people will know that he's a serious man."

"He's always going on and on though. He gives these long, long speeches," she said. "All the other characters do is tell him how great he is or how great he can be."

"He's a warrior teacher. That's his role in uniting the kingdoms. He's a reluctant hero. You read book one, right?"

"I did it in a day. I gave it right back to you," she said. "Remember?"

"So then you know the path of destiny he's on was

chosen for him by the dust spirits when he was a child making his way across the Narrow Wastelands with his family and people in their caravans."

Hearing my son defend his hero, while his prospective paramour voiced misgivings that so clearly mirrored my own was so compelling that I didn't notice that Daryl and I had drifted close together, and our swelled bellies were once again touching. I permitted myself to sink into his eyes for a second and allowed him into mine.

"When we eat?" he asked, wrapping his arms around me.

"About a half an hour," I said. "How long have you known about her?"

"Not long," he said, releasing me, surprised perhaps that I'd tolerated it for so long. "He didn't want anyone to know. He's not sure how much she likes him."

"So that's why you didn't tell me?"

"He made me promise to keep his secret and I figured either it would fizzle out or you'd find out."

"I don't like you keeping secrets about our son from me," I said and sat down on the couch with my arms crossed over my chest.

"I didn't mean to. I've been, like, reading those books of his off and on at work and stuff and we got to talking about them and then, it just kind of came out," he said, sitting down next to me. "I don't think he meant to say anything. It just, like I said, came out that there was this girl and like he liked her. Boys his age are just, like, you know, embarrassed. You're Mom. He doesn't want to talk about girlfriend stuff with you."

"Wait, you've been reading at work?"

"Yeah, at lunch and like it's also been slow there lately. David wants me to make him armor like the kind

Greylor wears when he fights the werelizards."

"How do you like the books?" I asked, finding myself engaged in something as close to a literary discussion with my husband as the school girl in me ever still dared to dream.

"The writer does a better job of, like, describing the werelizards than the armor."

"It does seem your little talk to him about hygiene went well. Too well. Now he's bringing home the school's hottest mathlete."

"I used his hero as an example. You know? I told him that to preserve his honor and promote the honor of others, here in, like, this land, he had to keep himself clean and stuff, as well as show others the proper respect."

"Really? What did he say?"

"David?" he asked.

"No. Greylor. Of course, our son."

"Ah, you know, like, I know I pointed out how the women in those books were all real helpless, dependent on men and, not that I used these words, but made to look real sexy on the cover because they're for boys and the writer's a man and like…"

"Daryl," I said, stopping him with closed eyes and a raised hand. "What did David say to all of this? What does it have to do with Vicky?"

"You shouldn't call her that," he said in a somewhat ominous tone. "She likes to be called Victoria. David told me."

"He did? Well, what else did he tell you about her?"

"Look the dude's my son, but he has a way of eyeballing me that, like, makes me think he thinks I'm a moron. And that he'll like shut me out if I don't do what he says, what he asks." He took a deep breath through his nose like he was struggling to inhale the right kind of air. "Just like you do a lot of times. Like lately I feel like..."

"So just, so I get this straight, let me, *like*, go over it," I said, curling up in the couch as much as a gal my size could without coming into contact with her husband. "You feel you cannot have a substantial discussion about our son with me because you sense he'll look down on your intellect, if you can't keep his secrets?"

"Gloria, I'm just trying to be honest with you here. God, you know, like, if I had a mirror right now, I'd hold it up and show you how you're looking at me. If he shuts me out, I'll be all alone here. No one will talk to me."

"Daryl..."

"And that's, like, fine for you and him. You two like being alone but I don't. I don't have anything else but you two."

"Do you feel like I've shut you out? Is that what you're saying?"

"Come on, Gloria. I'm not stupid. I know what's been going on here."

I hadn't thought he'd cared or noticed. I should've been more ashamed of hurting him but instead was angry that David had been sharing more of his life with his father. Only in looking back did I understand, that as much as I thought David and I were matches intellectually that wasn't what my son needed. He wanted to connect more emotionally, which wasn't something I had or have the capacity to do. He made fun of Daryl because that was the parent he felt closest to. I'd placed too much emphasis on being the audience for that impersonation when really anyone who knew his dad would've done almost as well.

"This's what makes it hard to tell you things," he said. "Like the way you are and how you react. And I've got something I should, like, tell you now. Something important."

"Is it about David?" I asked. "What else have you been keeping from me?"

"No. It's about work," he said, sipping from his beer. "There's something that's been going on there that I've been meaning to talk to you about."

By Sunday morning, the fight that had begun that Friday before diner was back on. Daryl sat up in bed, shaking his head at me. I pretended not to notice the sulky expression on his face. The sheets and comforter were pulled up to his chin. If he expected an apology from me, he knew me even less well than I thought. I'd let Saturday go by without saying anything more to him but I couldn't hold it inside any more. So I'd waited for him to wake up then harangued him some more. He got the bitch for breakfast. Not that any specific issue was at stake, not by that point. I was just reinforcing my displeasure.

The fact that he and David were getting closer and freezing me out meant there was some extra vinegar in the pissy mood I unleashed on him when he'd told me they might have to start cutting back on his hours at work, hours we needed. He then got pissy at me, perhaps fairly I might add, for getting pissy with him for something that he felt was beyond his control. So I came back at him for getting pissy at me for not telling me about both Victoria and work sooner. It'd all degenerated from there to the point where we just seemed to be pissed at each other for having the temerity to exist. Anything and everything was fair game. Can opened. Vial unsealed.

The first horseman was on the gallop.

"Don't go if you don't want to," he said, referring to the Easter service that we were to attend with his mother that morning. The battle over that had now moved from undercard to main event. "It's not like…"

"Like what, Daryl? Like marriage with you is little more than trading miseries with each other?"

"Oh, that's nice," he said, whipping the comforter and sheets off.

I left the room, shut the door behind me. Checking on David, I found he'd done nothing in the way of starting to get ready. At least, I wasn't going to be the one to make us late. Every movement my body made felt as though it was part of the battle Daryl and I were engaged in.

"David," I called to him; but he did not acknowledge me, his nose buried in the green knight book. I took a step into his room and maintaining my composure, called to him without quite yelling. Still, there was no reaction, the book did not move.

I suspected he was, like me, just pretending to read to avoid participating in the life of a family that was by then cutting sails for the seas of true, profound unhappiness. He'd read enough to know the rhythm of when to turn the page and obeyed it. It gave his mind the chance to be elsewhere. I know that's roughly what I was doing when I was 'reading' back in those days. He stretched out on his bed, the book blocking my view of his face. The one thing that gave him away was that he held it too close. As someone with a little more practice at that ploy, I could tell that he wasn't really reading. He was still an amateur phony. I'd gone pro years before.

I used his doorframe for balance as I put on my

pumps. A fantasy of taking the book from his hands and smacking him across the face with it was satisfying enough to just imagine for a moment.

"Come on, David. Get dressed. It's time. We've got to go soon," I said, holding one of my shoes aloft in what I thought of as a slightly threatening manner. "Put on some slacks and a shirt and get ready."

"Can't I stay home?" He whined the whine of a boy who'd actually benefitted from the tactic.

"No. We're going to Grandma's after." Having finally had my presence acknowledged, I put the other shoe on. "Get dressed. We'll have to stand if we're late, and then it won't just seem like torture, it actually will be very uncomfortable."

"I don't understand why we have to go. You don't want to."

"Just get dressed. We can debate it on the way there."

"Can't I please stay home? Please?" he whined and his voice cracked, chiming that perfect pre-teen note that made me want to tear all the teeth out of my skull.

"David, we do this every year," I said, forcing each word out. "Now, get going."

"I don't want to go to church," he said, striking that same note once again. "You can't make me."

"Daryl," I snapped, wishing I still had that shoe in my hand.

"Yeah," he said, peeking out of our bedroom.

"Help your son get dressed."

At the custody hearings, my attorney made great sport of the idea that I did much to keep Daryl happy. That I even went so far as to subject myself to his belief system, even though I found it absurd. That was a stretch. It was really Gail's belief system, if anything I was there to help Daryl make her happy. What I really found absurd was that the church didn't have air conditioning. In years when Easter fell late enough in April that some of May's just-settling thickness could already be felt, it was stifling inside. And, need I remind you how much we big gals can sweat? Never forget that.

I finished getting ready, strapping on a watch and swapping things from one cheap purse into another. The mumbling back and forth coming from David's room told me Daryl was half-assing his way through another argument. No doubt they were cutting some sort of deal. I always wished David drove harder bargains. He could've asked for a tree house or log cabin fort built to scale. The boy had no idea how much leverage he had with the old man. My son settled too often for trinkets, when Daryl, who was so desirous of winning the boy's admiration, would've done just about anything.

"How come we have to drive all the way to Grandma's church?" David asked later in the driveway, when I handed him a tray of cupcakes to hold.

"Cause we like Grandma's church," Daryl said, throwing me a look that begged for corroboration.

"We do?" David asked.

"Sure. Beautiful cathedral up on the hill. Nice music," Daryl said.

"Do we, Mom?" David asked, inviting me to join his side.

"It's the only church I'd ever consider stepping foot in," I said, "let alone sticking around for a service at."

As we neared the town of Daryl's birth, we came to a bridge. Beneath it, the high water flowed with purpose in thick brown currents. I loved that bridge for the sense of danger and trepidation that its height and narrowness inspired. Our car seemed so fragile compared to the mountainous crags that lay ahead and behind us. We'd followed a winding road that had been carved into the rock for so long that the open air felt like freedom, like I could fill my lungs with it again.

There wasn't anything special, as far as I could see, about Calvary Congregational. Modest and bland, it fit nicely with the general lack of imagination that was the area's architectural hallmark. The red brick building with a white-tiled roof, pitched at a sharp angle and topped off by a cross of silver, could've been constructed from a child's drawing of a church. Seated in the last pew, Gail swayed nervously from side to side until she saw us come in. Her face eased into a smile. With an impatient windmilling of her hand, she drew us to her. I walked into the pew behind my boys, all the better to get by with just a nod at her for a greeting.

The air was thick with the smell of incense and body heat. I felt a trickle of sweat run down between my breasts. At least, the window just above me was propped open. The organ wheezed to life and the choir, eight pink-faced middle-aged members of the congregation, lifted their voices in competent, if inelegant song. The pastor, Tom, had his unsmiling face fixed on all assembled. It was a relief when he asked us to be seated. Once he started to speak, my mind wandered.

I vowed there with my head down in mock prayer that as of that day I would read more and watch less TV, spend less time on the couch, spend less time feeling sorry for myself. No more would I turn on the tube to check the weather only to allow myself to get sucked into something utterly idiotic, then watch it under the guise of finding some feminist slant on it, while simultaneously dreaming of starting a blog, a tongue-in-cheek view of pop culture filtered through the lens of a frustrated suburban housewife. I would no longer watch things like that even to plan how my imaginary blog could be tailored to the always-bored, internet-surfing, overly-protective parenting crowd. Of course, reading too much from the computer screen did hurt my eyes. We needed a printer, if I was going to get serious about that. That would help me be the reader I wanted to be, the kind that kept up on current events. Maybe we should subscribe to a newspaper again. There was always the *Times*. I used to read it, when David was a baby. I'd start my day with it. I don't remember what'd happened there. I must've let the subscription lapse. I guess motherhood and keeping up with the paper at the same time were too much for me. At the time, it'd probably had felt like a relief. One less thing to worry about. I'm sure I told myself I could just go online to get the news. Daryl watched the local news before he left for work to get the weather. Sometimes he left the TV on. I'd hear a rumble coming from downstairs or a blaring down the hall from the little used set in the upstairs living room. I wanted to call him and tell him to come back and turn it off so many times. That was what Mother did to me when I was a girl. If I'd left the TV on, she'd phone me wherever I was and summon me home. "Your father and I are not your servants, dear. I think you are capable of turning it off yourself. You've certainly mastered the art of turning it on." So much of my trouble with David came partly, I'm ashamed to think, from my inability to emulate the disapproving chill of her voice. My blog could've been about the constant search for the middle ground between my idea of the ideal parenting strategy and memories of

how Mother did it. There must've been a huge reader-
ship for that -- all those women who, like me, get caught
in the swirl of our thoughts about a different life only to
find ourselves in the same place where we'd started once
the storm had passed.

"You seemed to really be deep in thought during the
service," Gail said to me in the parking lot after it'd ended.

"I guess the ritual of it makes me contemplative," I
said.

"That's the point. Not like those two." Her head
turned for a quick look at Daryl and David shuffling behind us. "Whispering and chatting away."

"Were they?"

"The whole time," she cried, sounding indignant.
"I don't mind a little chatter when Pastor Tom speaks
from off the cuff but the scriptures should be treated as
sacred."

Come on, Gail. I barely paid them any attention
when they spoke to me aloud, you can't expect me to
tune into their whispering.

"I wouldn't even know what to talk about during a
scripture reading," I said.

"Exactly. See, you get it. You're like me, you enjoy coming to the service for the right reason: the rev-
erential quiet. You should make it more of a habit," she
said reaching out and squeezing my hand the way a child
does when it wants to keep hold of an adult. "Why don't
you try to come once a month? Then, we could eat at my
house after."

"Why doesn't George come with you?"

"He does, sometimes. But since you all were coming, he stayed behind to make us a lunch. It should be

ready when we get there. So how about you becoming a monthly visitor here? Leave them at home. Just us *Anne of Green Gables* readers."

I pulled my hand from her grip and smiled my most worried, least committed smile. We followed her to her house, even though we knew the way. It made her feel good to lead us. She so often felt lost, I guess. Her car was small and grey and clung to the road desperately on a couple of sharp bends. Once we hit the main drag of her town, the traffic began to thrust itself at us from all directions. Many of the drivers were older -- their driving halting and uncertain.

"Turn in here," Daryl said as we approached a strip mall of pizzerias, nail salons and a huge Target. It'd once been a Super K-Mart. The outline of a giant, dirty "K" was still visible just to the left of the "T" in Target on the front of the building.

"Why?" I asked.

"I've got to get something."

"Daryl, we're on your way to your mother's house. What in the world could we possibly need at this place?"

"He's getting me a water gun," David said.

"A what?" I asked.

"I told him," Daryl said, "that I'd get him a water gun on our way to Mom's, if he didn't complain so much about going to church with everyone."

"Why now? Why don't you wait until we get…forget it," I said and pulled to a sudden stop in the fire lane and unlocked the doors. "Fine. Go then. Be fast about it. David are you going too?"

"No. Dad knows which one I want."

"Move quickly, Daryl. Your mother and George are expecting us."

"Relax, Gloria," he said. "It's just a water gun."

"You know the one, right Dad? The one we saw at the Target near our house."

Daryl nodded into the rearview mirror. He leapt from the car and raced through the doors dodging an obese woman loaded down with shopping bags and scrolling away at her phone.

"When did Dad take you shopping?"

"Once when you were napping, after I got home from school. He came home from work early."

"Oh yeah?"

"He came home and said you needed to rest from your busy day. We came home from Target with frozen pizzas. Dad burned one in the oven. Remember?"

"Mmmm…."

"The smoke detector went off. The other one was good. The one I made. I put the extra cheese on it. Remember that?"

"I do," I said, trying to think of when that might've been "That was a good pizza."

"Were you really tired?" Daryl's attorney would ask, years later, of such periods of lethargy. "Or could there have been something more, Mrs. Hytner? An emotional component, perhaps?"

"Objection," my attorney countered, "argumentative. She's answered enough questions on this topic. Can we move on to something new, Your Honor?"

Panting, Daryl returned minutes later with a white and red bag stashed under his arm. Part of the box poked out. *Sniper Soaker VII* read the label. As I pulled out, I watched David take possession of it with a look of joyful awe. Slowly, he unsheathed it. Measuring at least a foot and a half long and made of molded plastic with a large clear receptacle that was, presumably, for loading the weapon, it looked totally ridiculous. As we rode the short distance out through the back of the shopping plaza onto a rabbit warren of local roads, David ripped open the box and gnawed through the plastic ties that secured it to the cardboard. Turning onto Gail's street, I caught a glimpse of him sitting with the gun across his lap, like I was driving him to a hit. When we reached our destination, he attempted to jump out with it in his hands.

"David," I said, "leave the gun, grab the cupcakes."

"Can't I see if it works?"

"At home."

"What if it doesn't and we have to take it back?" he asked.

"At home," I repeated.

"Aw, Mom."

"Leave it, champ," Daryl said. "We'll take it out tonight. Hand me the cupcakes."

Daryl went first up the steep stairs that led from Gail's driveway to her front door. We hadn't made it very far, when from inside the house came the harsh sound of a raised voice -- Gail's. Her full-throated admonishments were punctuated by Fluffy, who barked and yelped and snapped at the air. We began to climb more slowly, as though if we were quiet ourselves, a collective calm might spread from us up towards the altercation. David took my hand. Squeezed. I squeezed back.

"When my family comes over! How many times do we have to talk about this?" she asked. Fluffy added sharp barks of disapproval.

George's reply was muffled. His slurred voice, a smear on the air. Loose syllables dropped unstrung from his mouth. A defense, it seemed, aware of its futility.

"It's barely afternoon, George! Look at the fucking clock!"

I'd never before thought of Gail as someone who would use the 'f' word. It didn't spill comfortably from her mouth. Those crucial two final letters tripped in a clumsy leap over her lips and likely gritted teeth. Daryl froze ahead of us. David took a firmer grip of my hand. His palm had begun to sweat. He turned back towards the driveway. Our car and escape must've seemed so very far away. Our leader pressed on, even more slowly. Fluffy's yapping had gotten worse. Rated R barking.

David didn't exactly try to hold me back. But there was the sensation that I was pulling him along, his body hardening into an anchor. I wished Daryl had called out ahead, fired a warning shot. The guests had arrived, barbed comments and recriminations could be put down for the moment.

"I feel," George started, his voice rising, but with words stuck to the roof of his mouth, "I'm fine. You'll see when we…when they get here."

"Will I? Will I?" Gail asked, her voice loud, cutting through the air.

David let go of my hand to cover his ears.

"How? They'll be here any minute," she said, her voice growing ever closer now even though we had stopped ascending.

Gail's shoes slapped across the floor, the growing nearness of their report telling of her approach. Daryl quickened his steps upward. David tugged at my sleeve, eyes wide and welling as they normally did before tears. Happily, he was unused to that kind of talk. Daryl and I were good at keeping our seething feelings at a slow, bitter simmer. Even later that summer, when our marriage was in its most acute state of decay, after Daryl had taken to sleeping on the couch downstairs, we never raised our voices at each other. The previous Friday's dinner with Victoria stood as a good example of a typical round of one of our bouts in that we said nothing to each other and even tried not to breathe too heavily in the other's direction. David had probably been too thankful to notice.

Our drifting was mostly icy, full of sharp glances, cloaked insults, and spidery silences that I could feel crawling inside of me. It was all often exchanged, as it had been that very morning, in the bedroom mirror so that we might both look and not look each other in the eyes.

Years later, during one of the interminable dinners I would have with my then college dropout of a son, David tried to explain that I was the source of the coldness that pushed him into the heat and excitement of drugs and drinking. He wanted a weeping *mea culpa,* I think. He'd felt the coldness, he said, and had internalized it. We'd projected it onto him and he'd lived most of his life since trying to warm up. I so wanted to point out to him at the time that he had just, very recently, failed Psych 101, making his assessment a little questionable but only nodded and sipped my wine.

None of the penchant for thrusting himself into excitement was apparent on his face on that expedition up the stairs at his Grandma's. He tugged at my sleeve and moved his head slowly from side to side.

"Daryl," I whispered as he reached for the door. "Do you want to take a minute with her?"

"What for?" he asked, backing down a couple of steps.

"I don't know. To talk to her? Calm her down a little?" I asked.

"What will I say when she asks about you guys?"

"We went to the car to get something. David has something to show her."

"Like what?"

"His water gun," I said. "Does it matter?"

David and I retreated down the stairs. It was a relief to hear the door creak and her invite Daryl inside. David leapt down the last few stairs ahead of me, two at a time.

"Can I really show Grandma Gail my gun?" he asked.

"We're going to have to show her something."

And should she've required a demonstration of the weapon's soaking power, I would've nominated my man even more enthusiastically then she would've hers.

20. The First Time I Almost Left Him

Despite not even being a full year old, David's retainer case was already tattered and on the verge of falling apart. The screws of its plastic hinges had rusted, bleeding a copper thread along the back of the bathroom sink. It smelled of a rotten onion coated in peanut butter. I dropped it, gagging.

"God, David," I screeched louder than necessary, as he was only a few feet away across the hall in his room. "Have you been cleaning this thing the way they showed you?"

He mumbled the aural version of a shrug.

"Could you come here please? David!" I called and directed him into the bathroom. "Does that smell like it might, just might, need to be cleaned? Smell it! What's that putrid odor telling you?"

"It's never smelled…like…good or… nice," he said taking a whiff. "It never smelled like something I would want to smell."

"Don't you rinse it out when you take it out of your mouth in the morning? Rinse it out with mouth wash like Dr. Burns showed you?"

"Not every morning."

"How often?"

"The mouthwash is way in the back under the sink. It's hard to get to. Sometimes, I, like, don't feel like reaching that far in the morning."

"David, are you being serious with me?"

"I'm tired in the morning."

"Maybe you should be going to sleep sooner, then. Spend less time reading beforehand."

"Mom," he whined.

"Leave the mouthwash on top of the toilet, then."

"Ew, Mom, that's kind of gross."

"No," I said and pointed to the case after forcing into his hand, "what you have there's gross."

"Victoria's getting one too."

Her name had a habit of coming up more and more, suggesting how often she was in his thoughts. She'd been to dinner twice by then and they studied together at least a couple of nights a week. Her father had taken them to the movies but hadn't gone in with them. I'd made the mistake of referring to that as a date, which earned me a reprimand and a small speech about how David found such a label cheap and not up to the standards he and Victoria were setting. I further enraged him by smiling during his lecture on the topic. My son the romantic, an idea that better allowed me to accept that Vicky was now a part of our lives. And I had her to thank for keeping him away from Jonny and Denny and Kenny. Once she came around, they just seemed to disappear.

I never believed it until I was older but life really does happen that way. Raising kids leaves one with such an elliptical memory that it can't always be relied on. One minute, they're crossing wooden swords with their father and saving their mothers from cages, the next, they're telling you how their feelings for a young woman cannot be captured by any commonly accepted labels.

By then we were running late for his appointment, so I had to hustle him down the hall and into the car. Saturday morning appointments were hard to get with Dr. Burns, if we were late, we ran the risk of getting on the wrong side of his elderly and officious receptionists, who controlled the good doctor's calendar. I couldn't be sure that they'd punish us for being late but they held too much power over his schedule to risk it. I drove reck-lessly enough to cause my son concern. He gripped his retainer case tightly as I took a turn too fast. David didn't complain outwardly on the ride but shot me looks in-stead that ranged from wounded to terrified.

The waiting room was full of the typical collection of mothers and their sullen dental disasters. I sent David ahead to check us in, urging him to hurry as we were right on time. A raven-haired girl with greasy splotches of acne on her face sat in the corner trying to pull off the impossible feat of remaining unnoticed while sport-ing an elaborate crown of head gear. Next to her and her mother, who was engrossed with her phone, were the only free seats. I took one and saved the other for David, who after announcing in a barely audible, almost sigh-like manner that he'd signed in, grabbed a magazine and read while leaning against the wall.

Sure, the girl looked embarrassed, but I spared a thought for the poor mother. Wearing that kind of con-traption's hard on the wearer but at least the glances of passing strangers are full of pity. When eyes are turned onto the parents, the look hardens into something almost accusatory. It comes from an underlying suspicion of anyone responsible for part of a genetic combination that would produce such a freak. Once the girl was called, she slid from her seat slowly, her mother having to help her on her way and hissing her a reminder not to slouch. The girl gave me a quick glance, her eyes dead like those of the condemned. I knew the feeling. I knew the dread. I'd once been in a much different waiting room, waiting for something just as inevitable but far worse than hav-ing some headgear tightened.

I will always remember the tile pattern of that waiting

room, four white squares surrounded by blue diamonds, spreading out in all directions, disappearing down long hallways and under doors. After checking in, I'd kept my head down, a hand on my stomach, waiting as the pain subsided. I was infuriated that they were making me wait. Something's wrong with my baby, something's wrong with my baby, I wanted to shout. It was the first time I thought of it as my baby.

Daryl wasn't much help. He kept trying to put his arm around me when we sat down. I kept leaning the other way. I wanted to tell him to go home, that I'd be alright. I regretted calling him in the first place.

"If it's, like, just gas like you said," he whispered, "you can, you know…right here. Maybe it's just the baby kicking or something."

I lived a good deal, too much, of my adult life in the shadow of that "or something." I hadn't really wanted him to come, but when the pain had started that morning it was so intense that I knew something was really wrong. I knew it from the first series of cramping spasms. They buckled my knees. I spent a lot of time and energy that day lying in bed trying to talk myself out of calling him. Maria was not around. Like any self-respecting city dweller in her 20's, she was surely quietly horrified at the sight of the still rather newly pregnant and yet somehow already expanding me, for I held the appearance of serious adulthood and no one moves to the city to be forced to bear witness to that.

When I'd first finally dialed Daryl's number, I wanted to just scream at him. It was his fault, after all. His phone rang. He hadn't worn a condom, every time. I should've been more insistent. The phone rang some more. We'd grown up listening to C. Everett Koop telling everyone to slap one on. I panted, quick breaths, praying he wouldn't pick up. Then there was a click and a pause. He cleared his throat.

"Uh? Hello?"

"There's something wrong with me!" was all I could get out, before another wave of pain contracted the muscles just below my abdomen.

"Is this Gloria? Who's this?"

I swallowed gulping down the precious moment of decision. The silence that buzzed across the line echoed through my mind. I was shaking.

"What's up? Are you um, like…did you take care of that…" he said, his voice trailing off.

HANG UP! HANG UP! HANG UP! a voice inside of me screamed. I swallowed again even though my mouth had gone dry. A wave of pain passed over me. I stifled a moan.

"I'm in a lot of pain. Don't know what it is, but I need to see someone. I need…"

"Oh," he said. Now, it was his turn to swallow and try to burrow his head in the silence crackling over the phone line.

"I need to go to a hospital. Any hospital."

"I'll come," he said, practically shouting. "I'll help."

I paused, holding the pain inside, the phone pressed to my chest. My heartbeat in his ear. I just so needed someone in that moment. The pain and fear had made me weak. Daryl rushed right over in cab. He helped me down the stairs and into it, shouting at the driver to take us to the nearest hospital. Giving myself over to him became easy. It even felt right and I thought I was getting closer to suddenly having that feeling for him, closer to truly requiting his declaration of love that seemed to have been made such a long time before.

Once the cab broke free of the traffic, I slid away from him to take on another series of cramps. It was like every period I'd ever had was happening at once. The cramps stopped for a while on the ride. My chest heaved as I couldn't get enough air into my lungs during that respite from the pain. Luckily, Daryl was burning off his nervous energy shouting instructions to the cab driver, who undoubtedly had a better grasp of the city streets, especially in that part of town.

When they finally called for David, I inspected the magazines on the rack hoping to find one that would help me pull myself from the unhappy moments my mind always was too keen to relive. None of them did the trick, though. Daryl's voice kept pulling me back.

"I mean you can fart. Just go ahead, if it'll make you feel better," he'd kept insisting, leaning towards me as if an ER waiting room was a place for secrets.

"Thank you, Daryl, but I feel better now."

When two nurses with a beat-up gurney finally came to take me, I found I could not get up from my seat. Daryl had to help me. His huge hand steadied me, pressing against my back. He smiled once they had me in place and put his hand against my sweaty forehead. I knew he'd be there to take me home, no matter the outcome. Waiting for someone's what a guy like that does.

I lost the baby within hours of our parting that day. I thought I'd made my decision about terminating the pregnancy but, as was my wont in those days, really just waited until it was made for me. For days after, I was unable to get out of bed. I couldn't eat, move or cry the way I would've wanted to. I just slept and stared at the ceiling, disbelieving what'd happened. Daryl was there so often when I awoke that I thought he must've been staying in our apartment.

Maria was around but busy with school so it had to be Daryl that helped hold me together. In the days, and I guess if I'm being honest, the years that followed, it could've been anyone. An anyone was all I was looking for and was all I really got. He was just there, just letting me know there was one person in the world who knew enough not to try and put into words the loss I'd suffered. We'd suffered. I did feel for him then and in my numbness sometimes mistook it for love or what I thought love was in my twenties.

You can't really tell someone not to show up to make sure you're okay, especially when you're so obviously depressed. You can't hold it against someone for caring about you. You can only wish it was someone else and that circumstances hadn't conspired to ruin your plans. Even on the rare occasions when I could vocalize my desire for solitude in the days immediately following the miscarriage, he reacted with such nauseating compassion that he made the desire seem selfish.

He'd lost a child too. I think that's the reason Maria receded from our life and let him do so much. At the time, she'd understood that better than I did. She went on and on about what a good guy he was, how lucky I was to meet a 'real' man, when so many males in the city were fakes or boys growing old who wouldn't have stuck around, who would've found it all too difficult to deal with. She even claimed that my life was taking the shape she wished hers would someday. I'd found a partner and purpose, was how she put it.

If I really did want to be alone, I could've told Daryl to go away. Pleaded with him to never come back. That we'd made a mistake in the first place and were only making it worse by brooding over what really was an out for us, furnished by my disagreeable womb. And I think I even tried to start a conversation like that, once or twice. I tried looking into those big, worrying, hazel eyes of his, feeling those work-strong hands, flecked with copper-colored freckles holding mine, protecting me, all of it sickening and cliché, telling myself I didn't need him but never managing to vocalize those thoughts.

Then before I knew it, Daryl and I were moving in together. It happened so fast and so long ago that it's become hard to see it as a series of discrete events rather than one ongoing catastrophe. One minute, I felt a severe cramp, so powerful it knocked me to my knees; the next he was there with me in the waiting room, holding my hand; then the next we're angling my tall oak dresser through the door of his basement apartment. It had all proved to be the opposite of being swept off my feet. I hadn't even been standing up for most of it.

Once they'd finished practicing their pricey version of sadism on my son, I was called to the back. Dr. Burns's office was a small room just behind the receptionist's desk. On its walls were pennants and pictures related to his alma mater, Syracuse. Above his head hanging on the wall was a picture of something called the Carrier Dome. It looked like a UFO made of trash bags. I took the seat next to my son. David moved his jaw from side to side, lightly touching his cheeks as he did so. Dr. Burns clicked a pen.

"Mrs. Hytner, how are you?" he asked, as though he couldn't be less interested in the answer.

"Good. And how's everything here?" I asked and bowed my head.

"I am pleased to report that David here has obviously been quite diligent about wearing his retainer."

I snuck a peek at David smiling at that.

"His jaw is settling into the proper position. His overbite will soon be fixed, completely."

"How much longer will I have to wear this?" David asked.

"I foresee you being done with this," Burns said, tapping the retainer's case which sat atop his desk, "in, say, another 8-12 weeks. From there we will fit you for a smaller device to make sure everything will stay as we want it and you don't backslide. That'll be for about another 4-6 months, I'd say."

"I just don't like having plastic and wires and shit in my mouth any more," David said. "I'm over it."

"David," I said sharply, resisting the urge to cuff him. The slap would've been as much for saying he was 'over' something as for cursing.

"You just keep doing as we've agreed, David. It'll be over soon enough."

"Soon enough," David said, slumping in his chair.

"Keep wearing it every night. It'll be over like that," Dr. Burns said and snapped his fingers.

"I hate it. I hate wearing this shit!" David cried and tipped his chair back then violently forward.

"Enough of the mouth, young man," I said, and my eyes may have asked Burns to look away so I could follow that up with a backhand. He didn't oblige.

"I'll tell you a secret, Dave. No one likes wearing any of this stuff. But, the ones like you, who triumph over their aversion to it, have to wear them for shorter stretches of time. You know what I mean by getting past an aversion?"

"Not mind it so much," David said.

See. David. Gifted.

"Good. This is a crucial time," Dr. Burns said. "We need to make sure your jaw gets set into the proper position because if it doesn't, it'll will be much harder to get it to do so from here on out. You understand?"

"Mmm…hmm," David muttered.

"You still reading those books?" Dr. Burns asked.

"He is," I said.

"We talk about them a bit. I told him that character, the hero. Greatlor was his name?" the doctor asked.

"Greylor," David said.

"Greylor, yes. I was telling Dave that Greylor probably has a stern jaw and straight, healthy teeth."

"That's probably true," I said just to annoy David.

"If there's nothing else, if you don't have any questions for me…" Burns shot up from his chair and extended his hand across the desk to each of us.

On our way out, the slender receptionist with a bob of white hair and a visible hearing aid stopped us at her desk. She smiled meekly, her teeth glowing blue from the reflection of the computer screen. I feared we'd been marked late and had an excuse and apology all prepared.

"A minute, Mrs. Hytner," she said. "There's something here…" she sucked her teeth and clicked the spacebar. "Oh, yes. Your insurance is under your husband's name, Daryl. Is that correct?"

"Yes. It's through his company."

"Yes. I see that. It looks like they have switched insurance carriers…"

"I have the new card," I said, digging into my purse.

"No. We have that number here. The issue seems to be that orthodonture is no longer covered."

"Oh…I…" I readjusted the strap of my purse, nearly smacking David with it. "I'll have to ask him about that."

"You owe the full amount due for today and the last two appointments now as well, actually."

"I'll have to talk to my husband." I only ever used that word when the thought of it might make me sick.

"We can send a bill. You're still at 114 Florence St. in Roslyndale?"

"We are," I said after a brief pause.

"So this way if you talk to your husband and get the insurance worked out, you can just tear the bill up."

Other than hearing my son use the word shit twice inside of five minutes and learning that we might owe upwards of $2,500, I'd enjoyed the afternoon reminiscing about my miscarriage. I felt I needed to hold the steering wheel extra tight to keep from swerving into oncoming traffic. I wanted to yell at David on the ride home but he had such a bored look on his face that I doubted he'd put up enough of a fight to make it worth my while. I stomped down on the brakes at the first opportunity which did send him flying forward then recoiling back once the seat belt caught him. He murmured an "ow," which felt good but the feeling was fleeting.

"Do you think Greylor has nice teeth?" he asked as we waited at the light, adjusting the seatbelt where it had grabbed him.

"I haven't given his teeth much thought, to tell you the truth," I snapped.

"They're never mentioned. Not once in any of the books," he said, taking no heed of the impatience in my voice. "And I think I would know. I've read them enough."

"I think if anyone outside of Mr. Ungrin would

know, it would be you. What do you think his teeth look like?"

"I don't know. I mean, I don't think they look that nice. The books never mentions, you know, like, dentists or toothbrushes."

"None of that shit, huh?" I said, turning to smile at him.

I know, Mother, I know. What will it say about how he was raised? How will it speak for his breeding? Rest easy, for in a few years, I'll walk in on him doing lines of cocaine from the top of the coffee table in my tiny living room sitting next to some naked boy, who couldn't have been more than sixteen, placing that day's transgression well amongst the ones I'd prefer to remember with a smile.

"Sorry about that," he said, smiling back.

"Let me ask you. Since when did you start saying 'like' so much?"

He shrugged.

"It makes you sound like…kind of an airhead," I said.

"You and Dad say it."

"*I* do not."

"Fine. Dad says it, though."

"Exactly," I said. "And why didn't you tell Dr. Burns what you thought of Greylor's teeth? You shouldn't let him go around thinking he knows about something that he doesn't. Doctors are know-it-alls practically by blood. It's truly intelligent people like you who need to keep them in line."

"He tries so hard to, like…sorry…to relate to me. I didn't want to ruin it for him."

When we pulled into the driveway, the sight of Daryl drinking beer in the garage as he sanded a block of wood clicked with something inside of me. I felt my pulse race, my forehead get hot. He waved at us, mouth agape as though it was the only orifice through which he could get oxygen into his body. I told David to go inside. Once he shut the door, I waited a few minutes, allowing Daryl to finish sanding down a hexagonally shaped piece of wood. He blew dust from it once, then twice and then held it up for closer inspection.

"Do the corners look right to you?" he asked. "Do you think they'll, like, fit under his arms?"

"Put the wood down, Daryl," I said.

"What's up, hon? Did the appointment go alright?"

"It didn't."

"He not wearing his uh…" he asked and stuck his teeth out over his bottom lip. "I told him to, like, be sure to wear that thing. Just last week I said to him, I said…"

"David's not the problem."

"Dr. Burns?" he asked.

"No. Not him either."

"What is it, then? What's wrong?"

"Daryl, have they said anything to you about your insurance changing at work or were you waiting to tell me about that as well?"

"You know, they like said something about, like, mailing something or…something."

"Nothing about why they sent a new card? Is that all you can recall? Something and something? Something or something? That's all?"

"Yeah, hon. Why?"

"They informed me at the doctor's office that since your insurance has changed, David's visits are no longer covered," I said, allowing my voice to get louder.

"How much is it?"

"Is this true about the insurance?"

"I guess, if that's, like, what they said. I remember this, uh, meeting when we talked about it but I didn't think it was, like, settled."

"Who's we in this case?"

"It was, like, back in the summer. I…"

"*Like*, *like*, who is we? Who were you talking with? What meeting are you referring to?"

"Tiny and Roger and a bunch of us. They, like, you know, administer the plan."

"Who?"

"Tiny and Roger."

"Can you ask them about the health plan, like, fucking soon?"

"Yeah, yeah, hon, first thing, first thing Monday morning. I'll even go in early."

As I turned away from him, I was filled by an almost overwhelming urge to get in the car and drive away somewhere. Anywhere. Just start again. Leave my clueless husband shaking in the garage, his face ruddy and sweaty, his arms coated with sawdust. I wasn't going to say anything. Just get in the car and go. I might've, purely as an act of penance, driven to Mother's to stay with her.

I wonder if he sensed any of the coming storm in that moment in the garage all those years ago. Sometimes, I hate to say it but, I look back in amazement that I ever had to talk to him, let alone negotiate any important parts of my life with him as my co-pilot. He was probably a lot smarter and more capable than I ever gave him credit for being.

As my eyes probed the car for the possibilities of

escape, he came up behind me. He laid his hand where my neck and back met and gave me a little massage that did feel quite good. He whispered a sorry and promised to work all the hours they could offer him. Things would be picking up soon he predicted, the spring was always slow. I turned around and hugged him. It was among the falsest of my many false shows of affection. In those days, I was still dependent on him for so many things. As we went inside and I began to get dinner going, thoughts of leaving faded.

Later that night, the notion even scared me a little. We sat around, the three of us, and watched a movie together. And, it really did seem that for a short while that the mini-crisis brought us together even if only for the night, just for duration of a Robin Williams movie.

21. **Experience With Firearms Not Required**

It took a while after the women's think tank summarily rejected me from what I had fantasized as my dream job -- *filing, ordering office supplies* -- and which I was certain would be my path to intellectual redemption, *--triaging phone calls, occasionally filling in to take the minutes at weekly staff meetings* -- before I found myself back at the desk in the basement, searching for another position that might nourish my soul and mind as much -- *other duties as needed.* I lowered my sights and clicked on any position that promised insurance benefits. Daryl had by then confirmed that the meeting back in the summer that had been, like, too long ago for him to remember clearly or some such bullshit, *was* in regards to the changes to his work administered plan. 'Changes' being a euphemism for loss of coverage pretty much across the board. He tried picking up extra shifts but Custom Cabinet Makers' Warehouse was clearly in full cutback mode at that point. For the first time in my life, I began to fear for my family's fiscal safety. We'd always lived paycheck to paycheck but in light of our changing insurance circumstances -- a euphemism of my own -- I understood fully for the first time how precarious our situation was.

We both took it out on David some during that time, I'm sorry to say. We each found, with degrees of varying subtlety, ways to remind him to wear his retainer. I wondered if he should wear it all the time every day so that he might be done with it more quickly. He balked at that. I reminded him that he'd said Victoria was getting one, which seemed to genuinely wound him. I think it was around that time that their little, whatever it was, had ebbed a bit.

As soon as I sat down that morning and began my search, I found a job bagging groceries. GOOD BENEFITS, it read. NO EXPERIENCE NECESSARY. It just got better and better. I took a moment to figuratively swallow, digest and then evacuate my pride through my bowels before scrolling to the bottom of the screen to find where to send a resume. There I learned that GOOD BENEFITS meant FULL WEEKENDS OFF, HOURLY WAGE, HEALTH CARE EXTRA. It seemed cruel to force someone to consider bagging groceries and then remind them at the end of the description that the job was barely fit for a high schooler. I was more than willing, hell happy, to debase myself a little if it offered insurance and got me out of the house during the day. I would've sung the verse of paper or plastic all year long, if they'd offered what we needed. I'd bagged groceries on my own once or twice and fancied myself quite adept.

Since I'd managed to consider becoming a grocery bagger without feeling a degree of self-loathing intense enough to make my hands shake and render the mouse useless, I slid that bad girl over and clicked on LUNCHROOM ATTENDANT. They wanted someone clean and polite to shovel out strained peas and diabetic mashed potatoes at the local special needs school. EXP W/MENTALLY CHALLENGED CHILDREN PREF. I wondered if I could use Sarah in the interview. Mention our talks. Fabricate some interest in her basketball team.

The Panek School required only a resume, no cover letter, so I sent mine along. They probably didn't have a lot of JD dropouts working the feed line. Though for all I knew, the place could've been crawling with people who had failed in gaining admittance to the law. A whole lunchroom staff comprised of those who been forced to reconcile themselves that the world would somehow keep on turning with one less lawyer in it.

I dreamed of striking up friendships with the highest functioning members of the student body. I'd take their "pleases" and "thank you's" with the warmest smile I could muster. My hairnet tilted at a jaunty angel, my hands sweaty beneath the rubber gloves. It might feel like real work. A labor, if not of love, then of appreciation at having escaped from the house.

Next, I found a job as a receptionist in a plastic surgeon's office. FILING EXP PREF. Easy to fake. TELEPHONE EXP REQ. Again, something I could say without hesitation that I had some experience with. They too wanted just a resume so I hadn't even the opportunity to ruin my chances with a cover letter. I fired another one off.

I wondered if the job might offer me the chance to become a kind of whispering counsel to the women there. Make them aware that they were paying for something they've only been made to think they need. Convince them of the pernicious role such doctors play in the worldwide patriarchy. Of course, I wouldn't get away with anything like that for very long. But maybe striking a blow like that for the sisterhood would've made it rewarding. I might've even been more effective for the cause there than working as a desk jockey at some WOMYN-friendly NGO.

I'd concentrate on the young girls that came in. I'd read an article around that time about the shocking number of women in their teens and early twenties getting work done. Apparently, in the eyes of the male-centered world, you're never too young to feel inadequate. Even if I worked just one day there, I would've had the chance to convince some young woman to stop playing their game, to reject the necessity to look a certain way, to no longer worship at the temple of the body but to instead seek happiness on her own terms.

It would've meant working for and, even if only for a single day, taking orders from someone who, at bottom, was surely the worst kind of chauvinist. Let's face it, no one gets rich in that business from lifting male jowls or giving width and length to puny penises. The doctor might very well have been a decent man, who flew to distant places to help the less fortunate but somewhere in his soul lurked the will of the objectifier. Hungry eyes that leered. A tongue of honey, practiced at holding forth on the ineffable yet readily attainable nature of beauty. No matter how learned and soulful and interesting the doctor was, I'd surely be working for a boob-man. I could barely stomach it, even then, even in my desperation. I regretted having sent my resume. If invited for an interview, I'd planned to decline and then, if it was Dr. Titties on the phone, give him a piece of my mind.

Most of the other jobs I found that day required experience of the kind I could not fake. EXP W/LOTUS NOTES. EXP W/AT RISK POPULATIONS. EXP W/ FIREARMS. EXP OPERATING 60-TON CRANE.

Once I was done, I went upstairs and made myself some tea and toast. The day's hunt had renewed my sense of purpose enough that I actually got some reading done, rather than switch on the TV. Then, David came in the front door, whimpering. I sighed when he sniffled. His breath caught as it always did, when he was trying not to bawl. I remained where I was, book still in front of me, allowing him the time he needed to collect himself.

When I finally rose to the day's task of being a mom,

he was on the living room couch, his head in his hands. Stepping closer, I called his name, trying to soften my voice so that it didn't sound like I was annoyed. He didn't look up. I went to rub the back of his drooping head. He flinched and raised his hand to shoo mine away. I sat down next to him. His face was flushed to a deep red. His cheeks moist with tears.

"What is it, honey?" I asked, almost whispering. "You can tell me."

Though I wish you wouldn't. Suck it up, kid. For once in your life suck it the fuck up.

"Nothing," he blubbered, wiping the back of his arm across his eyes.

When Victoria came along, we had a nice break from moments like those. And now it appeared that I was wrong to ever hope they were gone for good, just a part of some phase. The world was and would forever be full of stupid, malicious little bullies. A sensitive soul like David was always going to be at risk.

"It's okay. Whatever it is," I said. "We can talk about it."

Though, if you want to be quiet and just suck it up that would be fine, too.

"I don't want to," he said.

He sat back, staring straight ahead, his eyes blank. His eyelids red and raw, fresh bitten by tears. I put my hand on his knee and slid over to give him room.

"Kenny got on the bus with us today," he began.

"He did," I sighed, preparing myself for whatever horrible course this was about to take, to have my dwindling faith in humanity further eroded. "What was he doing on your bus?"

"He got on with us. Like he was waiting for us...

for me."

"Should've been on the high school bus," I said.

"I know. I know that," he whined, the tone of which diluted any motherly sympathy that I was at least trying to work up.

"Sorry," I said and lifted my hand.

He trembled. He was still a child. For a moment, I regretted every unkind thought I'd ever had about him, including the chafing I'd just mentally experienced at seeing him in this state.

"I can't…" he whispered, trying to control himself.

"Shhh…it's okay," I cooed just as I had when he suffered diaper rash as a baby. "It'll be better…it'll get better."

His body went stiff. The shaking ceased. The sob-soaked cheeks and running nose were wiped on each shoulder. Getting up from the couch, he kept his back to me as he walked towards the hall. I thought he was headed for his room and was trying to decide on whether or not to follow him.

"He was already there when I sat down," he said, pausing in the middle of the hall, his back still to me. "He'd never been on our bus before. The older kids are supposed to get out later but he must've cut. He was sitting in the back. He waved at me like I should sit with him. I didn't want to, but he acted like he was going to be nice to me. You know? Like he seemed different. He smiled at me. When I got back there, he patted at the seat. Denny and Jonny were right behind me and Kenny was acting like we were all friends. The Florence Street boys he said we were and I was so hap…" he paused to collect himself, his voice wavering. "I was so happy just to feel included. I thought we *were* all friends and I had just been, you know, overly sensitive like Dad says."

David turned, came back down the hall and then began to pace it. He kept his head down as though following some invisible line. I wanted to ask why he always fell for Kenny's friendship act. But I wanted him to keep talking and on an even keel, so I settled back into the couch.

"He started making these goofy faces and talking in these goofy voices to us. He was making fun of the bus driver, who has a little bit of a stutter and I didn't want to laugh, but I thought it was nice for someone else to be picked on for once, you know? To be on that side of it. He asked what I'd been doing, so I told him about Victoria," he began to get choked up but kept pressing on. "I told him she'd been my girlfriend and we'd broken up and I was trying to get over it. He laughed at me, laughed his mean laugh. He said that couldn't be because I was…a…faggot." By then he was shuddering and had to work to get the words out. "He…got…the…whole bus…to chant…Davey…is…a…faggot. All of them… the whole bus."

I didn't know which to console him for more: Victoria or Kenny. And like any typical dumb, dull-witted mother, I found I hated the girlfriend more. Wanted to do harm to her. She was the reason for this latest episode, not Kenny, who after all was just being as openly cruel and homophobic as teenage boys are allowed to be. I never would've seen it at the time, but the day was coming when David wouldn't get so worked up being at labeled like that and would, in fact, glory in it. He doesn't at all mind the world knowing that he can have the same sort of relationships with men and he does with women. The only labels that stick to my adult son are the ones he uses. I wish I knew how to tell him how proud that makes me, like we must've done something right in raising him, even if I can't pinpoint what exactly that was.

"The bus driver made them stop but…" he began to wail, crying as hard as I had ever seen him. I tried to take him in my arms but he ran down the hall to his room.

I followed arriving just in time to see him fling himself down on the bed and claw at the sheets. I stood in the doorway, watching but unable to bring myself to go to him. I just wanted scenes like that to stop, to no longer be in the position of having my callousness and emotional inadequacy repeatedly revealed.

"I could tell you they're just words but…" I said, "Do you want me to go down to his house? Call the school? The bus company? Get them to…"

"No, Mom," he said, sitting up.

"I will, though. Kenny's nothing but a bully and should be punished. What's that bus driver's name? He's the first who should answer for…"

"Mom. I don't want you to do anything." He wiped his face which was a red, wet mess. Snot had crusted under his nose. His eyes were totally bloodshot. "Don't do a thing. It'll only make it worse for me."

"David, I…"

"True courage, the kind that lays in the heart of every man, means nothing more than finding strength where you thought you had none," he said, pulling himself together. "It means letting your enemies see your weakness as a reflection of the weaknesses in them. Courage means facing the impossible and taming it like a dog."

"Greylor?" I asked.

He nodded his head, solemnly. I said no more and left him there, kneeling on his bed. Later when I passed his room on the way to mine, I peeked in. He was reading Book II, *For Honor and Greylor*. The look on his face was like that of a religious scholar examining the Talmud. I passed most of the rest of the afternoon in the basement.

I watched old game shows and tried to figure out a way of getting Daryl to do something about David. Maybe he needed to teach the boy how to fight or how to ignore things like that without seeming like a wimp. Maybe there was something a father could do that a mother couldn't. The women on the TV in their beaded gowns and huge hair were obviously having much more fun than me, like their only worry and biggest achievement was charming the host, Jack Barry. Just before the finale of *Joker's Wild*, the doorbell rang.

I began up the steps and heard David come out of his room and run down the hall. He pulled open the front door and murmured something.

"There you are, Davey. Your mom?" Sarah asked.

I stopped on the stairs, midway up. Hearing her voice made my skin crawl. Enough unpleasantness had visited my house that day. I wasn't prepared to face any more.

"No," David answered and I began creeping back down.

"There you are, Davey," she said. "Will your Mom be there soon?"

"I don't know," he said.

I felt worse about leaving David to handle it with each step I took back down to the basement. The murmur of their voices continued for what seemed to be a very long time. David ran down the hall back to his room, then the floor creaked as he crossed the hall into the bathroom where he ran the faucet. Curious, I crept back up the stairs. Once I'd reached the top, I heard the bathroom faucet go off and David come back down the hall.

"There you are again, Davey!" Sarah exclaimed.

The screen door creaked open. Dear God, I thought, he's letting her inside. I perched on the top step ready to shut the whole operation down at any minute, but there was no further sound. I took one more step and was back upstairs. I turned to the door but no one had come in. The living room was empty. There was no one on the porch either. I called for David. He didn't answer. I checked his room. He wasn't there. I went outside and stood on the porch.

From down the street came screams of rage and wet sneakers slapping on the blacktop. First just the top of his head crested over the hill, just the mess of blonde curls, then all of Kenny came thundering up, half-limping. His jeans were wet and clinging to his shins. The sound of tires peeled up the hill behind him. Sarah's flattop soon came into view, she stood up on her bike pumping the pedals. David sat astride the rack on the back of her bike, holding on with his legs somehow. In his hands was that preposterous water gun he'd forced Daryl to buy him. Once they got close, circling Kenny, he fired. Its stream was heavy and fast like a fire hose, soaking him from the waist down. Kenny lunged for the bike as they came near but missed. His body slapped against the street. She came around again and with Kenny curled up in the fetal position to protect himself, Sarah got very close. For a second, I thought she was going to run him over. Then, David hit him square in the ass with another torrent from his gun. Sarah yelped with glee. Kenny swore and rolled around on the pavement.

Across the street, Denny and Jonny were watching from the front door of Denny's house. Their faces pressed against the screen. They wore expressions of shock and even awe.

"Hey boys," I yelled to them. "What happened to Kenny? Did he wet his pants or what? Look! Look at him!"

"Kenny wet his pants, Kenny wets his pants," they cried out in jeering unison.

"Wet his pants, wet his pants," Sarah barked, joining in. "There he is, wetting his pants. His pants wet."

She and David rode up the block and around the bend out of sight. He had his weapon raised in triumph. Kenny climbed to his feet to the mocking chorus. He tried to glare at me but his eyes kept squinting shut. With wobbling, sloshy steps, he wandered the street, looking lost. The boys kept the chant going until Kenny turned his attention to them. He screamed and swore and threatened them.

I went back inside where I shook the crumbs from a well-used kitchen towel. As I walked outside, I noticed Denny and Jonny had retreated back into Denny's house and wondered what they thought of David now, if they'd been as surprised as I had by the boldness of his actions. Kenny was still out in the middle of the street, shouting at no one. He wore an expression of empty rage that was so close to sadness, I almost felt sorry for him. When I got near enough to him to hand him the towel, I flinched a little afraid he might hit me.

"Did you tell him to do that or something?" he asked as he snatched the towel away from me.

"No. He did that all on his own."

"You cheered him on though," he said, thrusting it

back at me after he'd wiped his face.

"Keep it," I said, "Tell your mom I'll get it back the next time we have one of our pleasant little chats. Or maybe, she can bring it when she comes to pay me a visit."

"Such a bitch," he said, then dropped the towel.

As he slunk back down the hill towards his house, I wanted to respond, but he seemed to have only that one insult for me, that one word. I found I'd never been as happy to be called a bitch or be thought of in that way. I knew that his mom would agree about what a bitch I was and hoped that he would pass the idea down to his children and his children's children. Anyone who wasn't a bitch to people like that, was on the wrong side of life.

22. In Peace

I had, quite accidentally, guilted Mother into joining me in visiting Daddy's grave on his birthday. The
week before I'd called to tell her my plan to go there.
Over the years, that call had become a part of the whole
guilt-spraying ritual. It was my way of daring her to acknowledge that she remembered him. On the phone that
day, I'd thought the silence that came back to me over
the line was that of her marinating a little in what, for
her, passed as shame. Then, she sighed as though overcome by the weight of an actual emotion impinging upon
her. An odd feeling that surely took a moment to identify.

"I've not gone back there since…" she said, breaking off. Her voice was creaky and hesitant, lacking its
edge. Sounding for the first time like an old woman.

It's an odd feeling, the moment you realize that time
has been slowly beating your adversary down more than
you could've ever hoped to. She became a widow for the
first time to me in that moment. Alone and aging with
only the abyss of ceasing to exist to look forward to.

"Mother? Would you like to come with us?" I asked.

"I suppose I could help show you the way. It is my
little corner of the world, so to speak."

"The way?"

"To his stone, dear," she said.

I didn't take up that point to argue. Save your energy, girl. I'd surely visited his stone many more times
than her and still wasn't sure I could remember its exact
location. I just told her I would be happy to see her, happy to drive her. Now that the day had arrived, I realized
how untrue that was. The prospect of journeying alone
with her to see his stone annoyed me to the point of ter-

ror.

By the time the tea kettle was boiling, the sun had just begun to peek over the horizon. A pale orange band lit the bottom of the kitchen window. I poured my hot water into a tea mug while I stood at the window listening to the morning stillness. *To the Lighthouse* lay face down on the table. The night before, I'd struggled my way through the first twenty pages or so. Sensing that I was actually close to losing my latest argument with Daryl, I'd retreated from the bedroom to the kitchen. Picking it up again that morning, I found myself even less able to concentrate.

Daryl's sudden keenness to go to the graveyard with Mother and me had made me wary. I figured he'd enjoy his time alone with David. But maybe it was just one more thing we could argue about. Maybe he was that much further from being done trying than I was. In any case, we'd reached a point where we rarely let the opportunity to contest something slip by.

"I should go, too," he had said. "It's a family outing. It's, you know, about the family."

"Since when do you care about that?" I asked.

"That's not fair. I've always cared. I've always wanted us to do things together."

"You didn't know him, Daryl."

"He's still family. He's still part of our family, yours and mine."

I recoiled mostly from the sense that it was like some rearguard action being used to pull me back towards him. I didn't want him to go because it would've meant admitting in some small shape or form that he was right. We were still a family and visiting my dad's grave was something we should do together. We were a family then. The phrase still sticks a bit when I force myself to admit the basic truth of it.

In the morning silence, the dread that that thought inspired had begun to consume me when Daryl made his grumbling way down the hall. He came into the kitchen, his face stretched in a long yawn. Once again, Daryl cropped up at an opportune time. I didn't really want to go with him but was realizing how much more I didn't want to be alone with Mother.

"Any coffee?" he asked.

I put out a mug for him and got the coffee maker going. The mug had been painted to look like it was made out of wood. Over the years it faded so that the wood was now white, most of the woodgrain barely visible. It had been a present from son to father years before, something I'd picked out.

"So I'm going to take you up on your offer from last night," I said.

"You are?" he asked.

"If you want to come with me you can."

"Should I?" he asked.

"I don't know, Daryl. You never met him but isn't it something a husband would do? Wasn't that your whole point last night?"

"You used to talk about him a lot. I feel like I kind of, like, know him."

"You do want to come?" I asked.

"Like I says, just cause he's dead don't mean he ain't family."

At times, he could use his upstate hillbilly English, skate around the rim of a confusing double negative and still make it all sound like poetry.

"What do we do with Davey?" he asked. "Leave

him here alone? We'll be gone a long time."

"He can join us," I said, figuring in the safety of numbers.

"Wow," Daryl said, blinking. "Like, really?"

"You were right last night. It's a family thing. We should do it all together."

He sat motionless, dragging his empty mug closer to him. The coffee maker began spitting liquid into the pot. Daryl sucked air in through his nose, his mouth hanging slack. I fought the urge to nudge it shut. He scratched at the stubble around his mouth, then yawned loudly.

"I can't believe I won an argument," he said, smiling at me. "Like, with you. I just cannot believe it."

"We should mark it on the calendar."

We laughed, holding each other's gaze. Daryl seemed truly elated. Perhaps, he thought that would mark a new beginning for us. Maybe he thought I was dropping my defenses, finally, after all the tight-lipped ugliness of that spring. Possibly and tragically, he sensed a closeness beginning anew between us. He was never good at judging such things and I, for my part, often erred in encouraging those sorts of feelings. On that morning, as I passed by him on my way out of the kitchen, I ran through his attempt at a hug like it was a turnstile. I told him I was going to take a long shower and charged him with informing David about our family outing.

After my shower, I cinched my robe and emerged from the bathroom to a battle occurring across the hall. I wondered at first what concessions David would wring from Daryl this time. I loved seeing Daryl squirm under the cross. David was so good at pushing him. I thought of it as preparation for my gifted son, who would one day learn to take full advantage of the world's fools and lackwits.

David sat on his bed, legs dangling over the side with his arms folded over his chest. Beside him, laying face down, was Book V *Bedray's Return*. Its spine was striated and worn. There was no telling how many times he'd read it by that point. I never worried about his obsession with those books after the water gun incident. They'd done the job that we, his parents, couldn't. They gave him the confidence he needed to survive the end of his early childhood. That harsh last chapter when the reality of the world, which the child has so longed to know, begins to overwhelm even the most ingrained of optimistic fantasies.

Daryl was seated backwards in the desk chair. His ample rump spilled off the sides and front. A pose copied from sitcom dads, who had an easy time getting their boys to understand the wisdom of a father's reasoning. His eyes were closed, his head bowed.

"Why do I have to go?" David asked, seeing me in the door.

"You don't want to go?" I asked, summoning every bit of false incredulity I could muster.

"I was going to go to Victoria's later. She invited me over. Remember?"

"No," I said.

"I told you about it," he said to Daryl.

I gave Daryl a glance that could've scratched glass. Not informing me wasn't as bad as learning again that my son had trusted him with information of that kind more than me. I sat down next to David on the bed.

"You know David, I regret that you never got to meet your grandfather. He really would have thought you were great. In so many ways, you remind me of him.

I know it's not your idea of a good time but if you would come, it would mean a lot to me."

"But he's dead."

David. My only son. Gifted. I wondered again if the test they'd given him had been properly calibrated.

"Yes, he is," I said, "hence the family outing to the graveyard."

"Come on, Davey. Do it. Your mom, she needs you, you know?" Daryl added, rising from the chair as though that represented his last and best effort.

"Can Victoria come?"

"I don't know, champ. We like…" Daryl said, squeezing by me on his way out the door.

"Can she, Mom?"

"You want to bring your gir…You want to take her to a graveyard?"

"I want to see her."

"Do you think she'll want to come?" I asked,

"I don't want to go without her. Grandma can be…." he began then lost the words.

Tell me about it, kid.

"Love to have her. Give her a call," I said.

Victoria lived not far from the train station that was situated between our town the next one. It was a newish development with large faux Victorian houses without an empty or abandoned lot in sight. Her home sat at the end of a cul-de-sac. The brick drive was a half circle that allowed me to drive right up to the front door, where lights in iron fittings like old gas-fired lamps hung on either side.

Rather than let us honk, my chivalrous son went to the front door. He rang the bell and stood waiting with his hands behind his back. Her parents were partners in the same law firm, apparently living the kind of life I'd once envisioned for myself. Even after I met Daryl, even after I married him, I used to fantasize about meeting my real husband, the one who collaborated on cases with me, who did pro bono work for poor immigrants on the side. We'd vacation on the Cape, not the Hamptons. We'd retire to pursue our joint dream of doing good works, helping battered women, while sacrificing little of our mildly ostentatious lifestyle.

Daryl drummed on the steering wheel along to AC/DC, taking breaks only for determined excursions with his right index finger up his nostril. I reached over and touched his hand, which got him to stop. Mother would've been proud of my gesture, though I suspect she would have counselled that a biting comment made just before the kids got in the car would've added to its effectiveness.

"Thank you for inviting me, Mr. and Mrs. Hytner," Victoria said.

"Sure thing," Daryl said.

"So glad you wanted to come for this unusual outing," I added.

"And I am sorry about your father, Mrs. Hynter."

"Thank you," I said, catching sight of her in the rearview. "He passed many years ago."

"David said he never got to meet either of his granddads. I think that's so sad."

"We don't really know where my real pop's at," Daryl added to make her feel better, I guess. "And my stepdad's long gone. How're things for you where, like, your folks' folks are concerned?"

"Both of my granddads are still with us," she said.

"Do you see much of them?" I asked.

"My mom's dad lives in New Jersey. He's semi-retired from Mars, the candy company. He comes for dinner about once a month."

"That's nice," I said.

"He always brings candy."

"Awesome," Daryl hooted.

"My dad claims it's to make up for the fact the he lacks an identifiable personality."

"Oh," was all I could say.

Daryl laughed and banged harder on the steering wheel.

"Her dad says that he's evidence that too much sugar rots the brain," David said. He and Victoria laughed as though it was part of the music they made together. I couldn't help but notice when I adjusted the mirror that they were holding hands.

"That's not very nice, David," I said. "You shouldn't talk about Victoria's grandfather like that."

"It's what her dad told me. I'm just repeating what I heard."

"You shouldn't repeat it, then."

"It's funny," he said.

"It's one thing when it's a member of your own family, but you shouldn't talk about someone else's even if you are just repeating something."

"You mean like when you said that grandma got her food out of the trash?" he asked, laughing hard now. I noticed Victoria had not joined in.

"Dumpster divers," Daryl added.

The drive out to Mother's was bearable that day. Maybe it was the young couple in the back, talking about school and literature. Maybe it was Daryl, trying to join in with them, asking questions, rather than trying to talk to me. Most probably, it was the knowledge that this meeting with Mother would be done at a neutral location. We wouldn't have to go into her home. Wouldn't be forced into servitude. Out in public, she didn't feel as free to attack. There was a less biting end to her barbs. She was not remarking territory that had once been mine. I even allowed myself to think she might keep her harsh asides about Daddy to herself. She wouldn't dare look like the bitter old widow in front of Victoria. Or maybe she would. The main thing was that I felt I was in for an easier go of it.

We arrived early at her home, which made the time we would have to wait longer. Finally, she appeared in her bedroom window above the drive, holding up a finger. Daryl honked to demonstrate her point had been made. I could just make out the scowl on her face as the curtains fell back together.

"Is she all alone in that great big house?" Victoria asked.

"It's not so big inside," Daryl noted. "The layout is weird. The space is, you know, used badly. The layout is um…how'd you say…."

"She's alone," I said.

She rarely, if ever, went into Daddy's study, even after he passed. Once a month, someone from the maid service would come to dust it and shake out the rugs. I probably was the last person to ever sit at his desk. He'd been in hospice care for almost a full week by that point. I'd gone home to gather some paperwork they needed because I didn't trust Mother to do it soon enough. I started by going through the bottom drawers of the desk. One side had nothing but reams of three-hole punched paper, the other old charts and graphs all placed neatly in labeled folders waiting for the proud day when they could join their compatriots in one of his cherished binders.

I slid open the middle drawer. In a slot at the front were paperclips caught up in snake nests of rubber bands. Behind these were stacks of legal pads, filled with numbers and Daddy's incomprehensible abbreviations. The last in that stack of those was a much thinner tablet. Many of its pages had been torn out and the top edge was jagged with scraps. On the top were words that I've never forgotten, words that I read again and again. I read it and reread it so many times, in fact, I can no longer remember what I'd actually gone in there for, what part of Daddy's life needed documenting so that he could die where he was staying.

Dear Edna,

This will be hard to read, perhaps as hard to read as it has been for me to finally write. Though, I suspect my difficulties in transcribing my thoughts may be partially due to my condition. Did we ever truly love each other?

I know you must be wondering why I am writing this, why I am offering you these cold, hard words. You may have already stopped reading this. You may think this all some melancholy manifestation of my illness.

You now have a lifestyle and obligations, which I suspect have never really fit the picture you once held of yourself; that young woman whom I lost my heart to at the regatta all those years ago. We have been trapped together for so long now in the same cage. Disease will soon see to my release. My wish for you is to wait no longer to find your own freedom.

There was no signature and that was something Daddy would have certainly affixed to such a piece of correspondence, once he felt it was finished. It bore no date either. I tore it out. I don't remember why, if I ever had a reason. I put it in my back pocket. There was a time in my youth when I'd pull it out and reread it after having a difficult call or interaction with Mother. As a young woman, I saw it as commiserating with Daddy. As time went on, I began to realize I read it as a way to try and understand her. I also wonder if some part of me was happy to think of her as being trapped, of wanting that to continue.

Mother's posture, so rigid and upright as she came to the car, said that today would not be one for tears, that by getting her to go, I had extracted from her all that she was willing to give in terms of concessions. Duty-bound, the work of a widow was never done. She opened the door behind me on the passenger side. I could feel the glowering examination she was giving the car's messy interior -- the clusters of leaves crunching underfoot on the mat, the stained upholstery, the young people huddling together in abject fear of her. She'd spent years perfecting that look, one that I never was able to perfectly copy.

"Crowded back here," she said, then grunted her way inside.

"Grandmother, this's my friend Victoria," David said, now wedged between them.

Mother nodded and exhaled her version of 'hello, nice to meet you.' Victoria's hand remained extended in the air just long enough for her to have to feel a tad insulted when it was not taken. Finally, she withdrew it.

"Nice to meet you, Mrs. Graham," she said.

"You in the habit of taking your dates to graveyards, David?" Mother asked.

"It's not a date. We're just friends," he said.

"Better than your father, I guess. He took his dates to city bars."

"Good to see you too, Edie," Daryl said.

"Did they tell you what you would be doing today, dear?" she said, leaning over David to direct her words at Victoria. "Did they tell you that a dead man was the guest of honor?"

In the rearview, I could just make out Victoria nodding.

"You didn't tell me you were letting him date at such a young age," Mother said. "A girlfriend already?"

"Mother, David told you, they're just friends. Just because two people enjoy each other's company doesn't mean they're dating. If his friend Denny was here, you wouldn't automatically assume he was David's boyfriend. Would you?" I asked, jumping on the grenade and pulling the pin before throwing it back.

"His boyfriend?" she cried. "Indeed, I don't believe I would."

"We're just friends," David said.

"Odd thing to be doing with any friend, boy or girl," Mother said.

"I kind of like graveyards," Victoria said, her head turned to the passing road.

I admired that. She had backed away from the hornet's nest but not so far she couldn't stick her hand inside to find out how much getting stung would hurt. Or maybe she was just the kind of person who can't keep quiet, whose opinions on everything have to be aired. God knows that if my son has a type, that's it.

"Do you dear?" Mother asked.

"I do," Victoria said, turning to Mother with that

smile of hers that certain people, people thoroughly unlike my mother, surely found disarming. "They're peaceful."

"No you don't," Mother said, leaning towards the girl so I could see the smile on her face, one so pleased at seeing the look of self-satisfaction disappear from Victoria's. "You only think you do. I expect you heard some adult say something like that and are now repeating it, believing it to sound like the words of someone wise and mature beyond her years. I have some news for you, whomever said such rubbish is undoubtedly an imbecile and you may tell them that Edna Graham said so. No one really likes graveyards, except for the incurably morbid and morose. And what those people need is time in the booby hatch. You aren't one of those people, are you, Virginia?"

"Victoria," David and I corrected her in unison.

"No, I don't think so," Victoria said, sounding more chastened than I would have thought possible.

Good thing it wasn't a date.

David slunk down in his seat. The result, however, was that it relieved Victoria of her shield and Mother now had a direct line over the top of his head at her. He should've sat up straight, changed the conversation or reached across Mother, opened the door and shoved her out into the ditch beside the highway. But he was simply no better than the rest of the Hytners that day, happy to be out of the line of fire.

"Watch out for this one, Davey," Mother said, pointing her chin at Victoria. "She likes to put on airs."

"Grandmother," David said, slowly doing a reverse slink back up the car seat. "I wanted her to come with us so she could see where Granddad was buried and I wanted her to meet you."

"She's certainly the nicest looking of your friends," Mother said.

"Thank you," Victoria said, uncertainly.

St. Leonard's Cemetery sat along a ridge off the main road well outside of town. The slope of it was steep and green. Seeing it from a distance with the sun hitting it at that certain angle made it look like all the stones were perched before open graves. At the top of the ridge stood a huge elm that offered ample shade to a chosen collection of souls in its shadow. We drove all the way around the tree twice before realizing we didn't know where to go. Daryl pulled off to the side, back down the hill by the entrance and we all got out. Victoria was fastest in exiting and putting distance between her and the car. David raced to join her.

"What're you all doing?" Mother asked.

"You know where he's buried?" I asked.

She shook her head.

"You don't?" I asked. "I thought you said you were coming to help us find the way."

"I don't recall saying any such thing, dear."

"Then, we'll have to look. I don't really remember, either."

Victoria and David walked to the top of the hill. Daryl was not far behind them. Mother got out of the car and leaned against it.

"We'll be here all day," she announced to no one in particular.

David lacked the decency to give everyone a long break from her. Within a few minutes, he and Victoria had found the grave. It was on the other side of the hill, deep in the tree's shadow.

"Over here. He's over here," he shouted.

Daryl glanced at Mother, then me before disappearing over the hill. She stood up straight and as though preparing for a hike, slung her purse behind her back. Walking a few more steps ahead, I caught a hint of the complaints that would soon be coming from her as though they'd ridden the wind from some near future when we were all back in the car with her and she was out of breath and unhappy.

"We can just get in the car and pull up and around," I said and walked back towards her.

"I want to walk, dear," she said. "I'm in good shape. Exercise is important."

She climbed the hill slowly, carefully putting one foot before the other. Once or twice, she reached out to steady herself on a grave. I walked beside her, offered her my arm. She didn't take it at first. Then just as the hill got steep, she grabbed at the sleeve of my blouse. By the time we'd neared the top, she had looped her arm through mine. We took slow steps as the hill got progressively steeper. Once or twice, it felt as though she was about to pull us both down but I managed to escort her safely to Daddy's final resting place. Once we got there, she kept her arm linked with mine. We bent over his stone almost as one.

23. Respect Smarts at Home

As that summer approached, I began walking around the neighborhood as often as I could find the motivation. I'd start down the street towards the Crumbrick's then follow the road as it twisted past the alternating empty lots and ramshackle homes of strangers. Under the power lines, I would stop and listen for the train. If it was running, I'd spend a blissful handful of minutes fantasizing about some alternate me, living some alternate life in some alternate, idealized version of the city. If, not, I just trudged on making this or that empty vow to myself about taking the steps needed in order to return me to my life, the one I'd promised myself so long ago.

One surprisingly hot mid-May day, the air heavy already with the punishing summer to come, I set out boldly in shorts. My pasty legs quaked with every step. By the time I'd reached the bottom of the hill, a good sheen of sweat had formed across my forehead and between my thighs. I stopped and doubled over, gasping for breath at the foot of the Crumbrick's driveway. Lynn was loading some brown paper bags, full of what I could only imagine, into the back of her rusted-out Chevy Nova. The back window had been replaced by a sheet of clear plastic, duct-taped to the frame. She scowled at me, then got into her car. It struggled to start, the engine turned over finally after several attempts. Then, it abruptly cut out. I heard her swearing. Before I knew what I was doing, I found myself banging on her windshield.

"Crumbrick! I want to talk to you." I gave the glass something in between a tap and a pound.

"Don't you touch my car," she warned. "I just had that window replaced. Get away."

Even from outside with the windows up, the air around the car smelled like an ashtray. She lit up a Newport and tried to start the car again. Again, the engine failed.

"Hey, I want to talk to you about something, something your son did. I've been meaning to tell you about it. Come on, get out of the car."

"Get away. I'm late for something else already. Something better than talking to you."

The engine came to life, momentarily. Then, it died once again, before she could put it in gear. A terrible, metallic whining made the car shudder in place.

"Crumbrick, listen to me. There's something you need to hear about your son. Something you should want to know."

"What do you think you know about Kenny?" she asked, taking the keys from the ignition and shaking them at me in a vaguely threatening way.

"He's a pervert. A sex offender."

"Ah, shit." She waved dismissively at me and tried the car again. "Get away will you? I don't fucking have time for this."

"He is. He pulled down my son's pants and underwear. I think he wanted a look at David's dick."

"Come on, quit taking it all so serious. Jesus. You oughta lighten up. They're just boys."

"I don't know. I'd be worried. Maybe he wanted to see what another one looks like because he heard how his father's too busy sticking his in waitresses half his age to come around."

"What!? What did you say?" she asked, cracking the window. "How's that?"

"I said, your ex-husband or whatever he is, as everyone knows, has been getting all around town with a fat girl from the diner. And, I mean, I hear she's *fat* fat, much fatter than me even. Two tons of fun. A grateful one. Is that why he left? You weren't grateful enough?"

"Get out of my driveway. Mind your fucking business," she screeched. "You bitches all like to talk. You should stay out of my business fucking, fat-ass bitch."

"I'd like very much to never need to talk to you again, Lynn."

"Soft's what your boy is. Soft and a crier to boot. Jesus, get out of my driveway and go toughen up your son."

"At least he's not a pervert like Kenny."

"You know what? I want you off my fucking property. Don't come back here bothering us."

"Doesn't he have any friends his own age? Is it maybe because, he's always trying to look at other boys' dicks?"

"Why don't you..." She wound the window lower now, her smoke-cracked face fixed in a truly unappealing grimace. "Just get the fuck out of here. Get off my property and don't never come back. Get, go on. And keep my name out of your bitchy mouth. I don't have to sit here and listen to this from some mother raising up a queer."

"It sounds like your son might be the gay one. Not that there's anything wrong with that."

"If you don't get out of here, I'm going to call the fucking police."

"Please do, go ahead," I said and bent over to look her right in her beady eyes, "I'm sure they'll be quite interested to hear about how Kenny's been sexually assaulting neighborhood boys."

"You come down here. Think you're better than me. Go on. Go, cry to someone like your faggot son. No wonder he still messes his drawers."

"I don't think that was what Kenny was trying to inspect."

She finally got the car started, threw it into reverse and sped out of the driveway, yelling at me, smoke curling around her face. I waved to her. She flipped me the bird.

"I want my kitchen towel back," I screamed as she pulled away.

That day, I didn't stop and wait under the power lines when I heard the train. I felt no need to fantasize. Much like a prison stay, suburban life offers its bright days when even from her cell on death row, a gal finds a moment or two of contentment. I paused to examine my vicious little soul and understood, just for a moment, that simply having one is enough. My pace on the walk back home was fast. It was like I was floating. I hoped to find Lynn returning when I passed their shack but she wasn't there. I flipped the house the bird, hoping Kenny might be inside to receive it. It didn't matter if anyone saw or heard me. I no longer cared. Part of me must've known that I'd soon leave that drab little neighborhood and Roslyndale all together. Part of me, by then, already had.

24. The Pasta Reckoning

For the last day of school in the middle of June, it was 80 degrees by 7 a.m. It would be like that almost every day from June until September that year. It was so bad, we even got an AC unit for our bedroom window. My idea. We couldn't really afford to buy it, but I could no longer lay sweating next to my even sweatier husband. We let David sleep on the floor there most nights. A real coup. Not only was I comfortable but went for weeks at a stretch without my husband trying to lay a hand on me. He'd soon take to the basement couch, the first signal that he, too, had finally given up.

David ate his Pop Tarts and drank his orange juice listlessly. It was more than a lack of sleep. I knew he must've been dreading the end of the school year. It wasn't only that he'd not get to see his non-girlfriend quite so often, she was going to be away for much of the summer, but also that he'd have to spend so much of the next three months in that house with me. Alone with me. And he couldn't yet know how bad that summer would be. I used the AC as a reason but really barely found the strength to leave the bedroom much that summer, and if he wanted relief, he'd have to be in there with me.

"Last day today," I said, hoping he'd make some effort at appearing excited.

"I guess." And a shrug was all he mustered.

His friendship with Jonny and Denny, which had become more distant that winter and spring, would seem a part of an almost forgotten past by the end of that summer. They'd all reached an age when it was becoming apparent how far apart they were in temperament and intellect. Denny, for example, was being held back. The story his parents told was that it was due to his being short and wanting to get bigger so he could go out for the middle school football team. That was all bullshit. He was an okay at sports, I guess. He was also more than a little dumb and Caroline probably came up with that story to avoid embarrassing him.

Jonny was transferring schools and getting more involved with the church. The poor kid's parents seemed determined to use him to somehow make up for all of the mistakes and sins of his sister. Rumors had it she was on drugs and living in the city, though no one knew exactly where or wanted to think about how she was supporting herself.

"You're going to miss your…school friends, huh?" I asked.

"Mmm…hmm," he said.

"You'll miss Victoria," I said, feeling as always the need to poke my little bear just so he could growl.

"Mom," he moaned as only a young boy who's ashamed of love can. "We're just friends."

"I know. I know. Can't I ask about your friends?"

"I guess," he said and bowed his head, making a study of the sugary crumbs and candy-colored sprinkles dotting his plate.

"Do you want to ask if she wants to come over for dinner tonight? It's a special day we should celebrate. You're going to leave the elementary school this year and go up to the middle school."

Middle school was where my son would have his heart truly broken for the first time. Victoria would drop him for some boy she met at choral camp. David was so crushed by it that he actually told me when it happened. I attended the Christmas Program that year just to catch a glimpse of the singing Romeo. He was tall with lashes for days and big almost doll-like blue eyes, an altogether more enticing package than my son, at least on the outside. I took some solace in the idea that Victoria was shallow, which was unfair. She was simply a kid, who like my son, was smart enough to daydream about better things, a better life, a boy like Doug Kelly. He dumped her later that same year. News which David also shared with me. And which we'd bond over, reveling in it a bit together.

"We never celebrated the end of school before," he said.

"It's a milestone year."

"All the sixth graders get picked on."

"Says who?" I asked.

"Everyone."

"Everyone at school?" I asked.

"Yeah, everyone."

"How would they even know, David? None of them have even been to middle school yet."

"Joe Sant said they locked his brother inside a locker."

"I don't think you'll have to worry about that."

"Why not?"

"You're too big to fit in a locker."

When he tried to pull his shirt down so that it further hid his belly, I felt awful for putting it that way. I just wanted him to relax and look forward to something, I didn't want him to slump away from the table. I guess I should've said the lockers were abnormally narrow at the middle school. That's life for us fatties, it's always the world that needs to stop shrinking.

"I guess we won't be inviting Denny to join in the

celebration," I said.

David smiled and handed me his plate as he got up.

"No," David noted. "He's being held back for sports."

"For sports," I said.

"But which ones?" he asked with playful incredulity lighting his face.

"You sound like you have doubts about this," I said.

"He seems a little slow compared to the rest of the class."

"I would say he more than *seems* a little slow."

Blackening his former friend's name had done the trick. At least, he no longer seemed so concerned with his appearance. Fat was a choice, stupid wasn't. At the door, I gave him a hug or he let me hug him, I should say. He endured it with a sigh that was a little overly dramatic.

"So should I count on four for dinner?"

"I guess," he said before running out the door for the bus. I took it as a yes.

I got out the rags, mop and bucket and went to work in the kitchen. It took a lot of scrubbing to get the grease up from around the burners on the stove. By the time I'd finished, my wrist throbbed. I lifted up the stove, propping it with the little bar inside. A debris field that spoke of nearly every meal we'd eaten in that house together in the previous year greeted me. After that, I was too tired to really scrub the counters or sink. The floor received, at best, an indifferent sweep and mop job but looked clean enough once I was done.

I busted out the Pledge and sprayed the dining room table and the china cabinet and wiped until the wood grain glittered. I found the cotton napkins, the good china and even some nice place settings. I guess cleaning rather than spending the morning lying in bed or sprawled out on the couch in the basement put me as close to being in the mood to be a good hostess as I could get.

When the kids got home, they noticed none of my labors, barely saying "hello" before going into David's room. I stood at the end of the hall listening to them and found the silence unsettling. I marched down the hall with heavy steps so that they would hear me. I really didn't want to walk in on them in the middle of anything that would embarrass all of us. They were on his bed, heads at either end reading *The Hobbit*. David's was a copy from the local library, the cellophane protected cover showed a dragon slinking around what appeared to be a mountain of gold. Victoria had a paperback that was worn and ragged, on its cover a man in a pointy hat was navigating a dirt lane in a green valley.

"Victoria," I began which earned a sneer from David as though I was about to ruin something, "do your parents know where you are?"

"Yes. I called them from school. They said it was okay. They said they'd like to have David over for dinner some weekend. Weekdays are hard for them."

"Sure," I said.

"They both work," she said. "Having two working parents makes dinner hard."

"You like spaghetti, right?" I asked with an undercurrent of "Tread lightly, you uppity bitch, you're in my house."

"Oh yes, Mrs. Hytner. Yours is so good."

"Excited for middle school?"

"Yeah. Pretty much. I'm going to try out for the choir."

"The choir? Will you be joining her, David? You have a nice singing voice." I'd never once heard him sing.

"Mom, can you leave us?" he asked. "We have to finish these."

"What's the rush?" I asked.

"Mom," David moaned.

"Okay, I'll go, I'll go. I've got to get the sauce going anyway."

"Do you make it from scratch? The sauce?" Victoria asked and I couldn't tell if she liked torturing David, as well or was just trying to be polite.

"In a way. I use canned tomatoes but it's not from a jar. It's sort of half from scratch. We're not Italian, so I can get away with it."

"My mother's Italian and she never cooks," she said.

"Not every woman does or should have to."

"She says she resents the thought that just because she's a female of Italian extraction that she must cook, that it's required or something."

"Extraction," I said with a laugh.

"It means she's of Italian stock," Victoria said with a smirk.

Don't call her Vicky out of spite. Don't call her Vicky out of spite. Don't call her Vicky out of spite. Don't call her Vicky out of spite. Don't call her Vicky out of spite. Don't call her Vicky out of spite.

"I know, Vicky. I know. It's just not a word I hear very often."

"Mom," David crowed, "you know she doesn't like to be called that. Call her by her name."

"Oh, I'm sorry did I say Vicky?"

"Yes," she said.

"Sorry, it is such a common diminutive, it just leapt to my tongue."

Feeling their stares, I thought it best to leave. My place, at least on that day, was in the kitchen. There I could cut and chop without offending anyone. I liked the work that day. It was one of those cooking experiences which allowed me to fantasize about becoming a chef at some point. I could go to culinary school in the city. There, I'd recapture my youth and somehow make up for all that had gone wrong in my life so far.

How I would've relished that conversation with Mother. Telling her I was going back to school, then pausing long enough for those steady, self-satisfied winds to fill her sails, before telling her the rest of my plan.

"You'll have to start from the bottom at some greasy spoon, when you're finished," I could almost hear her say in a voice tremulous with fear. "You'll work in filth like some common laborer."

Of course, I knew she'd not likely pass up the chance to inject some doubt-inducing cruelty into her counterargument when those initial salvoes failed.

"Don't you think you're a little old for that, dear?"
Or.

"Do you think, given your metabolism, that it's wise for you to work around food?"

The masochist in me wanted to enroll that very day just to run through the gauntlet of bleak emotions she would attempt to use against me on cross examination. I stirred my sauce, having that argument, hearing her voice in my head. I put my face in the pot and drank in the smell to chase her away. The meatballs were thawing on the counter. Once they were ready, I put them in a baking dish and popped them in the oven.

Picking up the book I was currently not reading, I sat in the chair at the end of the hall. I had gleaned only small snatches of the conversation that was periodically escaping from David's room, when Daryl came home. He slipped off his boots and staggered through the door. I could smell the alcohol on him from where I sat.

"Hon," he said, inhaling mightily and walking over to me on unsteady legs.

"You're home early," I said.

"They sent us all home early. I went out for a couple of drinks with the guys."

"A couple? It smells like more than that."

"Are you mad?" he asked, and I let him hug me. He belched as he did so. I practically got a contact buzz from the smell. "There won't be much overtime for a while. They said all of us will have to take an even bigger hours cut than the one we've already had."

"What?" I asked, shoving him away.

I had to hand it to him. He'd managed to produce an excuse that had totally taken my mind off of the fact that he'd been driving drunk. He sat down on the couch. Rested his head on the back of it and let out another belch.

"Not enough work. At least, they're not, like, laying us off," he said. "Not yet, anyway."

"What does that mean?

"I mean, you know, not right now…but…ah, look, I'm skilled labor. Worse come to worst, I'll find something."

"How much of a cut are we talking?"

"They'll let us know Monday."

All chatter, even the quietest kind, had ceased from down the hall. They must've been listening. What Victoria, with her busy professional parents, must've thought of that news.

"We'll, like, figure it out, hon," Daryl said. "We always have." He stretched himself out on the couch and closed his eyes. "What're we having for dinner?"

"Spaghetti."

"Smells good," he said. "You can really cook when you want to. Maybe we'll open a restaurant. I can build the tables. You'll cook. Down home, cozy, family style."

He had with a few words conjured a vision of hell that I'd never been able in my worst nightmares to consider. It so completely ruined the fantasy that I'd spent the afternoon concocting that I had to force myself to go back into the kitchen to finish up. When dinner was almost ready, I went to the couch to try and wake him. He would not be stirred. I gave up sooner than a wife might've been expected to, but if it were just me and the kids that would've been fine with me. We were just about to eat when a figure darkened the screen door.

"There you are," Sarah squealed, her hand raised above her eyes to see better inside.

I caught Victoria squinting, her eyebrows low and confused. It took a few seconds before she could rearrange her face back to its natural state of artificial pleasantness. Sarah's acne was as bad as I had ever seen it that day. Huge white globs of it dotted her cheeks and forehead.

"Hi Sarah," David said.

"Davey," she said, making brute music with his name. "There you are."

"Sarah," I said, stepping towards the door, "would you like to eat with us?"

"Dinner here?" she asked.

"Do you want me to call your dad and make sure

it's okay?"

I opened the door for her. She stepped inside, gazing with her mouth wide and licking the spittle from the corners of it with the tip of her tongue. I offered her Daryl's seat. We ate together, the four of us. Sarah was so overwhelmed that she said nothing the whole meal. And I was happy to have her. I should've invited her in long before that.

25. Next to Cake Logs, Epilogues are My Favorite Kind of Logs

The first taste of smoke in my mouth makes me cringe but I force myself to enjoy it. There's something faintly or, perhaps, seriously ridiculous about a woman my age picking up smoking again. David caught me doing it once not long ago. He called it weird, his thoughtless catchall for any human behavior that's beyond his comprehension.

My phone buzzes from the dangling pocket of my cardigan. I ignore it and finish my cigarette. Ms. Gray from next door is being pulled outside by that terrible little dog of hers. It's bridling at the end of its leash. I wave. She squints, which I take as her manner of trying to smile. She must be around my age but comports herself in such a stiff manner that it makes me feel young. I know I don't look like her, like my life has little purpose beyond handling a corgi's shit with only a thin plastic grocery bag between me and abject debasement.

My phone chimes and vibrates a few times. How like a child it is. I often wish I hadn't let David talk me into updating mine. My old phone gave up much more quickly. A gravely underrated virtue.

I click the button on the top that puts it in silent mode. I should just make sure that's the mode it's in most of the time. At least, I'm better than most people I see, who jump when their phone makes the slightest noise. David's like that, fumbling with that 'watch' of his every few seconds. I don't even know how he sees the screen. He says he can watch TV shows on it. I can't imagine. He tells me his father has one too, which makes my head spin. Daryl apparently texts him on a regular basis. In that case, the combination of medium and man makes for scintillating exchanges, I'm sure.

I only texted Daryl once, the day I left him. He'd just bought he and I matching emergency cell phones a few days before, even though we didn't need nor could really afford them. I woke up that morning as excited as anyone could've been for another stimulating day in the payroll office of Hans Paper Products, where I finally, after a summer of serious, constant searching, finally landed my first real, adult job. They'd wanted someone with more filing experience but settled for me instead. Luckily, my ego was pretty much armor-plated by that point.

I'd found the kitchen sink filled, as had become customary that fall, with at least a dozen upturned beer cans. Their silvery bottoms made them look like ordnances awaiting inspection. One by one, I began to pick them out of the sink, rinse them out and then drop them into the bin underneath.

Daryl came into the kitchen, yawing his warm, rotten beer yawn and asking for coffee. He then told me that his latest short-term employer no longer wanted him. I fought hard against the urge to put on a display of mock disbelief -- imagine that, someone not wanting you, Daryl?!

I picked up the last can and rather than rinse it out, I just dropped it back into the sink. The last of its contents spilled out into a pool of frothy, apologetic little bubbles. I didn't start his coffee. I grabbed my purse and without saying good-bye, just left. I wasn't dressed for work and just drove around for a while, coming to terms with what I knew had to be done.

I got on the highway and drove south for a while.

The farther I got from home and the more concrete the possibility that this was finally it became, the more exhilarated I felt. Around lunchtime, I stopped at a Friendly's. I texted Daryl. I can't say that I was aware of how telling my family I was leaving them via text would look to other people, nor did I care.

I sent two texts actually, one said I wasn't coming back and the other said that I would call David that night to explain. Daryl never replied. He did pick up the house phone that night when I called for David. I told him there was nothing more to say and we'd sort things out in terms of custody and all of that later. He didn't try to win me back, just grunted and handed the phone to our son.

I guess I was a little sad that David didn't get choked up or even ask many questions. It even seemed like he was anxious to get off the phone and start his exciting new life with me no longer quite so present in it. I don't remember blaming him for that. We'd had enough of each other during the course of that summer.

The night air's cool for the end of May. It feels like the summer is taking its time getting here which is just fine. It's easily the worst season to be living in the city. There were days last year, whole stretches of them in fact, when the Plexiglass enclosure where I wait for the bus felt like an oven. I have to walk there in the morning and often find myself a sweaty mess and totally out of breath by the time I make it down the street. I'll lose some weight, and I'll quit smoking; I keep saying. Someday soon. Not today but someday.

The usual morning rush hour driver on that route was, like me, a woman of some girth so that AC was blasting whenever I boarded. I'd wedge myself into a window seat along the back bench. The air coming in torrents from the vents above me produced the most ec-static chill when it hit my skin. It almost made baking in the Plexiglass microwave worth it. I always keep some deodorant in my purse for days like that. I'd actually first gotten into that habit of keeping a small tube of Secret on me the day I went to interview for the job I have now.

It happened on a November day that wasn't at all warm. Anxiety had me in a full lather, though. I was, for the first time in my then brief professional life, in-terviewing for a job I really wanted. I'd given myself plenty of time to get to the downtown office so when I got to my stop, I raced right into the Duane Reade, which conveniently was located right across the street. I put on the deodorant before I'd even paid for it. My nerves were working overtime. I could barely think straight.

I had a good rapport with my boss, Rosemarie, right off. She too was divorced and had learned the joy of work only in the aftermath of that. I pretty much knew I had the job before I left her office. When she called me the next day with her offer, I accepted without hesitation. I told her I could start right away.

Because of my age and how I talk sometimes, my co-workers think of me as an emblem of a different era, like I'm a foot solider from the more romantic bra-burn-ing version of our movement. Rosemarie asks from time to time if I've ever given any thought to getting my MSW and joining a response team. I tell her I'm too old. My job fulfills me. Of course, I daydream about do-ing it from time to time, about working my way through school then finding myself on a sharp upward trajectory, where I one day become the Commissioner of Family Protective Services, and then using that as a platform to launch a campaign for mayor. The dream usually ends with the bracing realization that it's not just an excuse, I really am too old. But in those daydreams during my commute, I still find space to realize how I've remade my life, how I'm close enough now to making something of my former dreams.

I crush out my cigarette, pick up the butt end and open the lid of the nearby trashcan just enough to slip it over the lip. Once I get inside, I make myself some tea and sit down at the kitchen table. I check my phone. The caller was David. He no doubt had a therapy session and wants to share his latest revelations with me. I'll call him back when I finish my tea.

Motherhood, I've at long last found, is like daydreaming; neither ever ends, and the sooner peace can be made with what's possible, the happier you'll be.

Author Bio

Born in a small town outside of Pittsburgh, Pennsylvania, **Jason Graff** is the author of *In the Service of the Boyar* (aka *The White Wolf's Secret*) and the forthcoming *heckler*. His passion for the written word was first well and truly ignited when he took a sucker punch for writing his high school crush a poem. He earned his bachelor's degree at Bowling Green State University and later, his MFA in Creative Writing at Goddard College. The intense nature of that program brought him into close contact with a diverse group of talented writers which included: Sarah Schulman, Richard Panek, Darcey Steinke, and Rachel Pollack. He has published fiction, poetry, and essays widely in journals around the world. With subject areas ranging from Darth Vader to conjoined twins to the death of language, his work explores the depth and breadth of the human experience. Jason Graff lives in Richardson, TX with his wife, son, and their cat. He is currently working on a science fiction novel about the end of the universe.

You can follow him on Twitter: @JasonGraff1, his author page on Facebook: Author Jason Graff, and on Instagram: @photograffing.

CPSIA information can be obtained
at www.ICGtesting.com
Printed in the USA
BVHW032201051119
563036BV00001B/7/P

9 781643 700120